THE REHEARSAL FLING

A SINGLE DADS' CLUB NOVEL

SOPHIE ANDREWS

CONTENT NOTE

The Rehearsal Fling is romance between a grumpy single dad and his daughter's dance teacher with multiple open door love scenes. While there are a lot of discussions about divorce and being a single parent, you can be guaranteed a happily ever after for this dirty-talking cinnamon roll and his lady love.

This one's for whoever runs the DILF of Disney accounts. You're a real one.

ONE
DYLAN

Saturday mornings at Imagination Station and Play Center were always wild. Kids everywhere, off-the-charts noise level, and there was bound to be at least one bloody nose. But once a month, we met to hang out in the jungle.

After we kept running into one another here with our children, we finally sat down together and realized we had a lot more in common than a couple of feral kids. We were all single dads.

"Fellas," I said, greeting the other two with a hand up.

Liam craned his head around his wiggling son and offered me a nod as he attempted to fix Finn's sneaker. Once he finished, he ruffled his kid's hair. "All right, guy, go on."

Finn took off in a zigzag.

Before taking a seat on our usual bench, under the window to the "doctor's office," I waved my daughter down. "Scar." She barely slowed to turn to me. "Watch out for your brother."

She rolled her eyes, like she was sixteen, not six.

"Hey." I crossed to her in two steps and sank to her eye level. "A lot of kids here are bigger than him, including you, and you know how he gets with the cars."

"Fine." Scarlett sighed, slanting her gaze toward the vehicle area where Tucker liked to park himself and was oftentimes run over by bigger children on the little peddle cars. I patted her back, and she ran off in Tucker's direction, so I took a seat on the bench.

Jude held up his travel mug of coffee. "Cheers."

Liam and I followed suit with our own coffees then dove into the donut holes Jude had brought. Among the three of us, we had five kids between the ages of two and eight. I was divorced, Jude widowed, and Liam never married, a regular old Single Dads' Club.

"How's everybody been?" Jude asked, crossing his right ankle over his left knee.

"Same old," I mumbled around a blueberry donut, my attention across the room on Amelia, Scarlett, and Tucker. The guys and I played zone defense, and right now, they were in my area.

Liam motioned to where Finn ran around. "Finally got his glasses sorted out."

Next to me, Jude let out a low laugh. "He's so cute."

"Sometimes," Liam added, brushing powdered sugar from his fingers. Finn was adorable.

An adorable tornado on two feet.

"Seb wants to try baseball this summer, so I signed him up," Jude said, his eyes on his eight-year-old son reading in the corner. Sebastian was a bit too old to enjoy all this imaginary play stuff, but he was satisfied to bring along a book or video game and hang by himself. Jude went on, "I was surprised since he's never shown any interest, but his best friend got really into baseball last year."

"Let me know if you need any help with that," I told him.

"Oh yeah? *The* Dylan Matthews is gonna turn my kid into a major leaguer?"

I huffed against my coffee cup. I wasn't *the* anything. A few seasons in the MLB, where I spent more time sidelined with injuries than on the field, wasn't much to talk about. "If he likes it, I'd be happy to help." I tipped my chin to Scarlett and Amelia in the "salon," where they pretended to put makeup on each other. "I tried to get Scarlett to play T-ball, but she was having none of it." I scratched at the few days' worth of stubble on my jaw, thinking about unloading the next bit of information. No doubt they'd give me shit for it. "I told you guys she takes dance lessons, right?"

Jude and Liam nodded.

"Well, apparently every year, the kindergarteners have a 'special someone' dance," I said, crooking my fingers into quotes over the words. "And she asked me to do it with her."

"You excited?" Jude asked.

"Yeah." I tipped my head to the side. "I was kinda surprised she picked me."

It didn't take long for my ex to remarry, and sure, Neil was… fine. And yeah, I was grateful he was a good stepdad to my kids. But with three parents in the picture, it was easy to feel like I was in a popularity contest.

This time, I won.

"How do I get tickets?" Liam asked. "I need to see this dance."

"Fuck off," I muttered. "I'm as graceful as they come."

"If you say so."

I was an athletic guy, could hit a line drive out to center field with my eyes closed, but I wasn't super confident about what I'd have to do in this class. Twirling and leaping were not my forte. Though, I supposed, they'd have to be for Scarlett.

Liam leaned over to meet Jude's gaze. "Hey, how did that date go?"

He puffed his cheeks up then blew out a slow breath. "I couldn't go through with it."

Liam and I both stayed quiet. I'd gone through a grief period when Paige and I split up, but I couldn't imagine grieving her death. Jude and his wife had been high school sweethearts, and although I'd never met her, I knew how much he loved her, how much he still struggled. Any person would. To be married and perfectly happy with your family one day then shattered the next.

I gripped his shoulder, giving it a squeeze, and tried for a joke. "You could do like I do."

The silent part was inferred. Easy one-night stands.

He shook his head. "I wouldn't even know where to start."

"Apps," I said, and Liam pulled a face.

"Meeting over an app. That's so…emotionless."

I raised my brow at him. Because, yes. "Exactly."

"Wouldn't you rather talk to someone in person? Get to know them?"

"What do you know about it?" I asked Liam because that dude was so involved with his work, he never went out with women.

"I know you can't learn all that much over a phone screen."

I shook my head, and Jude sniffed in suspicious amusement. "I don't know how you do it all the time."

"I don't do it *all* the time," I said. "It's every once in a while. To scratch the itch."

"You don't want to settle down?" he asked.

I angled my coffee in the direction of my two kids currently hopping over a rope ladder in the corner. "I can't. Not with them."

Liam crossed his arms and extended his legs out in front of him. "What do you mean? You were already married."

"Yeah, and I can't put them through that again." *That* being a not-so-friendly divorce. It felt like only recently Paige and I had been able to get to a place not littered with lingering resentments. Breaking up with Paige was the worst and hardest thing I'd ever had to do, even if it was for the best. And I didn't want my kids in the middle of something like that again.

"So what?" Jude circled a donut hole in the air. "You gonna have one-night stands forever?"

I shrugged. Then to change the subject of my miserable love

life, I gestured to Liam. "What about you? What's going on with the book?"

He smiled. "I got the deal."

I elbowed him. "Nice."

"Congrats, man." Jude extended his fist for a bump. "That's amazing."

Liam nodded in that self-effacing way of his. He was a professor at the local university and had been shopping his book about the history of the American government or something. All I knew was that he was super smart and taught history, but most of it went over my head.

"We should go out to celebrate," Jude suggested. "Grab a few beers at Walt's."

"Yeah," Liam agreed. "Sounds good to me."

"When?" Jude asked. "Next weekend?"

"I gotta make sure Tess is good." Liam nodded. "But it shouldn't be a problem."

I took my cell phone out of my back pocket, checking over the shared Google calendar with my ex-wife before saying, "Paige has the kids next weekend, so I'm free."

"Cool, mine can stay with their grandparents," Jude said.

"Dads' night out." Liam chuckled then called out a, "Hey, Finn, no," and jumped up to detangle his son from where he'd gotten his head stuck in the plastic mailbox. Again.

A moment later, Tucker came careening over, and I caught him by the waist to fly him up over my head while Jude rolled his eyes as Sebastian attempted to run over Amelia and Scarlett with a play grocery cart.

"Seb! Knock it off and put the groceries away."

The circus never ended with this crew.

Two hours or so later, after the kids had run out most of their energy, we all said our goodbyes and went our separate ways. Scarlett and Tucker had been begging me for Chipotle so we stopped for lunch, and they put down three orders of chips and guac, proving that they were, indeed, my children, then we headed back to my place for a movie marathon.

"Daddy, we has cupcakes for dinner?" Tucker asked from his perch on my lap.

"Cupcakes for dinner?" I jiggled his arms in the air until he laughed. "First of all, we don't have cupcakes. Second of all, even if we did, you guys would have to eat something of substance first."

Scarlett tipped her head back, gazing at me upside down from where she lay on the beanbag. "Daddy, what does substance mean?"

"It means…" My gaze drifted out the window until I thought of an explanation. "It means something of value or importance. You gotta eat something good for you…something of substance."

"Like pizza?" she guessed.

"Sure, like pizza," I said because Scarlett ate exactly five things—pizza, peanut butter sandwiches with no crust, macaroni and cheese, mashed potatoes, and, of course, guac and chips. I could occasionally get her to try a fruit, but she had yet to put any actual vegetables into her mouth that weren't hidden in something else. Tucker, on the other hand, would eat bird shit if it looked good enough to him.

"Pizzaaaaaa," Tucker howled, and I tossed him on the couch next to me.

"Okay, I'll make you guys pizza, but you have to eat it at the kitchen table."

Scarlett pouted. "Ugh!"

"Don't give me that look."

"Don't gimme dat look," Tucker repeated happily as I walked into the kitchen to grab two of the little frozen pizzas. I tossed them in the microwave then cleaned up a few dishes in the sink and wiped down the counter. For the most part, I thought I was a pretty clean guy, though I had improved a lot since the divorce. I had to, living on my own.

I was man enough to admit I hadn't been the best husband to Paige and had often taken her for granted, although that wasn't to say she was without sin. Nevertheless, I'd grown up a lot since we'd split. When Paige and I had started dating, I never would've imagined I'd be here, in a little townhouse, with the days I got to see my own children marked with hearts on a calendar stuck to the fridge. Yet, here I was.

"All right, come and get it!"

Scarlett and Tucker stampeded into the kitchen, fighting over who sat next to me with my leftover chicken and broccoli.

"Hey, hey, what're you two doing? You can both sit next to me." I pointed to the chairs on either side of me at the round table.

Tucker started to cry. "But I sit here!"

Grumbling, I set down my fork and nudged Scarlett to my left, giving in to Tucker's tears even as Scarlett threw out her arms in anger. I still didn't know how to react to tantrums sometimes. I had to pick my battles. The problem was I didn't always know which ones to pick.

"Look," I said, pulling their chairs close to either side of mine. "You're both sitting next to me, okay? Now eat your pizza."

After dinner and a dessert of popsicles, we headed upstairs. Each kid was bathed, brushed, and changed into their pajamas before we played for a bit in Scarlett's bedroom since she had a plastic princess castle they both loved.

"Okay, time for bed. Who's picking out the book tonight?"

"Me!" Tucker ran to the board books stacked in the corner. If the kids were bored by the limited choices, they had yet to show it. With my dyslexia, I was only comfortable reading the ones I knew really well, which were few and far between.

I cleared my throat and hauled both kids into my lap to read *Mr. Brown Can Moo*, giving it my all with the different sounds so they both giggled.

Afterward, I tucked Scarlett into her bed first, folding the covers under her chin with her stuffed rabbit. I kissed her head. "Love you, sweetheart." Then I turned on her night-light and sound machine before taking Tucker to his room. I tossed him into his crib, because he loved that, and bent to push his messy brown hair back from his forehead.

"Music, pwease."

"Yeah, yeah, I know." I hit the button for his music. "I love you, buddy. See you tomorrow."

With the kids down, I brushed my own teeth and changed into sweats then stretched out on my bed. I opened one of my apps but gave up after a minute with my friends' voices on repeat in my head. It wasn't like they disapproved of my choices —we were all doing the best we could—but it did sound like they were giving me a fair amount of warning.

Like, *okay, if that's what you want to do, but it's not what I would do.*

And I got it. They weren't into a hit-it-and-quit-it lifestyle.

I tossed my phone on my nightstand a moment before Scarlett peeked her head into my room.

"I can't sleep."

"Okay, sweetheart, come on. I'll lie with you for a little while."

And that was how I woke up the next morning, on her floor with a pain in my shoulder and a kink in my neck.

TWO
GENEVIEVE

alk, walk, hinge, hand flick, and freeze.

I glanced at myself in the mirror, making sure my angles looked good and my face was giving *it*.

Chaînés, chaînés, fan kick, step together.

Pursing my lips, I gave the next walks all the attitude I had.

Front battement, side battement, coupé, and tilt.

Here was the big finish. With my arms out to prepare, I took a deep breath and made sure to keep my spot, hold my center, and nailed a clean double pirouette before jumping out and in, striking my fists in the same direction. After stretching up tall in relevé, I tipped my body to the side and hit the final pose with my face toward the ceiling and arms behind me.

I waited a few beats then straightened as quiet claps sounded to my left.

Miss Amy was there, leaning against the wall by the entrance to the studio from the waiting room. "Looked great. As always."

I sucked air through my teeth, refusing to wince when I made my way toward the mirrors in the front of the room, where I'd positioned my phone on a tripod to self-tape. I stopped the recording and fixed the thin straps of my sports bra, tugging it down a bit, then snapped my leggings back into place at my waist. "The barrel turn felt off."

I could tell she didn't want to agree, but her smile slipped. "Afraid to land it?"

Of course she'd guessed correctly, and I wasn't about to lie to her. She'd know anyway. "Yeah."

I had completely healed from my injury, and even though I'd finally been released from my PT a few weeks ago, I still shorted some movements, subconsciously afraid to land wrong.

Removing my phone from the holder, I walked over to Miss Amy, my dance teacher since I was three. She was about six inches shorter than me, with a pixie cut dyed blond and a big smile. She hadn't changed much, other than the wrinkles she now sported and the fact that she was my boss. For the time being, at least.

I pressed play on the video, and we both watched as I completed the short audition routine. "What do you think? Do I need another take?"

"You look strong. Technique is sharp," she said, and I could hear the *but* coming. She tilted her head back to meet my eyes. "Do you really want to dance on a cruise ship?"

I huffed and let my shoulders slump as I removed my Split-flex character shoes. Barefoot, I made my way back to the center of the mirror, and it felt so good to press my feet flat against the floor. I needed to stretch. Whether the pain was phantom or not, I still felt it.

Miss Amy followed, her silence speaking volumes.

I folded up the tripod. "I don't have much of a choice."

"Of course you do." She extended her hand, gesturing to the whole of the dance studio. My second home during my childhood. This was the place where I gained confidence. Where I took out my frustrations. Where I found who I was.

"You could stay," she said. "Teach here. Take over."

Miss Amy had danced professionally throughout the '70s and '80s and moved into choreography when music videos became a *thing*. Her most well-known credit was as a dancer in *Footloose*. And yes, Kevin Bacon was exactly as amazing in real life as you'd think, she always said.

She'd eventually married and moved to West Chester, Pennsylvania, where she opened Rhythm Nova Dance Studio in the '90s after she had her two sons. I think Miss Amy had always wanted this exact thing—me taking over for her—but I'd never considered it seriously. I hadn't planned on staying here. Even this long. "I can't."

"Why not?"

I looked around. To the corner with the stereo system that was decades old. To the framed pictures of classes past, some including me. To the decals of tap and ballet shoes on the side wall. To the scuffed black vinyl floor where I'd shed literal blood, sweat, and tears.

"Because…" I swallowed past the lump in my throat. I didn't know the word for it. For needing something as much as I needed air. Performing made me who I was. Without it, I had nothing. I *was* nothing. "Because I have nothing else."

Miss Amy huffed. "Oh, come on, Evie."

Resting my hands on my hips, I pointed and flexed each foot in turn. "I don't have anyone here."

"You have me. Am I no one?"

"No, but you know what I mean."

She crossed her arms, brows narrowed. It would not be gloating to say I had been Miss Amy's favorite student. Also that I was possibly the best dancer to pass through these doors. She was the one to push me to go to New York. She'd encouraged me my whole life. So to have her talking me out of auditioning felt like a knife to the heart.

"Shouldn't you be telling me to get back on the horse?" I crossed my arms too. "Not give up on my dreams."

"I would never tell you to give up," she said with a tinge of astonishment. "Especially if it's something you really want." She released her arms and gripped my elbows so I would do the same. Then she held my hands in hers. "You worked so hard your whole life, and you made it. Can you imagine the number of girls who go to bed at night and dream of doing what you do?"

I nodded. I had been one of those girls. I had been the one in a million to *make it*.

"I was and will always be proud of you. But most of all, I want you to be happy. What happened to you was devastating, I know, which is why I'm asking you… Do you really want to dance on a cruise ship? Because if you do, then I want you to audition." She momentarily let go of my hand to gracefully flit her fingers through the air. "I know you won't have trouble landing the job. That's not the issue." Then she squeezed my hands together once again. "I want you to be happy. Wherever you are. Whatever you're doing, I want you to be happy."

I fought a quivering lip to smile, and she patted my shoulder. "I'll be in the office doing some work. Let me know if you need anything."

Fearing I'd give myself away if I answered verbally, I nodded and turned toward the mirror, blinking my eyes to clear them.

Staring at my reflection, I asked myself if I really *wanted* to dance on a cruise ship.

No, not really.

Who wanted to be stuck on a floating deathtrap?

I had seen *Titanic*.

I knew how it ended.

But I didn't have a whole lot of other options.

Growing up here hadn't been bad. It wasn't like my story was all that different from many other people with divorced parents who didn't get along and a school experience with a boy who broke my heart and a best friend who wasn't my best friend anymore.

But I always had dance.

When my parents screamed at each other, I closed my eyes and practiced the steps in my head.

When my boyfriend cheated on me with my best friend, I ran to the studio, where I took out my frustration and sadness on the floor.

When I didn't have anyone or anything else, I had dance.

It was the only skill I possessed. I couldn't go from the lights of the stage to those of an office. Or, more accurately, I didn't *want* to.

Miss Amy was right. I had achieved the dream, and I wasn't ready to let go of it yet.

I'd given myself until after the recital to find another job. To put my injury behind me and get myself back onstage, where I belonged.

Six weeks, that was all the time I had left on this self-imposed deadline. So, I'd take what I could get, cruise ship or Vegas or… amusement park parade.

But at least I had the possibility of finding my own Jack Dawson on a cruise ship. He could hand me my Dramamine pills and hold my hair back while I puked.

THREE
GENEVIEVE

pushed my hair back behind my ear, those few pesky strands by my temple refusing to stay put since they'd only ever been tamed by multiple bobby pins and an entire can of hair spray.

Nate sidled up next to me. "How's it going? You need anything?"

I smiled up at my older brother. "I'm good."

"You let me know."

"Yeah, yeah. Of course. Go away."

He shot me a playful look of warning before heading back to the kitchen. Nate had opened this place a few years ago. It wasn't quite a dive bar but also wasn't anything close to upscale, and since I'd been strapped for cash, he'd given me a job tending bar the last few weeks.

Walt's was named for our grandfather, Walter Kozlowski, a Polish immigrant who'd achieved the American Dream with a family and enough money to leave his grandchildren a little start-up funding. Nate had used that money to open Walt's, while I'd used it to subsidize my living expenses in Manhattan. Hindsight was twenty-twenty, but I probably should've put the money into a high-interest account—like my father told me to do

—instead of spending it at my favorite brunch spot on the Lower East Side with my best friend, Josie. Although I made okay money during the season, I sustained myself on side gigs, a few teaching jobs, and Grandpa Walt's nest egg, which was now completely depleted. It was one of the reasons why I was still here, saving up as much as I could before I left again.

I tugged on my black uniform shirt with Walt's logo in big white lettering then finished filling the order of tequila shots for the trio of twentysomethings probably barely out of college. They'd stuffed the jukebox full of Olivia Rodrigo songs before staking claims on their stools at the bar, hell-bent on "finding dick" tonight.

Good luck to them.

I never had much of it when it came to finding dick.

I hadn't attended college, so I'd missed out on parties, and by the time I came of legal drinking age, I didn't have the time or energy to spend on late nights and morning hangovers. Now that I was older, the time for those experiences had passed me by, and I was working behind the bar as opposed to sitting at it, catching a dark gaze across the room.

Walt's was narrow and long with enough room for booths to line one wall and high-top tables in the front windows opposite it. There was also a small stage in the corner that was used for trivia nights and the occasional live band. In the middle was the rectangular bar, where Miguel and I were currently working, until Tabitha would come in later to take over for me. Tab was a much better bartender than I was and always closed. I usually worked the quieter early afternoon shifts, but I'd recently picked up Friday nights. I mostly filled beers and shots since I could never remember the ratios for mixed drinks. Miguel was constantly rolling his eyes about how much money I gave away with my pours.

Swiping a tip from the back corner of the bar, I checked the time on the digital clock on the wall as a group of three white guys ambled in. The chubby one with a bushy beard and sandy hair in a bun pointed to the two open seats directly across from me, seeing as they were the only ones available at the bar. He sat and dragged over the laminated beer list. The second man, who was clean-cut save for a mop of wavy hair, claimed the second stool. I started toward them for their order as I laid my eyes on the third guy. He remained standing, although I was sure even if he sat down, he'd still have a good half a foot on me. He had to be at least six-two, with the shadow of a beard and green eyes that seemed to glow dangerously under an unforgiving brow.

"What can I get for you?"

The blond tipped his head to the side. "Do I know you?"

"I doubt it," I said, trying to rein in my irritation. "What can I get for you?"

He shook his finger at me. "No, really. You look familiar, but I haven't seen you around here at all."

I pressed my hands into the bar, my shoulders up by my ears. There was no way those lines actually worked on people.

"Do those lines really work for you?" the third one asked, backhanding his friend's shoulder, and I bit back a smile. Then I met his eyes, boring into me, and I was momentarily stunned, my heartbeat in my ears. He didn't move, didn't blink, a severe statue.

When I eventually forced my gaze lower, I couldn't help but notice his mouth. His lips were parted, revealing bright white teeth with sharp incisors, and my skin broke out in goose bumps. Between the mouth, eyes, and hair so dark it was almost black, he reminded me of a jungle predator. I tried not to shiver and turned back to the man still trying to place me.

"Yeah, I'm originally from here but was away for a long time," I said. "What can I get you to drink?"

He snapped his fingers. "Are you Nate's sister?"

I narrowed my brows. "Yes…?"

"I knew it. I told you you look familiar. I'm Jude Gray." He pressed his hand to his chest. "I graduated high school with your brother. We're old friends."

"Oh." I nodded, though I had no recollection. "Right."

He grinned as if he knew I was lying. "I'm sorry. What's your name again?"

"Genevieve."

"Of course. I'm so sorry I forgot." Jude smiled, bobbing his head. "Where's Nate?"

I glanced over my shoulder toward the kitchen, and when I brought my attention back to the men, the jungle cat was staring at me, eyes tapered to slits.

"Let me go check." A ghost of some emotion zipped through me, a mixture of fear and anticipation, similar to what I'd felt every night before I went onstage, and I practically sprinted away. I darted around the counter of the kitchen to the office, which had a couple of hooks to hang personal belongings, a little desk with an iPad, and two chairs for staff to take five.

My brother was typing out a text message on his cell phone, his feet up like he had nothing better to do.

"Well, it's nice to know you work so hard around here."

Without taking his focus off his screen, he extended his middle finger. There was only one person he would ignore everyone and everything else for.

"Tell me you're not texting Denise."

"I'm not texting Denise," he said.

"Nate," I sighed, but he didn't bother responding. "Seriously?"

"Stay out of it," he mumbled then jabbed his thumb on the screen, sending off a bible-length text message.

Nate had been dating this woman for a few months, and it'd seemed like they were getting pretty serious, until one morning my brother discovered Denise's roommate was actually her husband. It had been over a month, and Nate still wanted to work it out with her. But as far as I knew, she had dropped him like a hot potato once the truth came out.

I waited until he pocketed his phone to tell him, "Some guy's out there asking about you."

"Who is it?"

I pivoted away. "I'm not your personal assistant."

He was on my heels as I skirted back through the kitchen. "If you were, you'd be more helpful."

"I'm quitting."

"No, you're not," he said because I quit approximately three times per shift.

"Yes, I am." I stepped back behind the bar.

"No, you're staying. Hey!" Nate made his way to the trio of guys, clasping hands with each one. "What's up, boys?"

"We're here 'cause he got that book deal," Jude told my brother while pointing to the wavy-haired one.

"No shit!" Nate hugged the one with the apparent book deal. "Congratulations."

Since I didn't have any idea what was going on, I turned to the jungle cat. "Do you know what you want?"

"Yeah." He leaned on the bar, his biceps bugling with the movement. My gaze reflexively dropped to his forearms, muscular and veiny. "We're going to have the Hazy IPA and a Guinness," he said, obviously knowing his friends' orders, "and is that a seasonal Sam Adams?" He tipped his chin toward the taps. When I nodded, he pointed to it. "I'll have one of those, please."

"Coming right up." I spun away from him and his eyes and filled their beers, though my neck prickled with a sensation like I was being watched.

My stomach rolled with those stage-fright nerves again. I could only ever rid them by going out onstage and doing my thing, and I supposed that was what I had to do now. Face down the panther. I returned to the corner of the bar, where Nate had pulled all three of the men into conversation—my brother, the mayor.

I snagged the panther's gaze when he did a double take at me, and I offered him my stage smile. He dragged a big hand down his jaw, and I swore I could hear the bristles against his fingers, before he offered me the slightest curve of his lips. I didn't know if it could be categorized as a smile, but it had me dropping my stage façade anyway. I gave him my real grin, which was a lot less teeth and a little more crooked. In exchange, his lips pursed, his eyes shifting to slits again as if he was studying me for his next meal, and my cheeks heated, skin tingled.

"Hey." Nate lifted his hand to call for my attention then pointed to his old friend. "Evie, you remember Jude, right?"

I lifted a shoulder, and Jude laughed congenially at my lack of memory. "We were just catching up."

Nate gestured to the other two guys. "And this is Liam and Dylan."

Liam saluted me with his Guinness while Dylan peered steadily at me.

"Nice to meet you, Genevieve," he said, all smooth and silky. Better to catch his prey, I assumed.

I swallowed down the quaver in my voice. "You guys didn't go to our high school."

I sure as shit would remember someone like Dylan. Even a dozen years after graduation.

Liam shook his head. "No. The three of us—" he toggled his head between Jude and Dylan on either side of him "—met about two years ago and started coming here to hang out."

Jude smacked Nate's arm. "Because my best buddy here always gives us free drinks."

"You wish. But since we're celebrating O'Neil's book, it's on the house tonight."

Jude drummed his hands on the bar a few times as Nate laughed. Liam lifted his beer in a cheers, but Dylan was rather stoic.

"What have you been up to since you graduated high school?" Jude asked me. "Three years after us, right?"

I nodded and, out of habit, pressed the toe of my sneaker into the floor, circling my ankle, ignoring the dull ache. "I was working in New York City."

"What're you doing back here?"

When I didn't answer, because of the sudden pressure in my chest, Nate threw his arm around me. "Working for me."

I elbowed him off me as a crash sounded in the kitchen, like a couple of plates smashed.

"I better go take care of that. I'll be back," Nate said to his friends, and then to me, he added, "Get them whatever they want."

That had Dylan swiping a palm over his mouth, smothering what looked like wicked amusement, and I immediately thought about giving him plenty of things that were not on the menu. Maybe he was too.

And I dropped my chin toward my chest, wishing I hadn't cut my hair short. I'd at least have had some cover with my old, shoulder-length hair. This bob did nothing to hide my blush.

Nate stalked back to the kitchen, and I lifted my attention, splitting it between Jude and Liam. "So, food?"

Liam nodded. "Yeah, I could go for something."

I slid the kitchen menu in front of them, which listed the few offerings of the usual fried fare.

"I'll take an order of the sweet-and-spicy wings," Jude said without looking at it.

I tapped it into the POS system. "Anything else?"

"Order of fries," Liam added.

I glanced to Dylan, and he shrugged. "I'm gonna pick off their plates."

Liam absently swatted at him, his eyes on one of the televisions. "The hell you will."

Although he didn't smile or laugh, Dylan elbowed Liam then leaned in toward me. "What's your favorite?"

I instinctively leaned in too. I supposed this might be what it felt like to see someone at a bar you wanted to take home. This was what I'd missed for all those years.

Too bad, I was *behind* the bar.

"The crab dip is pretty good," I offered.

"Yeah. I'll take that." He quickly and gently patted my hand. "Thanks."

I finished putting in the order and moved on to serve other patrons, working for the next fifteen minutes on ignoring that corner of the bar.

By the time their orders were up, another stool had been made available, and Dylan had nabbed it, bringing him closer to my eye level. Close enough that I could see how his left eyebrow was slightly more angled down than his right, like he was permanently skeptical.

I set down their plates of food, along with napkins and utensils. Dylan's index finger brushed along the outside of my palm when he reached for them, and I didn't know if he noticed. I certainly did.

"Enjoy your food. Let me know if you need anything else."

I circled away from them to clean up some dirty glasses and take a few orders, needing to fill a draft at the taps, and my attention drifted to Dylan, where he had his elbows on the bar, listening to his friends. His T-shirt revealed deeply tanned skin, as if he spent a lot of time outside, and I literally paled in comparison.

After delivering a fresh beer to the older gentleman at the other end of the bar, I closed out another group. While the receipt printed, I chanced a peek at Dylan, and it was the worst possible time because I couldn't look away. Not when he had his thumb in his mouth, sucking something off it before licking his index finger. Catching a glimpse of his tongue had me hot all over, and I dragged in a ragged breath.

This was ridiculous. I had worked with fit, good-looking guys before, some of them even better-looking than Dylan. So why this particular guy had my skin pebbling with attraction, I wasn't sure.

As I was on my way to check on other patrons, he lifted his

fingers, the ones that had been in his mouth mere minutes ago, and said, "Genevieve, can I get another, please?"

Oh. Right. *That* was why.

Those eyes. That voice. Those long, thick fingers.

"Sure." I grabbed him a refill and slid it onto the bar.

"You work here every night?" he asked, accepting the glass from me.

"Usually a few afternoons, but last week, I started Friday nights too."

"You like it?"

I lifted one shoulder. "Could be worse."

He tipped his head to the side in a deliciously intimidating move, like he was getting ready to pounce. "That's true with everything, I guess."

I found my courage and asked, "You come here a lot?"

He nodded once.

"I've never seen you before."

"I've never seen you either," he said, and with the way he was looking at me, it seemed like he wanted to *see* a lot more of me. "I knew Koz had a sister, but I didn't realize…"

When his sentence trailed off, I was desperate to know what the end was.

Realize I was home.

Realize I worked here.

Realize… "What?"

He lifted a careless shoulder. "I didn't realize someone as ugly as him could be related to someone so pretty."

I curled my lips between my teeth, biting back a smile. It was tempting. Real tempting. To stand there and talk more, but I had a job to do.

I cleared my throat. "Let me know if you need anything else."

His only acknowledgment was a flick of his eyes down my body, and I spun away, tending to the other patrons.

The next time I glanced in his direction, he was angled

toward his friends like he was listening to them, but his gaze was on me.

I flushed hot and told Miguel I was taking a five-minute break.

When I returned, I swept down the length of the bar, checking on everyone to see what they needed. Dylan stopped me with his hand out, easing closer to me, lowering his voice, and I found myself sinking down on the bar as he said, "Can I ask you something?"

"Yeah," I breathed.

"I was talking to my friends the other day."

I raised my brow, unsure where he was going with this.

"About dating apps," he clarified, and I started to back away, but he reached out to me, briefly touching my hand to keep me in my place. "You ever use one? Of the apps, I mean."

I shook my head. In my previous life, I hadn't had a whole lot of time for relationships, and even if I had, the idea of swiping right or left didn't appeal to me.

Pitching his head toward his two buddies, he said, "Got me thinking that maybe they aren't all they're cracked up to be." His attention fell to where the tips of our fingers met on the bar. "Maybe it's better to get to know someone by talking instead of over the phone, you know?"

When he lifted his chin, his eyes back on me, I nodded since I couldn't answer with all the cotton in my mouth.

"So," he said slowly, his gaze never wavering from mine, "I was wondering if you would tell me what time you get off tonight. We could talk for a little while."

This was it. My moment to finally experience what I'd missed, what those twentysomethings did when they were "finding dick."

I could either take it and run, or disappear, what it felt like I'd been doing these past few months. I didn't want to disappear. I wanted to step back into the spotlight. What better way to do it than with *this* man?

"Nine," I told him, tamping down a smile as I backed away. "I get off at nine."

After having my career ripped away from me, I could at least give myself this much.

"Excuse me," someone said from down the bar.

And when I moved to serve the other patron, I swore I heard Jude say, "*Those* lines really work for you?"

FOUR
DYLAN

Jude, Liam, and I shot the shit for a while, all of us slowly slipping our second beers before moving on to water as Genevieve hung close by our corner. We chatted aimlessly while she filled drink orders until her brother wandered back out to chat with us. Then she tossed me a look as if she actually had to work instead of send me flirtatious glances and hightailed it to the other end of the bar.

And I had a real hard time keeping my focus off her ass.

Jude was the first to leave when he received a text from his mother-in-law informing him Amelia wasn't feeling well. Liam left shortly after with a pat to my back, and then it was just me. Watching Genevieve work.

Nate's brows narrowed, having caught where my attention landed, but he said nothing about it as he gave me a dap and a slap on the shoulder. "See you later, Matthews."

I kept my gaze on his sister. "Later."

When I'd walked in here tonight, I wasn't looking for anything. No woman to flirt with, let alone to spend any one-on-one time with. This was Dads' Night Out. I didn't expect to find a dark-haired beauty behind the bar. She was long-limbed and pale with glittering blue eyes and hair cut bluntly below her chin, but it was the way she carried herself that made me literally stop in my tracks. She was…elegant, sparkly almost. A shiny diamond, and I couldn't take my eyes off her.

Especially her mouth with ruby-red lipstick.

I knew I was coming in hot off the blocks by asking her to hang out after meeting her literally three hours ago, but I was basically doing what my friends told me to. Putting the apps away and meeting someone in person, right?

It wasn't my fault if that person was Genevieve, Nate's sister.

I also couldn't help that she was disarmingly pretty and had an even prettier blush whenever she noticed I was staring at her.

And I had a sudden itch that needed scratching.

She tucked a few stray hairs behind her ear and handed drinks over to a couple of young guys who were clearly flirting with her. It wasn't like I had any place to be upset because she was doing her job. But then one of those douchebags said something that made her laugh, and she lifted her chin to let out a soft chuckle, revealing a tiny mole behind her ear, and I had an irresistible urge to kiss it. She lifted her hand, as if telling them goodbye, and pivoted my way, holding up her index and middle fingers, mouthing, "Two minutes."

I nodded as a knot formed in my stomach. I hadn't felt the pregame butterflies for a woman in a long time. Yet Genevieve had me worked up like it was my first time on the field, especially when she waltzed out from the back with a zip-up hoodie on and a purse looped over her shoulder, smiling sweetly at me. "So…"

"So," I started, standing up. "Want to head out?"

She nodded, and we made our way outside, where we stopped in the middle of the sidewalk. "Normally, I'd ask if you wanted to grab a drink, but…"

"Yeah. Hazards of the job, I guess."

I circled my finger between us. "You run into this hazard a lot?"

"Never."

There was no way. "Never?"

Her top teeth bit into her lower lip as she shook her head.

"I don't believe you," I told her, and when she shot me a dubious look, I waved down the length of her body. "You have seen *you*, right?"

She popped a hand on her hip. "Contrary to what you may think, most people tend bar for the money, not for the hookups."

I bent my knees, lowering the few inches to meet her eye-to-eye. "You admit it, then? This is a hookup."

"Oh my god." She plastered her hands to her face as she whirled away from me with a laugh. "I'm leaving. Goodbye."

I caught her wrist, tugging her back to me. "I'm sorry," I said, completely unapologetic. "I'm in shock, that's all."

"Why? You're shocked your charms have worked?"

I might've been more amiable and approachable when I was younger, but I didn't spend a whole lot of time charming women now. It wasn't something I was interested in doing. All I needed was a few hours, and most women didn't care that the majority of my personality was surly asshole.

I planted my feet on the outside of hers, trying on a cocky smirk. "Charms, eh?"

She dropped her head back to her shoulders, exposing that mole again. "Honestly. For my first foray into this whole thing, I'm regretting it already."

"Wait, wait, wait." I leaned into her. "First foray?" I dropped my voice. "Into what? Sex?"

She pushed my shoulder with enough force that I had to step back, but I took hold of her hand as she said, "No, not sex. I mean, this..." She wore big pearl earrings and played with the one in her right ear. "This whole...one-night-stand thing."

"Right." I nodded, my stomach swooping. That was what I wanted, and yet I couldn't quite put my finger on it, the reason my heart rate spiked. Or why a wave of displeasure washed over me when she plainly stated what we were doing here.

A one-night stand.

"But, um, do you want to come to my place?"

I answered immediately. "Yeah, definitely."

She smiled, if a little timidly, so I took my time raising my hand between us, giving her a moment to say no if she wanted to. When she didn't, I curved my fingers around her shoulder, adjusting the strap of her purse. "We could go get something to eat instead," I offered with a shrug, providing her an out. "Or something else. Whatever you want to do."

Taking me by surprise, she leaned up and kissed my cheek, by the corner of my mouth. "I want you to come home with me."

"Okay," I said, because who was I to argue with the lady?

"I'm parked over there."

"I'm right here." I motioned to my SUV. "I can follow you."

She agreed and moved as if to walk away but stopped abruptly. "Just to be sure, you don't have a girlfriend or wife or anything, right?"

"I have an ex-wife, but none currently."

Her gaze dropped down to my left hand.

"I promise," I said. "I am nothing if not honest."

She met my eyes, her head bobbing. "Okay, and I trust you're not a serial killer since you're friends with my brother."

I tucked my hands into my pockets. "I would actually be more suspicious of your brother's acquaintances. I'm sure you know about D—"

"Denise! Yes! She's the absolute worst. Why is he so hung up on her?"

"I have no idea." Nate was holding out hope that she would leave her husband for him. Because, according to him, what they had was "special." Real fucking special if she was going home to her husband every night. "Your brother's living on a different planet."

She laughed, and I actually felt a smile tugging at my mouth. I kept to one-night stands because they were easy, and with this small commonality between us, it already felt like more. But I wasn't panicked about it.

It made me want her more.

"So, definitely not a serial killer," I said, holding up my hands.

"Good." Then she strutted away, and I had to force myself to stop staring at her ass in her tight jeans and get in my car.

Her apartment was in a two-story brick complex about ten minutes away, and I parked in her one visitor spot before snagging a condom from the box in my glove compartment. We didn't say anything to each other as I followed her inside and upstairs, where she unlocked her door. She flicked on the lights then closed the door behind us.

I surveyed her scant decorations. "How long have you been here?"

"A few months." She shucked off her hoodie and hung it on the back of one of the chairs at the small circular dining table. "I know it looks like someone just moved in. Nate tells me so all the time."

I shrugged. Most women had trinkets and framed photos, candles, and those wooden signs that said something like *Live Your Dreams*. Genevieve had bare walls, a rug, a faded sofa, and a TV.

"You want something to drink? Water or a soda?" she asked.

"Water's good." I met her in the kitchen, where I noticed a picture stuck to her fridge under a magnet. A group of women were all bunched together, with their hair slicked back and wearing red lipstick, like they were a cheer squad or something. It took me a second to locate Genevieve in the photo. She stood in the back, hand on her hip and head tilted to the side. But then real-life Genevieve reached her arm up to a cabinet above her head, her T-shirt rising a few millimeters. I took advantage and skimmed my hand along her side.

She let out an audible breath, thumping two glasses down on the counter like I surprised her.

"Is this okay?" I asked, and she nodded, moving to bring us closer together. When I brought my other hand to her waist, squeezing gently, her eyes flared.

"You're kind of intimidating, you know that?" she said, tracing her finger along the muscle at my shoulder.

"You think so?"

"Yeah, you have this…thing about you."

"Thing about me?"

"*It* factor."

"It factor?" I couldn't keep the corner of my mouth from twitching. "What does that even mean?"

"That's the point. You can't name it. There's something undefinable about you."

"I thought the same. I saw you and…" I had trouble finding better words besides, "I thought you glowed, were all sparkly and bright."

Maybe that was why this time felt special. Because I was so attracted to her. *Wildly* attracted to her. A can't-stop-gawking, punch-in-the-gut kind of attraction.

When she blushed, I stroked her cheek. My fingertips were callused and probably not even worthy of touching her soft skin, but I relished the difference. I brought my hand to the nape of her neck, dipping my face down to kiss her, though she slanted her head so my lips landed on her jaw.

I backed away from her. "We can just hang out, watch TV if you want. We don't need to do anything."

"No." She fisted my T-shirt, keeping me close. "No, I want to." Her eyes drifted back and forth between my own before she threw her attention to the side for a few seconds. "But I feel like I need to get to know you better." She bit into her lip, and I dragged my thumb under it until she released it from her teeth. "You want to play twenty questions?"

"Sure." I leaned against the sink, opposite her, and folded my arms and ankles. I was down for whatever made her comfortable. "You first."

She opened the refrigerator to retrieve a water filter pitcher. "Where'd you grow up?"

"Flagstaff, Arizona."

Her eyebrows arched. She was probably surprised I was living on the other side of the country now.

"I know this is your hometown," I said, "so I'll ask if you've ever traveled outside the US."

"I went to Paris with a school trip the summer before senior year."

I accepted the water from her. "How was that?"

"Uh-uh." She smiled behind her own glass, and Christ, she was pretty. "My turn. What did you want to be when you were little?"

"A baseball player. So, how was your trip to Paris?"

"Amazing." She closed her eyes, and I assumed she was back there in her mind. "The lights, the food, the people. I loved it." When she set her gaze on me again, it was dazzling, and the impulse to make her eyes glitter like that for a whole different reason overwhelmed me. I tightened my grip on my glass as she asked, "Do you have any siblings?"

"A sister, Haley." I took a gulp of water then crossed over to her, setting my cup on the counter. "Is your favorite color red?"

"No. Why?"

I stared at her mouth and ran my tongue over my lower lip. Her own tongue did the same to her lip, and my dick stirred beneath my jeans. "Your lipstick."

"Oh." She shifted her feet. "No, I always wore it for work." Then she cleared her throat. "Do you pick up random women from bars a lot?"

"No." Which was true. She was the first woman since my divorce that I'd met in person and wanted to get naked as soon as possible. I placed my hand next to her hip against the counter. "My turn. You already said you don't use dating apps. Does that mean you've had a lot of boyfriends?"

She shook her head. "I never had much time for a relationship. I worked a lot, and it was hard to meet someone. What about you?"

"I was married for seven years." I hooked my index finger around her belt loop. "Are you nervous?"

Her throat bobbed with a swallow, and I trailed my eyes back up to her face when she said, "A little," and then, "Do you have a lot of one-night stands?"

"I wouldn't say *a lot*." Which, again, was true. Even though I didn't want a relationship, it wasn't like I was with different women every weekend. Only on the rare occasions I had the time and energy to seek it out. Which made tonight even more different. I hadn't planned, been looking for, or even wanted a release tonight.

Until I saw her.

Genevieve pursed her lips, seemingly appeased by my answer. I wondered if that red color would rub off if I kissed her. Imagined where else it would look good. "Do you remember what number question we're up to?"

"No idea."

"In that case…" I lifted her onto the counter, settling between her spread knees. "I'm going to kiss you now."

But she shocked me by curling her hands around my neck and pressing her mouth to mine. I cupped her ass, bringing her flush against me, but otherwise let her drive for now. Her lips were supple, her tongue hot and wet as it slid against mine. She nipped down my jaw to my throat, her fingers dragging across my chest, her short nails scratching over my shirt, and I tightened my hold on her as I grew hard between her thighs. When she let out a little moan, her legs wrapping around my waist, my patience snapped.

I gripped the hair at the back of her head with my right hand, holding her so I could lick at her throat and that mole by her ear, while I sank the fingers of my left hand below the waistband of her jeans. I could feel she wore a thong and plucked at it, teasing my middle finger at the top of the seam of her backside. She wiggled against me, and I breathed my words into her skin. "Where's your bedroom?"

"Down the hall on the left."

FIVE
GENEVIEVE

Dylan followed my directions, carrying me to the bedroom, and he bumped the door open with his elbow. I reached out to knock the light on before going back to pawing at his chest. He'd been so sweet with me, playing along with my questions, though he never lost the glint in his eyes, like he was lulling me into a sense of security to set the trap.

And I happily sashayed right in.

He lowered me to the bed and grasped the back of his T-shirt to tug it over his head. There was something so masculine about that move, and I loved it. His chest was smooth and contoured, no hair at all, and I dragged my palms over the lines of his abdomen, barely holding back from scratching my nails down his golden skin.

"I knew it," I said.

He held himself above me, caging me in with his hands and knees. "Knew what?"

"That you're like an animal. A panther or something." I lightly scratched down his back. "All sleek and strong." Then I met his eyes. "And a little bit scary."

In answer, he sank his teeth into my neck, forcing a gasp

from the back of my throat. My hips canted off the bed, and he slid his hands up my torso, molding his palms over my breasts until my nipples were stiff peaks. He took his time, pressing hot, openmouthed kisses all over my throat and chest after he had my shirt and bra off. Every once in a while, he bit into my skin then soothed it with his tongue. He left marks on the undersides of my breasts, my upper biceps, below my belly button. I caught his gaze, and his eyes filled with that predatory gleam as his teeth dragged over me. I couldn't get enough, emitting a whimper of pleasure, and his whisper of a smile was pure sin.

I had a feeling he didn't smile often, but I thought that made what we were doing all the more enticing. I could elicit a grin from him, no matter how small.

When he got to the button of my jeans, he glanced up at me, and once I gave him a nod, he pulled them off, followed immediately by my underwear. I was completely naked, spread out on my comforter, and he stared down at me, shirt off, hands on his hips, his erection thick against his jeans. I was used to people watching me; it had been my job for almost a decade, and I'd certainly lost modesty long ago—living through puberty in leotards and tights and then quick changes for the show. But under his stare, I felt helpless.

Perspiration gathered at the back of my neck as my skin pebbled with goose bumps, and he licked his lips. A man before a feast.

"How long has it been?" I asked, because he truly did look starving.

"Twenty questions, still?"

I nodded and raised my arms above my head. His gaze followed the movement then slowly trailed back down to my face, lower to my breasts, and even lower between my thighs.

"How long has it been since I've been with someone? 'Bout three months, I think. How long for you?"

"A long time. Over a year. I went out on a few dates with this guy who was the nephew of one of my mom's friends. It didn't end up well."

He huffed out a response I couldn't understand as he shoved my thighs apart.

"What?" I asked, meeting his eyes over the valley of my torso.

"Why not?" he asked, and I blurted my first thought.

"He was too gentle, too soft."

If this was my chance to make up for the time I'd lost, I wasn't going to screw it up. I was going to be bold and honest and ask for what I wanted before I was relegated back behind the bar. Back to the life I didn't expect or want, back to the unlucky hand I'd been dealt.

Dylan let out a noise that sounded like a growl of appreciation as he scraped his jaw on the sensitive skin of my inner thigh and spread me wide open with his fingers to drag his tongue up my center. There was nothing gentle or soft about the way he used his lips and teeth on me, repeatedly stopping as I was close to going over the edge, only to nip at my legs or stomach. Then he'd start the process all over again.

"Oh god," I moaned, tugging at the sheets.

"Still scared of me?" he murmured against my skin, and when I shook my head, he slapped my clit. And—*dear god, yes*—I threw my head back, moaning. "Maybe you should be," he said and slapped my oversensitized flesh one more time.

I whimpered, already breathless. "You're going to kill me."

"Not yet," he murmured against me, and a tremor coasted down my spine.

He lifted one hand to my breast, rolling my nipple between his fingers as he worked my pussy over with his other hand, all the while still licking and sucking at my clit. He was nothing if not highly dexterous, and I was his willing play toy.

"Genevieve," he rasped, and I only ever wanted him to say my name for the rest of my life. "Do you know what my new favorite thing is?"

I panted, shaking my head back and forth, my body acting of its own accord as it tensed and flexed under his hands and mouth. My heart raced as the first wave of my orgasm crested over me.

"That," he said, and I could barely hear him with the blood rushing in my ears. "Watching you come is my new favorite thing." He crawled over me, color high in his cheeks, his lips shining with my arousal. "Will you do it again for me?"

I pushed my hair back from my forehead. "Is that part of twenty questions or more of a command?"

He bent his head down, sucking on one nipple and then the other. My breasts were small, but he touched them like they were the best things he'd ever seen. I writhed under him, and he let go of me with an audible pop. "Let's agree to call it a request." Then he nudged me over so he could roll to his back. "And now I need you to take off my pants."

When I laughed, he arched his brow and reached out one long arm to grip my hair, forcing me to his mouth, swallowing the sound.

I melted into the kiss, enjoying the rhythm we found with our tongues, before he let go of me so I could remove his jeans, revealing muscular thighs dusted in dark hair, and black boxer briefs.

"Dylan," I said, slipping my hand beneath the elastic of his underwear to feel the hard, thick length of him, "what's your middle name?" He didn't answer right away, so I shifted to straddle him, pushing the cotton down to stroke his cock, and he tipped his head up to the ceiling, eyes closed. I pouted playfully. "You don't want to play anymore?"

His abs clenched when I swiped my thumb over the head. "What was the question?"

"What's your middle name?" I repeated, scooting back to swirl my tongue around him.

His eyes snapped open, dark and piercing. "It's whatever you want it to be as long as you keep licking me."

Then his hand was on my neck, directing me with tight squeezes for the tempo he wanted. After a few minutes, he towed me back up to him and skimmed his thumb over my bottom lip. "It didn't come off."

I shook my head in confusion until it dawned on me. "Oh. It's lip stain. Stays on better than lipstick."

He frowned. "I was kinda hoping there'd be red all over my dick."

I snorted a laugh, covering it with my hand, but he pulled my fingers away to kiss me again, nipping at my lips like he was really trying to smear it. But he'd never manage it. This red had been tested over the years.

After one more lick to my lips, he stood to kick off his underwear and procured a condom from the pocket of his jeans before prowling back to me.

"What were you like in school?" I asked, tracing the veins in his arm with my index finger when he was close enough.

"Super popular." He kneeled between my legs as he tore at the silver wrapper. "I played baseball, and that's pretty much all I cared about. What were you like?"

"Quiet." I watched as he covered the glistening tip of his cock and rolled down the condom. My core clenched reflexively. "I had a few good friends, but other than that, I pretty much minded my own business."

Once he was sheathed, he sank down to lick me one more time between my legs then lined himself up at my entrance. "Any other questions before I make you come again?"

I shook my head, drawing my knees up to my sides, and he grunted as he sank into me. He had to inch himself in and out a few times, and my breath hitched at the snug fit of him. But when he was completely seated in me, he stilled as if giving me a few moments to adjust. "You okay?"

"I thought you said no more questions?"

"Such attitude." He smacked the side of my thigh before lifting it up, laying my calf on his shoulder. He rolled his hips, experimenting with different movements, all the while never taking his eyes off mine. I couldn't remember the last time I had sustained eye contact like this in a conversation, let alone during sex. It was intimate and overwhelming and…sexy.

But I didn't have long to consider my feelings because he found the spot that had my back bowing, and he doubled down, moving closer and closer to me until my leg was almost parallel to my body. He didn't seem to notice until he brushed his lips over my jaw.

"Fuck, kitten, you're so tight."

I moaned my answer, and he nipped at me.

"Flexible too." He pointedly stared at the angle of my leg. "I wish I would've known earlier."

"You never asked," I said with as much sass as I could muster, and his eyes narrowed to slits. He tweaked my nipple.

"Again with the attitude." He sucked at my pulse point, his hand moving from my breast to my collarbone, his long fingers gently squeezing the sides of my throat for a minute. As if I needed to know who was in charge here.

I already knew.

I was happy to give it up to him.

With a peck to my jaw, he moved back to a kneeling position, gripping my thighs tightly, holding them open. His thrusts were powerful and controlled, and I would no doubt have evidence of his fingers on me tomorrow.

His jungle-cat stare swept over me. "I like seeing my marks on you."

"It feels good when you put them there."

He rumbled out a sound of approval, his thrusts into me stuttering until he lowered himself to me, cupping my right breast and sucking at a spot near my nipple. He pulled all the way out of me, and I whined at the loss until he moved his other hand between my legs, circling his fingers around my clit, and I was coming again, sparks igniting all over my body. I didn't even have time to catch my breath because he plunged back inside me and light exploded behind my closed lids.

"That's it," he growled in my ear. "My new favorite thing." With a few more pumps, he shuddered and let his weight drop onto me, dropping kisses along my collarbone and shoulder. After a minute, he rolled off to the side of the mattress and grabbed a tissue from my nightstand.

I blew out a breath, gazing down the length of my body to see if I had permanent scars from the flames that had raced across my skin. I'd never had sex that good before. I was thirty years old, and it had taken me until now to have an explosive orgasm. Or, more accurately, two.

As Dylan dealt with the condom, I snagged a pair of sweats and T-shirt from my dresser on the way to the bathroom. I used the toilet and took stock of my appearance in the mirror, finding my lip stain still pretty well on, though my hair was a mess, and I had pink bruises all over from his teeth and stubble. I smiled to myself then covered it up with my clothes and made my way back to my room, where Dylan stood with his jeans on.

He turned, his unrelenting gaze on me once again. I wasn't sure what to do now, and I fidgeted, plucking at my pants. As if he knew, he closed the distance between us in two strides and wrapped his hands around my waist. He kissed the curve of my neck. "What's one thing you hate?"

That question freed the tension I'd been holding, and I had an inkling that his whole brusque intimidating thing was for show. I relaxed into his hold, thinking of my answer. "Traffic." I smoothed my hands around his thick shoulders. "What was your first job?"

"Working as a mechanic. My dad owned a shop, and I helped out on weekends since I can remember."

"Really?"

He nodded. "I think I learned how to change oil before I was even in little league."

I imagined young Dylan with his head buried under the

hood of a car. "That's cute, imagining you in overalls and with grease on your cheeks."

"Cute?" He towed me into him with his fist gathered in the cotton of my shirt, eyes blazing with heat I was now familiar with. "I'm not so sure." He kissed me once then stared at me, his jaw working as if he was about to speak, yet no words left his lips. Instead, he held me close, kissing me again. He teased me with his tongue, his teeth sending tingles between my legs.

"If you don't stop, I'm going to be begging for you to fuck me again," I told him.

His responding growl was nothing short of pleased. But still, he backed away. With his fingers wrapped around my upper arms, he dragged his gaze from my face to my toes and back. And I, for sure, was doing this one-night-stand thing all wrong if I was ready to ask him to stay the night, stay the weekend. Stay as long as he liked.

He leaned down to kiss my cheek, his mouth ghosting over my ear. "That was the most fun I've had in a long time."

"Me too."

He skimmed the tip of his thumb from my pearl earring down my jaw. "Maybe I'll see you around?"

Knowing my self-imposed deadline and impending departure from town was only weeks away, I shrugged. "Probably not."

I swore regret flashed in his green eyes, but I couldn't be positive because he skated his knuckles down my side, over the curve of my breast to the top of my sweats. Then he pulled at the elastic and moved past me. "Sleep well."

I followed him to the door, and he offered me one last kiss before turning away. Yet after only one step, he whirled around and held the nape of my neck to slip his tongue between my lips. He let out a hum, as if he liked the way I tasted, then nibbled my bottom lip. Finally stepping away, he squeezed my chin between his thumb and forefinger. "Honestly," he mumbled as he pivoted, "that mouth…"

"Hey," I called, and he paused with his hand on the railing at the top of the steps. "What's your favorite color?"

He tossed me a look. "Red, obviously."

I bit back a smile. "Bye, Dylan."

"Bye, Genevieve."

SIX

DYLAN

The good thing about owning my own business was that I could, for the most part, make my own hours. The bad thing about owning my own business was that I was the guy in charge, which meant if Mrs. Rabeiro's car wasn't finished tonight, I'd have to hear about it for the next few years of my life as the old bat would never stop complaining. She'd tell everyone who might listen to bring their vehicles over to O'Leary on Sutton Street for their tune-ups instead of here.

"You sure you don't want me to stay, boss?" Greg asked from his place by the door while I had my head buried in Mrs. Rabeiro's red Camry.

"Nah, I'm almost done here. She should be here soon."

"In that case, I'm gettin' the hell outta here," he said with an embarrassed chuckle.

Mrs. Rabeiro verbalized each and every thought that crossed her mind. She thought you looked like shit? She said so. Thought your baby was ugly? She sneered at it. Thought your prices were too high and your work not up to snuff? She not only told you, but also everyone around town. Which was why Greg snatched his stuff and hightailed it out of here. The last time Mrs. Rabeiro had caught Greg alone, she'd told him he could stand to lay off the pie and find better-fitting pants. She was terrible for a person's self-esteem.

I offered Greg a silent wave before double-checking the new belt I'd installed. Mrs. Rabeiro had informed me she was taking a drive up to the Finger Lakes with her friends and needed her car in top shape. I provided her a new serpentine belt, filters, and topped off her coolant, so hopefully she wouldn't be complaining about any more problems with her air conditioning.

After shutting the hood of the car, I swiped my water bottle from the counter and took a long pull, downing almost half of it, before thumbing my phone on, a reminder on the home screen that I needed to get to Scarlett's dance school in twenty minutes. Every Tuesday for the next month and a half, I would be attending class, and I knew Scarlett was pretty jazzed about it. She was excited for me not only to dance with her but to take her out to dinner, like I'd promised, just her and me, before returning her back to her mom's tonight.

Checking the time once more—Mrs. Rabeiro had eight minutes to show up, or I was leaving and she'd be walking to the Finger Lakes—I peeled off my coveralls and washed my hands.

Seven minutes and I opened the color-coded Google calendar on my phone, looking through the next few weeks, my mind taking a walk back to this weekend. To Genevieve.

Again.

Since I'd left her place late Friday night, or super early Saturday morning, depending how you looked at it, I couldn't help but think about her. Those lips haunted my dreams. The remembrance of the marks I'd left on her. I'd wondered if they'd faded by now or if she had any bruises. Then I took some pleasure in imagining at least one was still there.

That particular idea had had me jerking off in the shower this morning.

I *never* repeated performances for fear of falling into a relationship, either accidentally or on purpose. Although, all I'd wanted these last few days was to somehow find her. Quench my thirst. Then maybe I'd be able to function properly once again.

But I hadn't even asked for her phone number, so anything short of hanging out at Walt's, and I wasn't going to see her.

And I didn't know if I liked that idea.

Forcing all thoughts of Genevieve out of my mind, I slid my phone into my pocket and snagged Mrs. Rabeiro's car keys to drive the little red Camry out of the garage bay. Finally, five minutes before I had to leave, the old bird showed up. After running her payment through, I practically hurled the keys at her and pushed her out the door.

I rolled up to the studio with a few minutes to spare. Seeing as how I'd never taken a dance class before, I wasn't sure if I was supposed to bring anything or warm up...maybe do some stretches, touch my toes. But who was I kidding? I couldn't touch my toes. In my younger years, sure. Now? I was lucky to get out of bed without a charley horse.

Making my way inside, I lined up against the wall of the waiting room next to the other special someones. Except for one woman who appeared about my age, the rest were men. I guessed they were dads, although one appeared to be a grandfather, and there was one young kid, maybe in high school or college, probably a sibling. They all sort of smiled nervously at one another, lifting a hand in frightened greeting like they were about to be traded to a losing team.

The door on the right side opened, and a voice called out, "Okay, we're ready for all the special someones to come on in," which was followed by a familiar head of dark hair, a pair of sapphire-blue eyes, and those lips. Still stained red.

I stared at Genevieve in amazement as she greeted each adult crossing into the room where the girls shrieked in delight. I made sure to be the last one, and when she finally turned to me, her grin faded.

"Dylan?"

The tiny hairs all over my body stood on end. This had to be a sign, her being here.

I had been an athlete, and I had my superstitions. Most of all, I trusted my gut.

Right now, my gut was telling me to throw her over my shoulder and take her back to my cave. But I held back.

Barely.

"What're you doing here?" I asked, sticking my tingling hands into my pockets so I didn't curl them around her waist.

"I'm...I'm working." She darted her gaze around as if to make sure we were, indeed, at her place of work. "What are *you* doing here?"

"I'm here for class."

"Class?" She pitched her thumb over her shoulder, her voice low. "You're a *dad*?"

"You're the dance teacher?"

Her throat flushed, and dear Jesus, I wanted to lick her skin.

One night with her was not nearly enough.

"Oh my god," she said, placing her hand to her forehead. "Oh my god, I slept with a *dad*."

"Yeah, you did." I couldn't help it if I sounded smug. "And I'd really like to do it again."

The suggestion was out before I could think better of it, but now that I'd verbalized it, I knew it was absolutely what I wanted. A gut instinct. An innate need.

"*Again*?" She guffawed. "Absolutely not. And who's your kid?"

"Scarlett."

"No," she said after a moment of blinking those blue stunners at me. "We absolutely cannot have anything going on between us." She didn't give me a chance to reply as she gestured into the studio. "I've got a class to run, so if you'll please..."

I dropped it, for now, and made my way over to my daughter, who was grinning at me near the front corner in a light-pink leotard and tights. She wrapped her arms around my leg. "Daddy, you're here!"

I tugged her off me to lift her up so I could kiss her head. "Hey, sweetheart."

"I missed you," she said, squeezing me, because that was her new thing these last few weeks. She missed everything and everyone, even her brother.

"Okay. Let's get started." With a clap, Genevieve strutted to the front of the room, the wall behind her covered in floor-to-ceiling mirrors. Not only did I get an eyeful of the front of her in a plain black leotard that left nothing to the imagination, including her pebbled nipples, but I got a good look at her ass in those tight black pants, which were basically a second skin. As I scanned the room, I couldn't help but notice excited gazes from a few of the other men too, and my chest tightened.

I'd been in her bed days ago. I'd seen every inch of her skin, had marked it with my teeth and scruff. So, no, I didn't like the idea of these guys looking at her like she was their next meal. Or, at the very least, on the menu.

Not that I blamed them. I'd gotten a taste, and fuck, I was desperate for seconds. Thirds. A whole goddamn buffet.

"For those of you who don't know me, I'm Miss Gen," she said, all traces of her previous panic with me gone as she introduced herself with a hand on the delicate line of her collarbone. "I'm excited you're here to participate in our recital, and for you and the girls to make this memory together."

She pointedly ignored me. At least until Scarlett yanked on my hand, whispering loud enough for the whole class to hear, "Daddy, you're dancing in those?"

I, along with everyone else in the room, regarded my boots, and I winced. I'd forgotten about the email we'd received from the director of the dance school with information about class, including instructions to wear sneakers. Genevieve surveyed the room, evidently checking to see if I wasn't the only one who'd forgotten.

I was.

"You should only wear soft-soled shoes in dance studios," she chided with an impatient tone. "Do you have socks on?"

I nodded, and she lifted a brow in a clear direction. She was the one in charge here, and she wanted my shoes off. *Immediately.* I shuffled off to the side and crouched down to remove my boots, while Genevieve sashayed past me, the short heels of her tan shoes clicking with each step.

"We have six weeks for you all to learn this dance, and I know it sounds like a lot, but it really isn't," she said, talking from the back of the room as she fiddled with the stereo system. "I've only got you for three hours total before you have the dress rehearsal and then the recital."

She plugged in her cell phone—the same cell phone with the Manhattan skyline cover that I'd watched her place on her kitchen counter minutes before I'd sat her on it—and pressed something on the screen. Then she tugged a T-shirt over her head as she strutted to the front of the room, covering up all the good bits shown off by her leotard.

I normally went for women with more meat on their bones, but I couldn't stop staring at Genevieve, couldn't stop wanting to touch her again. Feel her under me, over me, however I could get her. Mostly, I wanted her to smile my way. I wanted to bask in her shine.

"Some quick instructions to start." She pointed to different directions of the room. "This is upstage. So when I say go upstage, I mean go to the back." She lifted her hands to the mirrors. "Downstage means toward the front of the stage." Then pointing to the right, she explained, "This is stage right. The actual auditorium will have curtains on both sides of the stage, and to get to stage right, you'll need to walk behind the back curtain since there is no entrance from the hall. And obviously," she went on, grapevining to the left, "this is stage left."

She assigned each pair of dancers a place to stand, telling us to "stay in our windows," then instructed us to "split down the middle, and head to either right or left to enter back onstage to your same spots."

The girls ended up pulling their dance partners to either side as Genevieve stayed in the middle of the room. "I'll count you in, and all you need to do is hold hands and walk to your spot before I get through two counts of eight, okay?"

It wasn't okay at all, but I tried to follow Genevieve's orders for the next twenty minutes.

At the end of class, she switched off the music and circulated around the room high-fiving each girl, with a "good job" or "great work" before smiling at the adults in the room. "I'll see you all next week. We have a lot of work to do."

Everyone filed out, but I hung back, waiting to talk to Genevieve. She positioned herself in the corner by the stereo, clearly trying to avoid me. "Scar," I said, bending down to my daughter, "why don't you go grab your stuff? I've got to put my shoes back on. I'll be out in a minute."

She skipped off, calling out, "Priya, wait for me!"

I stepped into my boots, not even bothering to tie the laces. "It's good to see you again, Genevieve."

"Yeah." She kept her focus on the stereo as her skin began to pinken. That blush set off an automatic response in my body, starting with kicking my pulse into high gear and ending with my blood heading straight to my cock. "I have another class about to come in," she told me.

"I wanted to talk about Friday."

"No."

"No?"

"No," she whisper-shouted, stepping close enough that I could smell her soap, feel the heat radiating from her. "I cannot talk about how we had sex Friday night."

"*Really great* sex," I added, and she rolled her eyes.

"Really great sex." Her face glowed bright red. "But now I found out you're Scarlett's dad."

"So?"

"So…" She waved her hands wildly, apparently at a loss for words.

I wasn't. "I think we should do it again."

"No. I told you. No."

"Why not?" Usually I was the one denying a double dip. I didn't know what to do with this woman refusing me, and if I was honest, it stoked my competitiveness.

She heaved a sigh like I was a stain she couldn't get rid of. This diamond had hard edges. "I…" She dropped her eyes from mine. "You're Scarlett's dad. I'm her teacher. It's inappropriate."

I knew she wasn't telling the truth, and I let my attention drift around the room, to the white walls and photos of past dance classes that hung along the top. I thought I spotted Genevieve in one of them, but I couldn't be sure. "Is there some rule against it or something?" When she didn't answer, I knew I had her, and I bent my knees, forcing her gaze to mine. "Gen, come on, you going to tell me you didn't have fun?"

She bit into her lower lip, and I chanced a touch, tugging it out from under her teeth. Her breath caught, and I guessed I wasn't the only one who'd been thinking about what we'd done all weekend.

"You going to tell me you didn't feel something between us?" She still refused to answer, and I hunched over, closing the few inches between us, breaking her hard shell open with our game. "How tall are you?"

The corner of her mouth twitched. "Twenty questions?"

"It was your idea."

She crossed her arms and turned her foot out, chin lifting proudly. "Five-eight and three-quarters. How tall are you?"

"Six-three and a half. Did you have pets when you were a kid?"

"Dylan," she whined sweetly, standing up to her full 5'8 and ¾". "We can't do this. Your daughter is right out there." She threw her hand toward the door as a trio of middle schoolers strolled in, giggling about something, all three in tights and leotards, and I had a flash of what Scarlett's future would be. They glanced up, blandly eyeing Genevieve and me, before going back to talking about whatever…something about a kid named Garrett.

Garrett was a player, I wanted to warn them. All guys named Garrett were. I was friends with a Garrett in college, and he was basically a walking genital wart. I played with another Garrett in the minors, and he cheated on every girlfriend he had.

"So, later then," I said.

She shook her head and turned on the music, effectively putting a stop to any more conversation. But I wasn't about to give up that easy. I only needed to regroup.

I had to get her alone. Get her out of my system and my head right again.

I didn't need another relationship, but I did need to scratch at this growing and ceaseless itch. From Genevieve's reaction to me, I figured she was feeling the same way.

If we'd be seeing each other for the next six weeks, it seemed like a logical answer to our little situation.

In the waiting room, I held out my hand to Scarlett, with her jacket on and little pink dance bag over her shoulder. "Ready?"

"Ready!"

As we ate dinner at a diner, Scarlett regaled me with the lowdown on kindergarten this week, before we swung by Jude's storefront for a couple bags of candy. Gray's Candy was like an old-school shop straight out of *Charlie and the Chocolate Factory*, and Scarlett chose peach rings and wax bottles, along with some tart lollipops for her brother. That kid would eat anything, including tart lollipops.

He was a brick shithouse.

Once I pulled up to Paige and Neil's house, Scarlett raced ahead of me inside. "Tucker, look what we got you!"

When I entered the living room, Neil glanced up from his spot on the couch and nodded toward me before he said in Scarlett's direction, "Slow down, hon, or you'll trip and fall."

Paige sidestepped our daughter as she walked out of the kitchen. "No running in the house."

"Tuck, look!" Scarlett shouted, ignoring both her mother and Neil to run up the stairs to where their rooms were located.

Paige blew out a breath then looked to me. "How was it?"

"Good."

"I assume she's all hopped up on sugar?" she said in a tone that was only *faintly* condescending. Because *she* was allowed to give the kids treats. But I couldn't because it turned them into gremlins.

Mom good. Dad bad.

"No, but Tuck might be soon. She brought lollipops for him."

Paige draped her long ponytail over her shoulder. "Okay. Well, thanks for taking her."

I tried not to roll my eyes. "You don't have to thank me. It's what we're doing. We're learning a dance together."

She shrugged as if it didn't matter, but it mattered to me.

"I'm her dad. You don't need to thank me."

Paige lifted a staying hand, mumbling a, "Yeah, right," and I hated that.

Yes, I was forgetful on occasion, and I was the first to admit I'd taken advantage of her while we were married, but it was never on purpose and definitely not premeditated. I'd wanted to be a better husband to her, but by the time I was able to pull it together, she was already over it. That didn't mean I wasn't still trying to be a better dad to our kids every single goddamn day.

Although, I supposed there was no use in starting that argument tonight or any other night. The time for defending myself was over. I only had to stay in my lane. Life was easier that way.

"I guess I'll see you Thursday," I said. "I'll be over to get the kids after work."

She nodded and turned around. "Close the door on your way out, please."

"Night, Scarlett! Night, Tucker!" I hollered toward the steps, and they both came rumbling back downstairs to leap at me.

Tucker was already dressed in his dinosaur pajamas. I kissed them both. "Love you guys. Sleep good."

"Night, Daddy," Tucker said, a purple lollipop in his hand.

"I'll miss you," Scarlett said, and I kissed her once more.

"I'll miss you too."

Once the kids raced upstairs, Neil offered me another head nod. I gave one back.

And that was that.

SEVEN
GENEVIEVE

"But really, how are you?" Josie asked on speakerphone, my cell resting next to my head while I had the backs of my legs pressed up against the wall.

"I'm fine."

"No, you're not. Stop lying."

I didn't answer, but I didn't have to. Josie and I had been best friends since we were the new kids on the kickline, both of us earning two of the few coveted spots the same year. She was still performing. And I was...here, on the floor, stretching out the aches of my injury.

"I figured you were probably stalking our socials," she said, and I cringed, hating that she knew me so well. Josie had been named a dance captain this year, which meant she had helped out at auditions and appeared in a lot of social media content. I was really happy for her. And so disappointed for myself.

That could have been me too, but everything had all fallen apart right before this past season. After so many years of wear and tear, one wrong landing and my Achilles tendon snapped during rehearsal in late October. My tenth season was over before it started, and by the time my monthslong recovery was over, the audition process had already begun for this coming year. So, my career was effectively over as a Rockette.

After surgery, I'd had to be on crutches for two months and in a walking cast for a month longer, so I couldn't stay in Manhattan. Between mobility issues and the depression I'd found myself in, my brother had convinced me to move home. I told myself it wasn't for the long-term. That I'd get back on the stage. But it was months later, and I still hadn't found my way back. To Radio City or otherwise.

"Can we talk about something else?" I asked.

"How's the teaching gig?"

I dropped my forearm over my eyes. "Anything but that."

"Lemme hear it."

I swiped my palm over my cheeks, warm at the mere thought of Dylan Matthews. "I met this guy."

"Ooh. Yes, okay. And?"

"He came back to my apartment."

"And you had sex?"

"Yeah. It was…" Even though Josie couldn't see it, I exploded my hands in front of my face, imitating the sound.

"Yeah?"

"Mm-hmm. He's tall and really tanned, *really* muscular." When Josie hummed, I drew the picture of him with my fingers. "He's got the V, and these green eyes that look a little bit like he could be the bad guy in a superhero movie. He seems kind of grouchy but is really sweet underneath the intimidation."

"So what's the issue?"

There were multiple, but I went with the easiest one. "He's the dad of one of my students."

Josie gasped in delight. "You're kidding."

"No. We hooked up on Friday, and I never thought I'd see him again, but there he was Tuesday afternoon."

Josie laughed. "What are the chances?"

"Apparently with me, pretty good odds to mess my shit up."

What were the odds that one misstep in a move I'd done hundreds of thousands of times would sideline my professional dancing career? What were the odds that the man I had an incredible night with was the dad of one of my students? What were the odds that I met a really great guy when I only had a few weeks left here?

With other people, maybe slim to none. But me? I must've broken a mirror or stepped on a crack.

"What was he doing there? Picking up his kid?"

"He's in the special person dance we do every year. The kids bring someone to dance with, and since it's mostly girls, they usually pick their dads."

"Aww, adorable."

"I know," I wailed, remembering him smiling down at Scarlett as they turned in a circle. He had dimples. Two nice-guy dimples carved into the middle of his cheeks, reframing all that tough-guy bluster into a boyish grin. No one would ever suspect it from his hard stare, but he was soft on the inside. All you had to do was see him with his child. "I'll have to be with Dylan every week for half an hour."

"Dylan? That's the guy."

"That's the guy," I confirmed with my eyes closed, picturing how he'd strolled into the studio in his ass-hugging jeans, a black T-shirt, and those boots, like he'd just gotten off work. He had that blue-collar look about him, and those hands? They were the hands of somebody who worked with them every day and not only to staple papers and send emails. Those callused fingers scratched so deliciously along my stomach and thighs.

"Well, maybe that's a good thing. You could hook up with him again," my best friend said, and I huffed.

"I can't."

"Why? Is there some policy against it?"

"No." I pulled my bottom lip between my teeth, imagining Dylan nibbling on it.

"Then what's the problem?"

I rubbed my palm against my forehead as my stomach roiled with the same nauseated feeling I'd had when I'd spoken with Miss Amy last week. "I won't be here much longer."

Her voice perked up. "Did you get a gig?"

"Not yet, but I did send in a tape to a cruise line."

"A cruise ship?"

"What?" I snapped because it was impossible for me not to get defensive. There weren't many jobs available for dancers who weren't a double or triple threat. I couldn't act or sing, so my options were limited, even if I was more than proficient in tap and jazz, and had a decade of professional experience. "It's work."

"Yeah, but…it's a boat. Don't you get seasick? You puked on the ferry to Staten Island."

I rolled my eyes. She had to remember every little thing. "Can you, for once, not have perfect recall?"

She snorted. Her perfect recall was part of the reason why she was such a phenomenal dancer. She could watch a combination twice and repeat it flawlessly. It was incredibly annoying. And stunning to watch.

"I was DMing with Jeremy Montana the other day," she said. "Remember him from that master class he taught a few years ago?"

I hummed. "Doesn't ring a bell."

"He helped put together Britney's show in Vegas. He also did—"

"Oh!" I snapped. "Yes, yes, I remember him. He wore that one long earring."

"Yes."

"The cross," we both said at the same time and laughed.

"He's choreographing for some acts in LA. I can see if he has anything happening right now."

Although I thought I was a pretty versatile performer, I wasn't sure how suited I was for hip-hop.

"I know it's not really your thing," Josie said because she could read my mind, "but if you want me to, I can see what's up."

"Yeah, I guess. Why not, right?"

"Don't sound too excited about it."

"Well…no. I mean, yeah, I am."

She stayed quiet. Too quiet.

"*What?*" I asked after a while, irritated that she could make me emotionally squirm even over the phone.

"I think it might be time to reevaluate."

"Reevaluate?" I balked. "What's that mean?"

"It means you should think about what you really want."

What was with the people closest to me questioning my desire to dance? As if they didn't know who I was. "I don't need to think about it. I want to dance. I'm not giving up my career."

"I'm not talking about giving up your career. Come on," she said on a sigh as if I were the one being irrational. "I mean that sometimes you use dance as an excuse. Usually what we do in the studio and onstage is the hard part, but I think everything you do outside of dance is the hard part. So you use it as an excuse to hide."

It felt like she'd hitch kicked me in the chest, and I choked on a rebuttal. Because, yes, dance was my comfort, my protection, my safe haven. Singularly focused on it, I didn't have to face my parents who lived on two different planets or my fear of opening myself up to someone who could hurt me. Dance was easy. Confronting the other stuff in life was hard.

"So, anyway," Josie said, and I blinked back into reality. "You like this Dylan guy?"

"Yeah, but I'm not going to do anything about it."

"Why not? It's not like you have to marry the him. There's nothing wrong with getting a little D on the down-low."

"It's not little," I told her in a moment of mania, and she shouted at me.

"Why are you on the phone with me and not with him right this second?"

"Because," I said, waving my hand around to an imaginary audience, proving my point, "I'm not staying here."

"If you're not staying, then what's the harm in having a little fun while you are there? You deserve to treat yourself with a hot guy who can dick you down. It's just sex, right?"

I swallowed the lump in my throat. "Yeah."

"Then I say do it up. Have fun."

I combed my fingers through my hair, mumbling a quiet, "Maybe."

"No maybe," she said then lowered her voice. "Go get your daddy."

"Oh my god, Josie! I'm hanging up now."

"I love you," she sang.

"You too. Talk later."

"Bye, toots," she said and hung up, leaving me to stare at the ceiling for a moment before opening my legs to a straddle. I flexed and pointed my toes, heels and backs of my thighs still against the wall as I recalled the way Dylan's voice had growled in my ear about how flexible I was.

"Damn it," I mumbled, dropping both of my legs to my right side, rolling to my hands and knees before standing up with a couple of pops in my joints. Josie did have a point. This was just sex.

I had always put my career ahead of my romantic life, although even calling it a romantic life was a stretch. Ever since my high school boyfriend, I hadn't much been interested in losing myself to another relationship. There were short-term boyfriends in the off-season, but no one I'd ever felt particularly connected to. No one who'd given me a high like the one I'd gotten from the stage.

Except for Dylan.

And that scared the shit out of me because I didn't want anything or anyone to hold me back from leaving, whether it was to LA or on a godforsaken cruise ship or back to New York.

I was going.

No matter how good the sex was.

Even if it was the best sex.

With his eyes and hands and mouth and—

I needed to get out of the house and stop thinking about Dylan. With a quick intake of my kitchen, I grabbed my purse and car keys and headed to the grocery store. I wouldn't be reminded of him there.

Quietly singing along to the Whitney Houston tune playing in the background, I filled up my little cart with fruit and veggies then moved over to the cereal aisle for my favorite comfort food. I reached for the biggest box of Froot Loops there was when a familiar voice called out, "Miss Gen!"

I spun to my right, spying Scarlett Matthews running full bore at me.

"Hiiiii!" She crashed into me, hugging my legs, as my eyes snagged on another figure, her father sauntering up the aisle with his shopping cart.

The universe was conspiring against me.

"You doing some shopping?" I asked Scarlett, yet I couldn't pay attention to her answer. Dylan's eyes were obscured by the shade of a baseball cap, but I knew they were staring at me from the goose bumps that rose on my skin. With each step he took, I instinctively moved two steps back.

The guy was lethal.

"Genevieve," he greeted me with that panty-melting voice. "How are you?"

"Fine." I nodded and cleared my throat. "Good."

"Good." The corner of his lips twitched, and I hated he could see and was amused by my awkwardness. Josie's voice echoing in my head about getting *my daddy* didn't help either.

"Scar," Dylan started, bending down to his daughter. "You can't go running into people like that. I know you're excited to see Miss Gen, but you gotta slow down, okay? You could hurt yourself or someone else, and I don't think my insurance would cover it if you broke your dance teacher."

I refused to give in to a laugh as Scarlett nodded.

"Sorry about that," Dylan said to me, standing to his full height. He tipped his hat back a bit, his gaze sweeping over the length of me then landing on the huge box of cereal still in my hand. "This is our favorite aisle too."

"Ooh, I want!" the boy in the cart crowed, and I knew he was Scarlett's little brother from all the times her mother had come to pick her up from class with him in tow.

"What?" Dylan pointed to the Cocoa Krispies. "These?"

"Yeah! Yeah! Yeah!"

Dylan tossed the box into his cart.

"Good choice." I smiled at the boy. "I don't think I know your name. I'm Miss Gen, what's yours?"

"Tucker," he said, and with his dark hair and dimples, he was the spitting image of his dad.

"Nice to meet you, Tucker."

"We shopping," he told me.

I gestured to my cart. "Me too."

"Miss Gen, you want to shop with us?" Scarlett tugged on my hand, and I took in her pleading face and then Dylan's impassive one, his head tipped to the side, waiting patiently.

Something told me this man's endurance was unflappable. If he wanted something, he was willing to work for it.

I should have said no since I knew I wouldn't be able to escape Dylan if I said yes, and yet… "Sure."

Scarlett grinned wide, her ponytail bouncing as she hopped alongside me. "I love grocery shopping. I like to put it all in bags."

Behind me, Tucker beeped a few times, and I glanced over my shoulder to smile at him while he cruised a truck back and forth along the side of the cart. Then I looked to Dylan, who shot his focus up from where it had been below my waist. Like he'd been checking out my ass.

He gave me a shrug, totally uncaring that he'd been caught, and I refused to find his confidence endearing or adorable.

"Daddy," Scarlett said, pivoting to walk backward. "Did you know Miss Gen was a rocket?"

Dylan's brow pinched for a few moments, his gaze bouncing back and forth between his daughter and me as if putting pieces of a puzzle together in his mind. Then his eyes perused me once more, evidently fond of whatever was going on in his brain. "Ah. I was thinking she wanted to go into space." He tugged on Scarlett's ponytail. "You want to be a Rockette, not an astronaut."

Then he nodded at me, his tongue running along his lower lip as his eyes darkened, and it wasn't difficult to guess what his mental images might be. Me onstage. Maybe me performing just for him.

I liked that idea too.

"Makes sense," he murmured after a long moment in which it was hard to breathe in the stifling air between us.

I faced forward, aimlessly chatting with Scarlett in an attempt to ignore her dad as we all made our way down the next few aisles, and I reached for a small bottle of olive oil as Scarlett skipped around. "I made Daddy practice the dance with me."

"Oh yeah?" I turned up the next aisle, slowing until Dylan was next to me. "You gonna be the star student on Tuesday?"

"You should see my jazz squares," he said with that dry humor that never failed to make me smile.

I bit back a laugh, and Tucker shrieked in delight. "Cupcakes!"

"No." Dylan snatched the boxed mix out of his son's hands. "Sorry, buddy."

"Pweeeeeeeaaaaaase."

"No. I don't bake, and we don't need any cupcakes. We're getting ice cream." When Tucker wailed in frustration, Dylan shook his head then lowered his voice to explain to me, "We never come up this aisle, but I wasn't paying attention."

I never shopped the baking aisle either, but here we were, evidently walking each and every row.

"You cook a lot?" Dylan asked me when I placed two jars of spaghetti sauce and whole wheat pasta in my cart.

"I usually make one big pot of something that I eat for a couple of days." I pointed to what I had in my cart. "Like pasta with veggies." Moving to the next aisle, I asked, "You cook?"

"I grill."

"Even in the snow!" Scarlett added as she twirled in front of us.

"You grill in the snow?"

"It's either that or microwave pizza, so…" He trailed off as we passed all the pet food and turned down the paper products aisle. "Scar, grab some tissues."

Scarlett picked out two tissue boxes with pink shapes on them and threw them in the cart, explaining to me, "I have al…algergies."

"Allergies," Dylan corrected, and I nodded at her.

"I have them too. I'm allergic to pollen, dust, and cat hair. Do you know what you're allergic to?"

She scrunched up her face, silently asking her dad to answer.

"She's allergic to anything and everything that grows outside."

"I take grapie every night," she told me. "To help my algergies."

"That's good," I said, realizing we were now in the personal hygiene aisle. I nabbed a box of the multipack tampons, waiting to see if Dylan would have a reaction, but he stared blandly at me. As if we did this all the time, grocery shopping.

For tampons.

With his kids.

I didn't know anything about being a parent, but this whole

thing felt oddly domesticated. And I wasn't sure what to think of it.

When we arrived in the frozen section, Tucker—over the cupcakes meltdown—chanted, "Pizza, pizza, pizza."

Dylan placed a bunch of boxes in his cart while I absently reflected on what the hell I was doing with my life. In this supermarket. With this *daddy*.

When he caught me nibbling on my bottom lip, he narrowed his gaze. "Stop teasing me."

We rolled on to the ice cream, and with the kids' attention otherwise occupied by deciding what they wanted, Dylan sneaked his hand around my hip.

I glanced over at Scarlett as she repeatedly opened and closed one of the freezer doors, before meeting his eyes, back in their panther slits. I grew hot where his palm found my bare skin under my shirt, and I was falling under his spell again.

"I haven't been able to think about much else besides you," he said, his gaze taking in every inch of my face.

"Me too."

"So, let's do it again." He squeezed my hip, so much gentler than I knew he could be. "It doesn't have to be a big deal." He bent down, brushing his lips along my ear. "I need to tame this pussy one more time."

"Dylan," I breathed, my nipples pebbling. "You can't say stuff like that here."

"Why?" He cocked his head back, brow raised in challenge. "Because you like it?"

I shook my head.

"Then why not? Give me one good reason."

I tipped my chin to Scarlett, who was attempting a pirouette.

"What does she have to do with it?"

"I don't know, Dylan." I huffed at his incredulous tone. "I don't have kids. I don't know the rules about what we can and cannot do. I don't want to damage her."

"Don't leave them alone in cars and make 'em wear life vests in water. Those are the rules."

"What if she finds out?" I asked. "Wouldn't that be weird to explain to her?"

"She's not going to find out because nobody has to know. What happens between us is between us."

I couldn't argue against him. Or, rather, I didn't want to.

"We set the rules," he told me with finality, sliding his palm down my ass for a squeeze before he dropped his hand and backed up like he didn't just light me on fire in the middle of the ice cream aisle. He turned to his kids. "What are we getting? A tub of cookies and cream or popsicles?"

"Cookies and cream!" Scarlett shouted while Tucker smacked one of the freezer doors.

Dylan put the ice cream in the cart then ruffled his son's hair and reminded Scarlett to watch where she was going. He was a parent. A *dad*.

I tugged at the collar of my long-sleeved T-shirt, mentally warning my hormones that we were in public, and pushed my little cart ahead to the next aisle. I dropped a carton of milk into it as Dylan grabbed cheese and yogurt, then we walked over to the cash registers, where I lined up in front of Dylan's cart and loaded my items onto the belt.

After I finished paying, he scooted to the end and lifted Scarlett onto the edge of the counter so she could help him bag their groceries, and it annoyed me that I really liked seeing him like this. Between Dylan the jungle cat and Dylan the dad, I was becoming addicted to each side of him, and I wanted to learn what others he was hiding.

"Well, thanks for shopping with me, guys," I said to Scarlett and then Tucker once we were all outside. "It was really fun."

"Yeah! We should do it all the time," Scarlett suggested, and Dylan angled his head in a silent question to me, like it was an open invitation.

I ignored him as Tucker told me, "I have pizza for dinner."

"Well, you enjoy your pizza." I held up my hand for a high five from each kid. "Scarlett, I'll see you on Tuesday." Then I took off in the direction of my car. "Bye."

"Bye, Miss Gen!" Scarlett called.

"Bye, Miss Gen," Dylan repeated in a low rumble that set off another frenzy of hormones.

Damn him.

EIGHT
DYLAN

carlett's dance class was one hour, but since the special someones were infiltrating for the last half, they'd spent the first bit practicing their recital dance, which was a tap number to "Little Bitty Pretty One." Genevieve spent a fair amount of time attempting to get the girls to snap and walk on beat at the same time. How did I know this? I watched.

I watched Scarlett light up any time her teacher spoke to her and how she struggled to balance as she shuffle-hopped on one foot. I also watched Genevieve demonstrate the moves in her black tank top and tiny shorts with beige tights underneath. She had them folded up on her calves with heeled tap shoes on her feet, and her dance "uniform" had me thinking about engine rebuilds so I didn't get a semi in the middle of the waiting room.

Genevieve was an athlete. Long and lean and gorgeous. Not to mention those lips.

Those goddamn lips.

Since it was Paige's night to pick up the kids and take them for a few days, we agreed she'd meet me at the studio so Tucker could sit in her car with his iPad while I danced with Scarlett. Which allowed me the opportunity to ogle Genevieve as much as I wanted without seeming like a creep. I wasn't about to pass it up.

At the end of the half hour, she gathered all the girls up to the center of the floor in a semicircle then played some snappy pop song. They all started clapping and wiggling around, and I assumed this was something they did every class. Every team had one. A ritual to get them pumped up or, in this case, come down.

Genevieve pointed to one girl who stepped to the middle of the group and swung her arms back and forth, not quite on beat, but the others cheered her on. Then she pointed to another girl, who took the center position, laughing and gyrating. It went on like that, each girl having a turn to be center stage. Even Genevieve got in on it, stepping up to the middle to do the Macarena, and I blew out a breath, disappointed that I didn't get to see any moves from the professional dancer.

"She's great, right?" some dad next to me said, and I grunted in agreement. "Hannah loves Miss Gen." He leaned into me like we were pals. "Makes it easy to come to these classes when she looks like that too."

I glowered at him, even though I had no leg to stand on since I'd been objectifying her mere moments ago.

"Oh, sorry." He backed up a step. "Do you, like, know her or something?"

Without answering this dickweed who was about to learn the taste of his balls when I shoved them down his throat, I moved toward the door, so I was the first one in when Genevieve finally opened it to us.

"Miss Gen," I said, surreptitiously grazing my hand along her hip.

In answer, she pressed those pretty red lips of hers together, intentionally turning her face away from me, though she tossed out an "I'm glad you wore the appropriate footwear" my way.

I bit back a grin at her then let it loose when I crouched down to hug Scarlett.

Once we were all inside the studio, Genevieve sauntered to the center of the floor. "It's wonderful to see everyone here again, although I know CiCi's brother couldn't make it tonight. I'll be filling in for him now, but in case anyone else has to miss classes, I filmed the dance for you. Miss Amy will be emailing you with a link to the video so you can practice on your own. But for now, let's get started by going over what we did last week. We'll try it a few times up to speed and then add on."

She crossed over to the sound system in the corner and cued up The Temptations' "My Girl" before prancing over to where CiCi stood. This class went much like the last, Genevieve demonstrating the moves, the girls giggling at us, and me trying to look cool. When it came to the jazz square portion, I flicked my eyebrows at her, vying for her attention. I wanted her to see how good my squares were. I mean, I was probably the best dancer in class.

When it was time to leave, she once again gave each girl a compliment and high five before sending them on their way out of the door, and I really had to hand it to her. She was an excellent teacher. She was able to keep the behavior and attention of a class of kindergarteners for an hour, as well as turn a bunch of rhythmless adults into suave dancers.

I waited until I was the last one in the room and met Genevieve by the back wall while Scarlett gathered her stuff in the waiting room. "What're you doing this weekend?"

"Covering some shifts at Walt's."

"You want to hang out?"

She eyed me as she took a bobby pin out of her hair and did something to it with her teeth that was too quick for me to see before sticking it back in her hair. "I can't. I'm working."

I wrapped my fingers around the ballet barre attached to the wall. "What about before? Or after?"

She only arched her eyebrow, and I liked when she got a bit of an attitude.

"You're gonna make me work for it, huh?"

She pursed her lips for a moment, really tempting me, then murmured, "Something tells me you can handle it."

And fuck, she was so pretty, but that raspy whisper? Good god in heaven, I was desperate for her. "I can handle it." I licked my lips, and her gaze dropped to my mouth. "Can handle *you* too."

Her chest rose with an audible inhale, and she folded her arms, but not before I spied the sweet little pebbles of her nipples. When it was clear she wasn't going to answer me, I nodded and tapped the barre right next to where she leaned her hip on it. "I guess I'll see you around, Miss Gen."

Then I spun around with my hands out, exactly like she'd taught us tonight, and strutted out.

"All right," I said, opening the back door to Paige's car to get Scarlett buckled into her seat. "I'll see you two in a few days." I gave each kid a kiss on the head. "Be good. Love you."

Scarlett and Tucker both grinned at me, shouting their *I love yous* as I shut the door. After I knocked on the roof twice, Paige pulled away, and I meandered back to my car. Genevieve wanted me to work for it? Well, I loved a good challenge.

If she was bartending this weekend, I'd go to Walt's. Back to where it all started. I was lucky there, anyway. If I had to, I'd go every night and sit my ass down in front of her until she gave in.

But for now, the only place I was going was home.

It was the end of April and the days were getting longer, so without the kids around, I took my time grilling up a perfect piece of Alaskan salmon while I sipped on a pale ale. I ate at the table on the small porch that was still littered with balls and empty containers of bubbles from when Tucker and Scarlett had played out here yesterday. My cell phone buzzed, interrupting the music I had on, and I swiped my thumb across the screen to answer. Jude was one of those people who actually preferred to talk on the phone like some weirdo, but since my texting skills were subpar, it was fine with me.

"Hey, Gray. What's up?"

"Hey. You got the kids tonight?"

I stretched my legs out in front of me, crossing my ankles. "Paige has them until Saturday."

"All right. Well, listen. You said you'd help out with Sebastian's baseball team if he needed it, right?"

"Yeah."

"You sure?" he asked.

"Yeah."

"Okay, so… Long story short, the coach hurt himself in some freak lawn mower accident, and he won't be able to finish out the season, and they need someone. Are you up for it?"

Setting aside the reason for his call, I had to ask, "Freak lawn mower accident? What?"

"Yeah, man," he said, like he couldn't believe it himself. "I heard some piece of rebar or something flew out and hit him in the head. Knocked him out cold, but their property's on an incline, so he ended up falling and rolling downhill, and he fractured his elbow."

"Holy shit."

"Right? He's got a concussion and is scraped up pretty good." But before our conversation could devolve any further into gruesome freak accidents, as they sometimes did, he brought it back. "So, can you do it? Can you coach?"

I scratched at my chin, thinking.

"You don't have to," Jude said hurriedly. "I didn't mention anything to anybody, but I figured, who better to take over?"

I tried to remember what he'd told me about Seb's team. "These are all seven- and eight-year-olds? How often do they practice? Twice a week?"

"Yeah, Mondays and Wednesdays, with games on Saturdays or Sundays."

I nodded to myself, thinking about how that could work. If I had the kids on those days, I could take them with me. They wouldn't mind. Tucker would probably love it. "Yeah, as long as I can get someone to cover for me for Scarlett's recital."

"When's that?"

"First Saturday in June."

"That shouldn't be an issue. The games are in the morning, but if you can't be there that day, I can do it."

I stayed silent.

"Or get someone else," he amended with a laugh.

"All right. Pass on my info to whoever. I'm in."

"Awesome. Seb'll be stoked to hear. I'll talk to you later. Thanks, man."

"No problem," I said then ended the call to take my plate and garbage inside, where I made my way upstairs, my phone still in my hand as a new email notification came through. It was the link from Miss Amy with Genevieve's video.

I flopped back on my bed and opened it up, pressing play. The studio was empty save for Miss Gen, talking through the dance in counts and steps while the song played quietly underneath. She completed the whole dance, demonstrating parts we had yet to learn, and then said to the camera, "Now, I'll show you from the other direction in case it's easier for you to learn it that way." The video cut to a different angle, this one of her back. She called out the moves to the mirror, the reflection showing how she had her phone placed on a tripod. This time when she finished, she curtsied adorably, grinning at the mirror, her hands out like she held up a skirt, and that was when the video ended.

I immediately replayed it.

I didn't care about learning the dance. I would eventually. All I wanted to do was watch her. I didn't have to hide how I kept my eyes glued to her chest or ass as she danced. She was completely covered in black leggings and a T-shirt, but she might as well have filmed this naked for how my blood heated and surged south.

Before I knew it, I had my hand down my pants and my hard dick in my palm. This girl was driving me out of my mind, to the point that even hearing her say, "Slide up two, three, four, and back, six, seven, eight," had me closing my eyes in ecstasy.

I thought back to how her tongue and lips felt on my swollen cock, how she'd writhed against my fingers, let out her tiny hiccupping breaths when she orgasmed. And there was nothing as sweet as when she bit into her lip nervously. She carried herself so confidently, I liked that I made her a bit anxious.

With her face frozen on my phone screen in a smile, I pumped my fist until I came, her name falling from my lips.

NINE
GENEVIEVE

I should have known he'd be here, but my stomach still flipped when Dylan strolled into Walt's at a quarter to eight on Friday night, in his usual T-shirt, jeans, and boots. He sat down right in front of me, his hands folded together on top of the bar.

I tossed a coaster in front of him. "Funny seeing you here."

"Is it, though?" He tipped his head to the side. "You have to know you have me by the balls." When I sputtered a laugh, he shrugged. "It's true."

I disregarded the butterflies in my belly. "What can I get for you?"

"Since I can't strip you down right here, I guess I'll have a Sam Adams and some crab dip."

As I filled his beer and added his food into the POS system, my brother appeared from the back. He made his way over to Dylan, and I pretended I wasn't eavesdropping.

"Hey, Matthews." They clapped hands. "What are you doing here? Where're the other two?"

"Here by myself tonight."

"Really?" Nate sounded surprised, but Dylan didn't respond. "Trolling for a chick?"

I frowned not only at the question but the accusation in it. Had Dylan lied to me when he said he didn't pick up a lot of women? I could feel his eyes on me, but I refused to turn around, emptying the dishwasher.

"Fuck off, Koz," Dylan grumbled, and my brother laughed.

"Hey, man, no offense. I just know how you are. I thought maybe you were putting your night off from the kids to good use. Hey, Evie." My brother smacked the bar to get my attention, and I pivoted toward them. "Drink on me for this guy," he said with his hand on Dylan's shoulder.

I looked from my brother, with his easy grin, to Dylan, with his arms crossed and surly face set in stone under his baseball hat. They made quite a pair, and even though I wasn't sure how I felt about their short exchange, I couldn't refrain from smiling.

Nate patted him on the back a few times then shuffled away, leaving me to deliver the crab dip to Dylan.

"So," I started carefully, "you seem to get along well with my brother."

"Likes to get all up in everybody's business, that one."

I sank my elbows to the bar. "Tell me about it. He practically dragged me home and set me up here."

His eyes stayed on mine, maybe waiting for more of the story, but I wasn't about to tell him. When I stayed quiet, he sniffed. "We're only friends 'cause he gives me free beer."

"Fair enough." I laughed and helped myself to steal a piece of the toasted bread.

His eyes fixated on my mouth as I chewed. "And to be clear, I don't *troll* for chicks here or anywhere else."

I played it cool. "I didn't ask."

"You didn't have to."

And all my cool flew out the window with how he could read me so well. So instead of responding with something that would give me away, I stole another one of his chips.

He lifted the brim of his cap and arched one eyebrow. "You always eat off your patrons' plates?"

"Only the ones I've slept with."

"Attitude," he warned, though his mouth trembled in amusement. He picked up his own piece of bread and scooped up a bit of the piping-hot dip, blowing over it. "How was your week?"

"Not bad, but I can't get rid of this guy who keeps showing up while I work, at the grocery store, even in my dance class."

He widened his eyes in faux outrage. "Want me to take care of him for you?"

I curled my fingers around his wrist, bringing his food to my mouth to eat it. I took my time chewing and swallowing. "He might be growing on me."

He sluggishly lifted his gaze to mine and let out a deliciously sinful hum that vibrated in my bones. "You think you can be cute and I'll share my food with you?"

I sucked my lips between my teeth to keep from grinning.

"You're right." He pushed his plate to me. I helped myself to another bite, and he seemed to like my sharing his food. "What time are you here till?"

"Ten."

He leaned back, bringing his beer to his lips. "Me too."

A big group strolled in the door, and I reluctantly straightened, hauling my attention from Dylan to the other customers. I supposed I had a job to do.

While I worked, Dylan watched some baseball game on one of the televisions, his chin in his hand. But whenever I had a minute with him, we continued our game.

"Do you like savory or sweet better?" I asked as he rubbed the tip of his index finger along the bar top, and my mind went soaring back to our night together. To his fingertip rubbing my clit until I was a panting mess under him.

"More savory," he answered slowly, his voice like a physical caress. "But I'd never turn down a donut."

"I love sweets," I volunteered, plucking at my T-shirt, trying to air out the perspiration suddenly dotting my skin.

"I bet," he murmured, deliberately trekking his gaze down

the length of me, and I pushed at his shoulder at his cheap flirting. He gave in to a quarter of a smile, catching my hand when I retracted it. "Are you close to your parents?" he asked, drawing his thumb over my palm and index finger, keeping me on tenterhooks.

"Not really," I said, and once he finally released my hand, I snatched a rag to wipe down the bar for something to do that wasn't thinking about his rough fingers on me. "My parents divorced when I was in middle school, and they're both remarried and don't speak to each other anymore. It's pretty awkward with holidays and birthdays and stuff, but..." I trailed off, afraid to say any more. I knew what it was like to be the child of divorced parents, so it was just one more reason to stay away from him. And yet, I asked, "What about you? Are you close to your parents?"

His biceps bulged as he stretched his arms up behind his head, the bottom of his shirt hiking up an inch to reveal golden skin and finely honed muscle. "It's hard because they live on the opposite side of the country, but yeah, we talk on the phone a lot." Then he leaned forward again, elbows on the bar, chin in his hand. "I usually take the kids out to see them during the summer, and they fly over here occasionally. We make it work."

The next time around, he asked, "How old were you when you started dancing?"

"Three, with Miss Amy. I grew up in that studio. Went from high school straight out to auditioning." I set down the glass of water he requested. "What do you do?"

"I own Matthews Mechanics. Opened it about five years ago."

I smiled, crossing my arms in self-satisfaction. "I knew you did something with your hands."

"Yeah?" He pressed the tip of his tongue into his sharp incisor, his gaze coasting over me, and it prickled like his teeth gliding over my skin. "How?"

"A hunch." I swiped my palm over my heated cheek and

occupied myself with taking the order of the lady at the opposite end of the bar.

When I next checked on Dylan, a redheaded woman was sitting awfully close to him, batting her eyelashes as she gestured to his empty glass with her own beer, and some animal instinct had my hackles raised. I filled a new pint and placed it in front of him then dragged my hand over the side of his head.

"Did you get a haircut?"

His eyes narrowed to slits, his nose sliding along my inner forearm as I let my fingers drop to his neck.

"There's barely anything left to tug on," I said, and I swore his chest rumbled with a growl. The redhead spun around on her stool as he let a lopsided smile loose in my direction, a shadow forming in his dimple.

My knees went weak.

"You jealous, kitten?"

I pretended the pet name didn't make me want to drop my pants right there. "No."

"That's funny." He picked up my hand from his shoulder and bared his teeth against the pulse in my wrist. "Because it looks and sounds like you are."

I wrenched away from him, fearing for how fast my heart raced.

"All you have to do is say the word, and I'm yours," he said, unblinking, and I whirled away from him and his eyes and his voice that dripped with a mix of sin and sincerity.

I knew he didn't mean it like *that*, but it affected me as if he did. So I stayed at the other end of the bar for the rest of my shift, though it didn't escape my notice how he stared at me over the next hour.

When Tabitha showed up to relieve me, I grabbed my things from the office, but Nate stopped me before I could make my escape.

"I noticed you were talking with Matthews a lot. What's that about?"

I shrugged. "My job."

With one arm crossed over his middle and the other up, scratching at his trimmed beard, he squinted at me.

"Don't give me that look," I snapped.

"What look?"

"The overprotective, big, bad brother look. You couldn't even scare a fly."

"That's hurtful, Evie. The tattoos should, at least, earn me some suspicion of violence."

I fluttered my fingers at his geometric designs. "Yeah. The triangles and swirls are super scary."

He straightened from his slumped position against the wall. "Look, I'm just saying… Watch out for him."

"Who?" I asked innocently.

He dipped his head, rolling his eyes at my tragic acting. "I know women dig the whole grumpy vibe, but he's got baggage. You've been through enough already, and—"

"And let me stop you right there." I held up my palm. The one Dylan had slid his thumb along. "First of all, it's *hilarious* that you want to give me dating advice when you're hung up on a woman who's made you the *other* man."

He started to argue, but I cut him off.

"Secondly, nothing is going on with Dylan and me." I spun toward the door. "Even if I wanted there to be, I'm leaving in a few weeks, so it's not happening."

"Whatever you say," Nate muttered to my back, and I waved my middle finger behind my head. "Only looking out for you!"

I ignored my brother and made my way out to the front of the bar, where Dylan was waiting. He gestured for me to walk ahead of him, and I quickstepped out to my car.

"Hey, hey…" He easily caught up to me, his long fingers curving around my elbow. "You joining a track team or what?" His brow furrowed as he stood in front of me. "You all right?"

"It feels…" I shook my head, hoping to shake the fog away after that warning from Nate. I didn't care what he had to say, but it was difficult to push his words aside when Dylan was standing in front of me. My body needed one thing, while my heart screamed another, and my head swam. I leaned my back against my car door, accepting the one truth standing firm through the storm of emotion. "I thought it was going to be a one-time thing with you, but I can't..." When I refused to meet his gaze, he forced me to with his hand gently shaping around my jaw. "I can't stop thinking about you," I confessed.

He closed the space between us by a few inches. "I can't stop thinking about you either."

My hands found their way to his chest, and I nuzzled my face against his throat. He smelled of clean cotton and some spicy soap, like he'd showered right before he'd shown up at Walt's tonight. "But I'm leaving."

"Leaving? Like, right now?"

I lifted my head. "In a few weeks. After the recital."

He nodded slowly, his eyes never leaving mine. "Where you headed?"

"Depends on where I get a job."

His gaze made a circuit of my face, though he didn't say anything.

I filled in the blank. "That's why I can't do this with you."

"What do you think we're doing?"

"I don't know." I shrugged. "A relationship or something?"

It was another long moment before he said, "It's good you don't want a relationship. I don't either."

"Oh." I didn't know what else to say, both relieved and a little let down. But that couldn't be right. I was leaving.

In five weeks.

"Why'd you make that face?"

I jerked back. "What face?"

He cupped my cheeks, smoothing his thumbs over my fore-head. "You got all crinkly here and wrinkled your nose like you smelled something bad."

I tried to relax in his hold, schooling my features.

"What's wrong?"

"Nothing," I said, maybe a little too quickly because his brow lifted. "Just…you know…"

"No, I don't know."

I settled my attention over his shoulder. "It's really nothing. Only that I'm leaving, so I'm not looking to get into anything with anyone. No attachments to hold me back, you know?"

He held my chin between his thumb and forefinger so I'd look at him. "I think it's perfect."

"You do?"

"Yeah. I'm thirty-four and divorced. Not exactly relationship material."

I scratched the tip of my index finger along the collar of his T-shirt, right under his throat. "Was that supposed to convince me of something?"

"Yeah, that we should have more sex."

I muffled a laugh. "What part of I'm leaving don't you get?"

"Genevieve," he intoned, and the stern way he said my name had me ready to bend over for a spanking. "It seems like you're being difficult on purpose."

I shook my head, and he slipped his hands around me, making himself clear. "I want you. You want me. And neither one of us wants a relationship, so let's just have sex. No big deal. Feelings don't have to be involved."

"You want, like, a no-strings-attached…fling?"

He answered by bending to suck on the slope of my neck.

It was going to be impossible to avoid him until the recital, and it was already impossible to ignore the simmering attraction between us, so it did seem like a good solution. "Do we shake on it?"

"How about you let me give you an orgasm, and we'll call it settled?"

I took his baseball cap off and combed my fingers into his hair. "Well, all right. If you insist."

Then he pressed me back against my car, his mouth finding the sensitive spot behind my ear. "Your place or mine?"

I felt for the handle behind my back and opened the door. "Neither."

He raised his brow, confused.

"I don't want to wait," I explained in a moment of wild honesty and even wilder spontaneity.

He skirted his gaze around then threw a filthy glance my way. "You have a thing for voyeurism?"

"Not particularly."

"Just my dick, then?" He dropped into the passenger seat, yanking on the handle to adjust it, making room for his long legs.

"Exactly." I tossed his hat onto the dash and sat on his lap, closing the door after me, feeling the hard length of him between my legs. He wasted no time kissing me, his hand delving under my T-shirt, molding to my breasts.

"Did you go to college?" I asked as he licked and nipped at my throat.

He hummed an affirmative against my skin. "Arizona State. Baseball scholarship."

"Wow." I gasped when he sucked on me, and I ground down on him. "So, you were really good."

"I played professionally for a few years."

"No way!" I slapped at his shoulder until he backed away from me. "You never told me."

"You never asked." He repeated the words I'd spoken when we were in bed together in a mocking voice, and I tried to pinch him, but he clasped my hand and forced me to turn around so my back was against his chest. Then he unbuttoned my jeans and slipped his hand beneath my panties, groaning in response to how wet I was. "Did you go to college?"

It took me a while to answer because he circled my clit with leisurely strokes that had me rocking up into his hand. "No. I moved to the city to start auditioning right after I graduated high school. I became a Rockette when I was twenty."

"Every time we're together, every new thing I learn about you, I'm more impressed." His teeth scraped over the shell of my ear, sending goose bumps skittering over my skin. He tucked his other hand back under my shirt to tug the cup of my bra down so he could play with my nipple, and I was already so close to an orgasm.

"You were the professional baseball player, and you're a dad." I tilted my head, allowing him better access to my neck. "I hear it's really hard to keep kids alive, so that alone impresses me."

"You should tell that to my ex-wife."

I froze, and he sighed heavily.

"Ah, fuck. I made it weird, didn't I?"

Even though I'd agreed to this friends-with-benefits situation, it didn't mean I wasn't still well aware of the dynamics of ex-spouses who didn't get along. And I didn't want to get into the middle of it. Especially when this was "no big deal."

Removing his hand from my pants, he shifted so we could see each other better. "I mean—I… This is why I'm no good for relationships." He let out a rough breath and scrubbed his hand through his hair. "Shit, Gen… Look, we went to couples therapy, and obviously, it didn't work for us, but I learned a lot about myself. I actually still go to therapy and—"

"Really?" My jaw went slack.

He shrugged like it was no big thing to work on himself. "Mostly to talk through strategies with my kids and my work. I'm dyslexic, so sometimes I struggle with day-to-day stuff and—"

I threw myself at him, kissing him like an absolute savage, and it took him a moment to recover before his hands were back on me.

"That's so hot," I panted between licks and nips at him.

"You like me going to therapy?" he asked, squeezing his

fingers around my rib cage as he tilted his hips up so his erection rubbed against me. "Wait until you hear how I make checklists and change my bedsheets every week."

"So grown-up," I murmured against his jaw, his stubble like tiny needles against my lips. When he ventured his hand down below my waist, he parted my slick flesh with his fingers, and I moaned. "Dylan, I need you."

"Do you have a condom?" he asked, ruthlessly tugging on my nipple, my back arching away from his chest.

"No, do you?"

He stilled. "In my car."

Then I stilled. "Shit."

"I can go…" His words trailed off as he slipped two fingers inside me.

"Just…just keep doing what you're doing," I panted, already too close to the edge to pull back and stop. He wrapped his left arm around my waist, holding me tight to him so I couldn't move. He shoved my pants down a few inches, granting him more room to press and push and slide his fingers in and over me, all the while kissing and sucking at the spot behind my ear, murmuring words about how he couldn't stop touching me and how he couldn't wait to get me naked again.

I writhed in his lap, the hard ridge of him against my ass, nearly too delirious to hear a car door slam not too far from where we were.

"There're people coming this way," Dylan rasped against my ear. "You think they know what we're doing in here? That I'm getting you off with only my fingers. That I can feel you pulsing around them."

I cracked my eyelids open to spot a pair of younger guys headed toward the entrance of Walt's, and though we were probably in their line of sight, it was dark out, and their heads were bent in conversation. Still, it didn't stop me from shuddering in pleasure at the thought of being caught.

"You were meant to be onstage," Dylan said. "You love being watched, don't you?"

His words were both a balm and stinging pain, and when he slapped my clit, I threw my head back, moaning as my muscles tightened, dancing on the edge of release.

"Yes, you do. Go ahead and scream when you come so they'll know exactly what we're doing."

Falling over the precipice, I shouted Dylan's name, all of my pleasure bubbling up from the back of my throat. Along with the knot of anxiety he had relaxed. Before I could catch my breath, he had my jeans off and my body turned again, this time face-to-face, my legs straddling his thighs. He unbuckled his pants, lifting slightly to shuck them down enough that his cock sprang free. Then he cupped my jaw in his big hands. "Grind on me, kitten. I need to feel you."

I held on to his shoulders and rolled my hips back and forth, gliding my already overly sensitized sex along his length.

"Yes," he groaned. "Like that."

He kissed me, one hand in my hair, the other on my lower back, simultaneously pushing and keeping me steady. His mouth was territorial, taking more and more of me. Or maybe I was offering myself up. I didn't know, couldn't tell who was pushing or pulling anymore.

But I somehow found myself leaned back with my shirt up, his lips on my breast, and his cock leaking between my legs.

He moaned out my name, and we both stared down at the mess we'd made. Our skin and clothes covered in him and me.

"So fucking hot," he murmured, pulling me close to him. I tucked my head against his throat, and he gently stroked my spine. "You feel better?"

I nodded. "Do you?"

He hummed, and I felt more than heard it. "I don't know."

I forced myself away from him, carefully maneuvering my legs off his lap, and I dug through the console for a few tissues for him.

"You don't know?" I repeated, putting myself together as best I could.

He wiped off his lower stomach and balled up the tissues, slipping them into his pocket before tucking himself away in his underwear. He zipped up his pants, plucked at his T-shirt a few times, then angled his gaze toward me in the driver's seat when I handed him his baseball cap. "I don't know why I can't get enough of you. After what we just did…" He wiped his palm over his mouth and hair, staring out of the windshield. "I shouldn't want you this much. I shouldn't…"

His jaw ticked, and he left his sentence unfinished.

Which was just as well. I wasn't sure I could handle it otherwise.

He shook his head once then reached a long arm to the back seat, where I'd thrown my purse. Setting the small black bag in his lap, he helped himself to paw through it until he retrieved my cell phone. Then he held it up to me. "Passcode."

I tapped it in, and in return, he typed his phone number into my contacts before tossing it back into my purse and setting it all in the back seat. Then he leaned over and pressed a chaste kiss to the corner of my mouth. "Heads up that I'm not great at texting since I can't spell for shit, but message me when you get home, okay?"

"Would a proof of life picture be better?"

"Only if you want to know what your tutorial video did to me," he said, as if that would turn me off.

"Maybe I do," I said, all sass and confidence.

I didn't know where it was coming from, this sexual freedom. Or maybe it was always there but locked up tight. I'd been so career-focused my whole life, I needed someone to let it loose. Let *me* loose.

And if there was ever a reason for me to agree to this fling with Dylan, it was *that*.

He was letting me loose.

"Another night," he promised and stepped outside before shutting the door, knocking on the roof twice.

And as I drove away with the sight of Dylan Matthews in my rearview mirror, I had to remind myself I was leaving.

I was absolutely leaving.

TEN
DYLAN

"All right. Good eye, Angel. Good job. Who's up next?"

Angel, in his shirt that was way too big on him, dragged his bat behind him as he headed to the back of the line. I needed to figure out a way to get some pep in his step.

I accepted the balls Tucker had fetched from behind home plate. He was my little ball and bat boy, running equipment for me. I'd tried to wrangle Scarlett to help too, but she wasn't at all interested. She preferred to stay in the stands, playing on an iPad.

Motioning to the kid at the plate, I flicked my fingers side to side. "Widen your stance a bit, Austin."

"I'm Ashton!"

"Sorry. Ashton, step out a little more. Good. Now, keep your elbows up and eyes on me."

I tossed the ball toward Ashton, and he was a few seconds late on his swing. "Good follow-through, but keep your eyes on the ball, okay? Here comes another pitch."

On the next swing, he connected, sending it out toward me.

"Nice. Great job."

Ashton moved to the back of the line, and the next player

stepped up. This one for sure was Austin.

"You're looking good, Austin. Great stance—"

"I'm Axel."

I sighed. "How 'bout I call you all Adam?"

A peewee of a boy raised his hand. "But I'm the only real Adam!"

I inhaled and exhaled nice and slow. "You're right, Adam. I'll work on getting uniforms soon, and everybody will go by last names, agreed?"

They all nodded, and I turned back to the one at the plate. "Okay, Axel. Here it comes."

After each player had a few turns hitting, I instructed them to set their helmets and bats down, so they could run the bases.

"Pump those arms," I reminded them as I trekked over to the fence, where Jude stood.

"What do you think?" he asked me, his gaze out on Sebastian who was at the back of the pack.

I folded my arms over my chest. "Too many A names. What about, like, Bobby? Or Tommy?"

He snickered quietly then held his hand out to Tucker, who wound up and crashed his palm against Jude's.

"Dang, little dude." Jude shook his hand, and Tucker grinned happily like the brick shithouse he was. "But, seriously," he said to me. "Thanks for helping out."

"It's nothing."

"Well, your time with your kids is precious, and you're spending it here at practice."

I shrugged. "Tuck loves it, right?"

My son plopped one of the helmets on his head and slapped at it. "Yep!"

I turned over my shoulder to check on Scarlett. "Hey."

She glanced up.

"Only a few more minutes, okay?"

"I'm hungry. Can we go to McDonald's?"

"No. Your mom's making you guys dinner."

She pouted but went back to her screen.

"How's dance class going?" Jude asked once I faced forward.

"It's all right." I swiped my hat from my head and scratched at my scalp before replacing the cap. "But I slept with Nate's sister."

"Evie?" he asked, his voice high-pitched and annoyingly worried like I'd broken *his* little sister's heart. Which was stupid. He'd barely remembered her when we were there. I gestured for him to keep his voice down so Scarlett didn't hear. He leaned in to whisper-shout at me. "If you're telling me we can't go back to Walt's, I'm gonna be pissed. I really like it there. Plus, I'm not picking sides between you and Nate."

I huffed at his dramatics. "Of course we can go back there. And no one is picking sides. Jesus." I crossed my arms. "Everything's fine, but she's Scarlett's dance teacher."

His eyes widened to the size of dinner plates, swiveling his head between me and my daughter.

Ignoring him, I cupped my hand around my mouth to alert the team. "Last lap!"

Jude only stared at me.

I glowered at him. "Don't look at me like that."

A slow smile spread across my friend's face, and he took his cell phone from his pocket. "I gotta text Liam. This is too good." He typed away on it, muttering, "One-night stand with his daughter's dance teacher."

"Actually," I said quietly. "It was more than once."

He froze mid-text to meet my gaze.

"I saw her this past weekend too. And…" I wagged my head back and forth, contemplating how much to tell him.

"What? Are you dating her now?"

"No." I jerked my head back. "What? No. Not that I wouldn't want to if that was something I did, but it's not, so…"

Jude quirked a brow at my rambling, and I attempted to rein myself in.

"How it was between us…it was good, but she's moving

away in a few weeks, which is kinda perfect. Neither one of us is looking for anything, so we're just going to…"

He circled his hand for more explanation. Of course he wouldn't understand. The guy who had been with one woman his entire life would have no concept of a short-term fling.

"We're going to spend the next few weeks together, no strings attached, and then when she leaves, no hard feelings." I clapped a few times to call for the kids' attention. "Great work. Grab some water and make sure you pick up all your equipment."

Then Jude and I started in on stacking the bases into a bin that I needed to lock up behind the dugout. He shook his head a few times. "I don't get it, man. How could you not expect to catch feelings for someone you're having sex with?"

"Easy. You set boundaries and remember it's only sex. She knows I don't do relationships, and I know she's not staying, so there's no need to get sentimental about it."

Brief memories of our time together floated through my mind to the more recent text messages we'd exchanged, continuing our twenty-questions game. I now knew her favorite movie was *Footloose*, her favorite food was strawberries, and she'd had a pet guinea pig growing up named Cookie.

And since Friday, she'd sent me a "proof of life" picture every single night. They'd all been rather innocuous yet wildly sexy. Like the one of her applying lipstick or a selfie in the mirror at the dance studio when she wore a light-blue leotard or just lying in bed with her head against the pillow and no makeup on her face. If I were a different kind of person, I might've made that my home screen, but I didn't get attached. Besides, I already had a picture of two little ones on my home screen.

"Genevieve's a great girl," I told Jude. "But she knows the score."

He dismissed me with a soft sound. "If you say so." He patted my shoulder a few times. "I'll see you Wednesday."

As other parents shuttled their kids away, I waved Scarlett

and Tucker over. "Before we leave, do either one of you want to try to hit?"

"Yes!" Tucker immediately sprinted off to grab a bat and stood at home plate.

Scarlett cheered for him. "You can do it, Tucker!"

I lobbed a ball his way, and much to my elation and not so much surprise, my son smacked the shit out of the ball. I whooped and laughed as he ran as fast as his little three-year-old legs could carry him.

"Home run!" Scarlett clapped.

"Way to go, buddy!" I picked him up when he crossed home plate again. "Nice hit."

"Go again?" he asked, and I ruffled his hair.

"Not today. I gotta get you home to your mom. But we'll play again. I promise."

He sulked but took my hand when I put him down. After I locked up the equipment and loaded my car, we were on our way.

After I parked in front of Paige and Neil's house, the kids raced to the door, shouting about how they were starving. I trailed them at a much slower pace and ambled into the kitchen, where Neil was in the middle of setting the table. He gave me the usual nod. I offered him one back.

Meanwhile, Paige divvied out green beans onto plates next to meatloaf.

"Oh no!" Scarlett crossed her arms. "I hate green beans."

Tucker followed suit, imitating her. I pointed at him. "Don't you start. Just because your sister acts like that doesn't mean you do too."

Paige glanced over her shoulder at our daughter. "And you've never even tried green beans, so you can't say you don't like them."

Neil cajoled Scarlett, "Try them, you might like it." When she started to argue, he tipped his head. "One bite, that's all we're asking. One tiny bite."

She responded with a growl and smacked her forehead on the table, so I took that as my cue. "Okay, I'm gonna head out. Love you two."

Tucker waved with this fork in his hand, too excited over dinner to give me a hug, but Scarlett flung herself at me. "Daddy!"

"I'll see you tomorrow at dance class."

"Promise?"

"Promise." I kissed her head and shooed her back to the table, but Paige stopped me halfway to the front door.

"Hey. I need to talk to you."

I turned, lifting my cap. "What's up?"

"I'm going to have Scarlett's birthday party here."

"I thought she wanted to have it at the pool." I distinctly remembered her telling me she wanted to have it at the pool where she took her swim lessons.

"She did, but by the time I called, they were all booked up."

"Oh. Okay."

Paige folded her arms defensively. "*What?*"

"Nothing."

"Then why'd you say it like that?"

"What?" I raised my hands, not sure what she was talking about. "I said okay because...okay. Her birthday party will be here."

She rolled her eyes. "You said it like it's my fault."

I rubbed my hand over my face and sighed. "I don't care where the party is, here or there or on a goddamn spaceship. As long as Scarlett's happy, I don't care. And I'm *not* blaming you for anything."

After a moment, she relaxed. Though, she didn't apologize for her...misinterpretation, so I didn't either. "I'll need the number of people you want to invite. I'm assuming your friends from the play place?"

"Yeah."

"Text me their names, and I'll give you the invitations next week."

I nodded. "Is there anything else you want me to do?"

Her face pinched, and then it was my turn to be offended.

"I can help. If you're hosting the party, the least I can do is pick up supplies or whatever."

She still didn't look convinced, and this was the shit that really pissed me off. I knew I'd fucked up while we were married, but I was different now. I was trying to be better for our kids and our co-parenting relationship. "So, you're gonna get mad at me because you think I have some kind of tone when I say 'okay' to having the party here, but you won't even let me help with it. How is that fair? That you blame me for everything, but don't give me a chance to do anything."

In answer, she did that infuriating head-tilt thing and lifted her hands, like she hadn't instigated this. Like I was the bad guy and she was the innocent one. "Fine. You need to text me the names of all the people you want to invite and pick up the cake and catering."

"Great."

With that, I stalked out of the door, trying not to slam it on the way.

Once I was in my car, I opened up my text thread with Genevieve and asked if I could see her tonight. I didn't receive a reply until I was home, informing me that she had her period and was teaching class tonight anyway.

So there went my plans for the next few nights that I didn't have the kids.

Until a new photo came through. This one of Genevieve looking theatrically sad with her red lips pouting. But the part that really caught my attention was how she had her body angled, leg positioned up on the ballet barre, head inclined up toward her phone, as if stretching like that was nothing.

My dick thought it was *everything*.

Seemed like I had a date with my hand and my new favorite picture.

ELEVEN
DYLAN

Being the third week of class, I thought we should have been getting better. The portion of the dance Genevieve taught us tonight was without the girls, and we were supposed to send them off for a bit while we kicked and grapevined across the stage. But most of these people couldn't even keep time.

It was a mess, and she shot me a glare on the multiple occasions I grumbled in irritation. But, goddamn, how many times did she have to say it was step kick, *not* kick step.

As usual, when class was over, I hung around for a minute alone, following her back to the corner with the stereo. As she toyed with the controls, I toyed with the waistband of her black pants. "What're you doing tonight?"

"I'm going home to take some pain relievers for my cramps and sit on the couch."

"You don't feel good?" I asked, and she shook her head. "Because of your period?" I guessed, and she nodded.

"I always have a lot of back pain," she explained and then asked, "What about hanging out this weekend?"

"I have the kids."

She wrinkled her nose. "Oh, okay. Well, I guess…let me know when you're free?"

I nodded and backed away a few inches, playing it cool. Hoping I didn't sound as desperate as I felt. "Of course."

She offered me a smile, and I pivoted around to Scarlett, who was watching Genevieve and me with her soft brown eyes. Her soft and *knowing* brown eyes. I tugged on her ponytail, forcing her gaze from her teacher and hopefully away from any suspicions she might've been dreaming up.

Hurting my children was the number one reason I didn't have relationships, and Scarlett's attention on the two of us was a reminder that I needed to be extra careful. So I supposed that I needed to keep my hands and eyes to myself for the remainder of the classes to be sure I didn't let on to the arrangement Genevieve and I had.

After Scarlett and I went out for dinner and I dropped her back home, I slipped into shorts and sneakers. I wasn't sure where the sudden restlessness was coming from, but I needed to run. Although not even the three and a half miles helped in clearing my head of the woman who'd taken up residence there.

I didn't know why I felt so cut up about not seeing her tonight. It wasn't like the two of us had plans or anything. The whole point of this was to *not* make plans, yet frustration coiled tight in my chest.

Even worse was how I was moving on autopilot, scrolling through my phone for my DoorDash app, ordering food that wasn't even for me. I hoped a hot shower would do the trick and get my mind right.

I tugged on a pair of clean shorts and threw myself onto the couch as my cell phone rang with a FaceTime call. I didn't have to look at the name I'd programmed with the red lips emoji next to it. I knew it was her. Because I'd sent her food like some fucking love-sick chump.

"I guess we come to the part where you tell me why your

marriage didn't work out," she said, skipping pleasantries, "because if this is how you treat girls you're just fucking, you must go all out for the ones you're actually with."

I ignored her question. "Say fucking again."

She grinned at me then rasped real slow and gravelly, her red lips forming the word. "Fucking."

I blew out a long and agonized breath. "You sure I can't come over? I'm not afraid of a little blood."

Her eyes went wide. "Believe me, you don't want any part of this right now."

The part that I couldn't believe was that my first instinct was to go to her place to hang out. And *only* hang out. Like a goddamn boyfriend.

Then she stuffed her mouth full of food, and I'd never seen a cuter food monster. Fuck me.

"How those tacos working out for you?" I asked.

"So good. Thank you. Hits the spot." She slurped a splash of salsa off her hand. "Okay, back to your story. I need to know."

"You're leveling up twenty questions."

"Mm-hmm."

I scrubbed my hand over my face, not particularly interested in confessing all my faults. I already paid my therapist enough to do that. But I supposed it would be good to clear up some things between Genevieve and me. Or, rather, me and myself.

This wasn't new, giving Gen information. I'd been divulging tiny pieces of myself for the last three weeks, but nothing as huge as this. And it wasn't like I had trouble telling the truth—obviously, I didn't with Dr. Manascalo or the guys—but just like I didn't do repeats with women, I also didn't invite them into my personal life.

Although, as usual, there was nothing *usual* about Genevieve.

"I guess I have to go back to before I met Paige," I started, muting ESPN on the TV and tucking one arm behind my head. "I was never good at school, but my mom's a teacher and she wanted me to go to college. I would've rather gone into the draft early, but she made me promise to get a degree because she said baseball wasn't a sure thing, and she was right."

"But you played in the major leagues, didn't you?"

"Yeah. I was the fortieth draft pick."

"Is that good?"

"Yeah." Back then, I was so full of myself. Not that I thought I was the best player in the league, more that I considered myself untouchable. That nothing could bring me down. But I'd found bottom eventually. "I played first base and spent three years in the minors, which was when I met Paige. When I played for Philadelphia's farm team."

"How old were you when you met? Twenty-two, twenty-three?"

"Twenty-three, and I was used to how I was treated through high school and college, like…"

"A self-important jock who had everything handed to him on a platter," she finished for me.

"Harsh, kitten."

She laughed. "But fair?"

"It's fair." Getting more comfortable, I readjusted my hold on the phone and rested it on my stomach, so my upper chest, shoulders, and head were in view.

Gen paused with a tortilla chip covered in salsa halfway to her mouth. "Dylan, are you not wearing a shirt?"

"No."

"Let me see."

"You take your shirt off and show me so we're even."

"I can't. I'm too busy eating to let you ogle me."

"Then no ogling me if I can't ogle you."

She heaved out a sigh and shoved her chip into her mouth, her words ordering me to continue with my story a bit garbled.

I went on, "I was used to having a lot of people help me, especially with my schoolwork. I really did need it. I mean, you know I'm not faking it."

"No." She snorted. "I got that when you couldn't spell Australia after a few tries and then sent me a bunch of kangaroo emojis."

"Hey, you got the message." Over the weekend, while we had texted a bit, she'd asked where I'd like to travel to one day. I'd butchered the name so badly, spell-check didn't even work.

"I did. So, you were getting a lot of help in school, and what? You got spoiled?"

She spoke so plainly about me that my usual self-consciousness didn't come into play. Not even a little bit. I was telling her a story, and she was listening, interested but not judging.

"Yeah," I went on, "you could say that. When me and Paige got together, she sorta took over that role. She was making sure I got everywhere on time. She was cooking my dinners. She was keeping track of my stuff since I tended to lose it." I rubbed at my forehead, knowing this was the part that would turn her off. Which was what I wanted to do. I wanted to draw the lines in the sand. Let her know I was no good for her.

Skipping over most of the details, I told her, "I didn't realize all the weight I'd been putting on her, especially once we had kids. It was just always how it was with me. She eventually told me she didn't want to parent me and the kids. And that was the end."

"But you seem so together now."

"I had to get it together. I only spent five years in the league, but most of that time, I was on the IL."

"Is that like DL?"

"DL?" I repeated.

"Down low," she said, and I gave into a small smile.

"No. IL is the injured list."

"Ah. I'm learning so much."

I envisioned her tossing a ball back and forth with me. "Soon I'll have you talking RBIs."

"RBIs? Stands for really big instrument…?"

"You thinking about my really big instrument?"

She hummed. "Maybe."

"Maybe you're nothing but a really big tease," I said, and her answering laugh was light and airy.

"You're the one who brought it up."

"Because it needs attention."

"Oh my god," she giggled. "It's only been since last week. Are you that hard up?"

"Yes, kitten, I am. Very hard. Up."

She blushed a pretty pink and shook her head so her hair swayed, as if trying to cover it up. All she did was make it worse.

My addiction to her.

"Back to baseball," she chided, though she couldn't mask her amusement.

"RBI stands for runs batted in," I explained.

"Okay. RBIs and IL, got it."

I ignored how adorable she was. "I had a hairline fracture and high ankle sprain my first year. Second year, I needed shoulder surgery, and after that, I was pretty much bouncing back and forth from the minors to the majors, depending on my injuries…or reinjuries."

She made a sound like a wounded bird.

"You all right?" I asked.

"That's why I'm here," she said quietly—too quietly—and I sat up, watching as she crumpled up the foil paper from her tacos.

"What?"

"Last year, I tore my Achilles. We were rehearsing the kickline, something I could do in my sleep, but… I don't know… One wrong landing and something snapped. It was the worst pain of my life."

I winced, having heard horror stories of torn Achilles tendons.

"There is no IL in the dance world. If you miss an audition or job because of an injury, that's it. You're out. I was out for the whole season, and I lost my spot."

"Ah, Gen, I'm sorry. That fucking sucks. I know how it feels, and I'm so sorry."

"Yeah," she said after a while, snapping the lid onto the small plastic container of salsa. "But I don't want to talk about that. What else can we talk about?"

"I don't know." I eased back down to the cushions. "But why don't we talk while you take your shirt off."

"No," she snickered.

"All right, then. Even exchange. I told you my story. You tell me yours."

"Uh, I think I'd rather show you my boobs." She started to move like she was really going to take off her shirt, but I stopped her.

"Genevieve," I said, gentler than I felt. I didn't like her hiding from me.

"Hm?"

"You owe me. I told you my story. You tell me yours."

I could see she was walking out of the kitchen from the movement of her screen. "I told you already. I tore my Achilles. That's my story."

"Nah." I held my hand out in front of me, curling my fingers in and out of a fist in an attempt to get rid of the tension buzzing through my veins. "That happened to you. Like my injuries happened to me. It's not your story."

It was a long time before she answered as she cuddled up on her couch and settled under a blanket. And that was long enough to drop my hand to the middle of my chest and count my heartbeats underneath it. Almost thirty. I was a patient man.

Eventually, she gave in. "My story's not all that interesting."

"I very much doubt that," I said.

"It's true," she snapped. My kitten had claws.

"Genevieve, you've lived in New York City, been to Paris,

and I'm sure you've danced everywhere. How did you get there?"

I hated myself for asking. For giving in to the thing I knew I shouldn't want and the terrible knowledge that the more I knew about her, the harder it would be to keep my line in the sand. Every minute talking with her was another wave threatening to wash it away.

"I got there by working really hard," she said, and I should have left it there. Whatever she was hiding was her business, but after offering up my past on a platter to her, it felt like we were on uneven footing. Like I was in this deeper than she was, which couldn't be true.

Because I couldn't feel anything for her.

But if she let me in on whatever she wanted to keep hidden, then we were simply two friends helping each other out. At least, that's what I'd tell myself.

"You're a professional athlete. Of course you worked hard," I said, and she sniffed a laugh.

"I never wanted to do anything else," she explained. "I wasn't particularly good at or interested in school. I'm not sure what came first, me not being interested or me not being good at it, but I was *good* at dance."

Goose bumps raced down my arms because I knew exactly what she was talking about. Finding your *thing*. The one thing you excelled at above all else. The one thing you'd give up anything to do.

"You're still good at dance," I said because I felt like she needed to hear it.

Again, she didn't say anything for a long time. "My parents divorced when I was ten. It was ugly."

Her reactions and reluctance to me made a lot more sense now. "I'm sorry."

"Yeah." Her voice was bland. "But I dealt with it."

"Through dancing," I assumed, understanding how to focus emotions on to that *thing* you're good at. How helpful it could be, while also being a crutch. My crutch was yanked out from underneath me when I was released from my contract and unceremoniously dropped from major league baseball. I imagined that was how Genevieve was feeling. Like the thing that had held her up for so long wasn't there anymore, and she was struggling to stand on her own.

"When I was in high school, I started dating this guy. His name was Brent," she started.

"I hate him," I said, earning a laugh.

"We were together for two years. He was my first love, first everything, and…" She inhaled audibly. "I was ready to give it up for him."

"Give what up? Dance?"

"Yeah. I was caught up in Brent. I couldn't see my life without him, and I was ready to follow him wherever he went. Until I caught him with my best friend, Alyssa."

"Oh shit," I muttered. Because I knew how that felt. To be shattered by someone you loved. Not exactly in the same way, but enough to commiserate with her. "That's… That must have been really hard."

"Yeah. It was, and I couldn't believe I'd almost thrown it all away for him. A few weeks later, I moved to New York."

I didn't need her to explain any more to me. I could connect the dots myself. Dance had saved her. And maybe that was where we differed. She used her good thing to hide and rebuild, while I used my good thing as an excuse. I hadn't tried very hard in any other aspect of my life because I'd been trying so hard at baseball, but it sounded like Genevieve tried so hard in dance because when she tried at everything else, it failed her.

In my case, I was the letdown.

In her case, other people let her down.

I made an attempt to brighten her up. "Well, when you get back onstage, I might have to pay you a visit. See if I can distract you with my really big instrument."

"Dylan."

"Yeah?" I loved how she said my name.

"You'd have to try awfully hard to make me lose focus."

I agreed with a hungry sound from the back of my throat. "Challenge accepted."

TWELVE
GENEVIEVE

Since it was the tail end of my period, and I had absolutely no plans because Dylan had his kids for the weekend, I laced up my sneakers for a walk early Saturday afternoon. Sometimes I did my best choreographing while walking. I'd visualize it all in my head as I pumped my playlist through my earbuds, but with all of my classes' routines basically done at this point, I had nothing to work on and listened to a podcast instead.

I was on mile three and a second episode of Kate and Oliver Hudson's show when I came across a park with two baseball fields on one end, two soccer fields on the other, and a small jungle gym and pavilion in the middle. But what caught my attention was the familiar figure standing at the chain link fence in front of the dugout closest to me. He wore sneakers, athletic shorts, a T-shirt similar to the uniforms the team had, and a hat.

Without consciously thinking about it, I made my way closer. Dylan's team was seated on the bench, with one player at the plate and another on first base.

After our long and emotional conversation Tuesday night, we hadn't communicated much. I think we'd both needed time away to remember what we were doing wasn't serious.

Although it was nice to talk to someone who could relate to what I was going through, I knew it wasn't good for my heart.

Because of how that stupid, stupid organ was currently fluttering wildly in my chest.

"All right now! Come on!" Dylan shouted, clapping a few times.

I stood at the end of the fence, close enough to hear what was going on but far enough away that I wouldn't be a creep. Adults and a few kids were scattered on lawn chairs behind the fence, cheering, and I noticed Jude Gray. He had two little girls next to him, one of them being Scarlett.

"You got this, Seb!" he called. A moment later, the pitcher threw the ball, but the batter missed.

"Hey!" Dylan poked his hand around the fence as if his message needed to be physically sent. I automatically took a few steps in his direction. "Shake it off! Eyes open and anticipate! You can do it!"

The batter nodded and got back into position. This time, when the pitcher threw, the batter connected and sent the ball flying toward third base. Everyone cheered, including me. And I didn't even know the kid. Didn't know anybody.

"Miss Gen!"

A little body crashed into me, and I steadied myself on the fence, patting Scarlett's back with a laugh. "Nice to see you too."

"What're you doing here?"

"Came for a walk. Are you here helping your daddy coach?"

She wrinkled her nose. "I hate baseball."

I bent down to her level. "Well, it's nice you're here to support him anyway."

"Want to sit with me?" She took my hand before I could answer and led me over to the bleachers. Jude grinned when he saw me.

"Hey, Evie, how are you?"

"I'm good. What're you doing here?"

He pointed to the kid now at first base. "That's my son, Sebastian, and this is my daughter, Amelia."

She smiled at me with messy pigtails on either side of her head, a stuffed unicorn under her arm.

"Amelia's four, and she's my best friend," Scarlett said, "but she doesn't like dance."

I lifted a shoulder. "Well, that's okay. Not everyone likes baseball or dance. I bet Amelia has something she really likes." When the little girl nodded, I asked, "What is it?"

"Unicorns!"

"Of course you like unicorns. Who doesn't?" I tugged on the one she held. "What's this one's name?"

"Small Unicorn," she said in a voice fit for a pixie.

"Small Unicorn." I nodded sagely. "Perfect name."

She bent to pick up two more stuffed unicorns. "This one is Sophia," she said, showing me the blue-and-pink one then the tiny rainbow one, "and this is Purse."

"Purse?" I bit back a laugh as I turned to Jude, who shrugged. "Purse is a great name," I told Amelia.

"My birthday is-is-is in December," she told me with excited breaths.

"Oh yeah?"

She nodded, squeezing all three of her unicorns tightly. "And Daddy's gon-gonna get me a big, *big* unicorn cake!"

"Obviously, he is. You can't have a birthday party without a big, big unicorn cake."

She bounced up and down excitedly, and Jude elbowed me lightly. "Now I won't hear the end of it today."

"But how can you say no to that face?"

"Real easy," he said then looked at his daughter. "No."

She grinned and threw herself at him, smothering him with kisses.

"Love you, Daddy," Amelia squealed, and he wrapped her up in his arms.

"Fine! Three-tier unicorn cake it is."

I laughed while Scarlett crawled into my lap, and I tipped my chin down to her. "You girls got your daddies wrapped around your fingers, huh?"

She held up her index finger, examining it. "No."

I squeezed Scarlett a little tighter and shifted my attention out to the field as another kid hit the ball almost right to the pitcher. He caught it and chucked it to the player at first base.

"Out!" the umpire called.

Dylan clapped a few times. "Hey, that's all right!" The boys made their way toward him and their bench. "You guys did great. You got on base. You did exactly what you're supposed to do. Good work."

He knocked them on the shoulders as he turned, his gaze absently lifting. He took two steps and then paused with a double take in my direction.

Scarlett waved madly. "Hi, Daddy!"

I ticked my head to the side at his curious brow raise and shrugged.

He answered with a smile he wiped away with the palm of his hand, though Jude noticed, if his quiet but interested hum was anything to go by.

As the game progressed, I talked with Jude about my dance classes and the end-of-the-year school events for his kids. He was friendly and easygoing, though there was an aura about him, a distance in his dark eyes that I couldn't quite cross, but he was kind and funny all the same. I liked being around him, and I was glad Dylan had a friend like Jude. And the other one... Liam? He seemed nice, too. Then there was my brother.

It made me feel good to know Dylan had close friends. So that when I left, I'd know he was well taken care of. Not that I thought he'd be heartbroken or anything, but I cared for Dylan.

As a friend cared about another friend.

Whom I sometimes slept with.

And I wanted the best for him.

When the game ended, Dylan's team lost by one run, and after the two teams shook hands, he brought them in for a huddle, imparting what looked like words of encouragement from the head nods. Then they all stuck their hands in the middle and shouted something together that sounded like "Go Bears!"

But it was hard to tell with how Scarlett was tugging on my hand, demanding that I watch her leap. Tucker appeared, collecting all the balls, then reached for a helmet, but Dylan caught him around the waist before he could get it on his head. I smiled to myself, watching him carry Tucker in one arm then easily hug Scarlett to his side when she ran to him.

I never thought I'd be into a dad, and yet Dylan was just so… capable. And big. And handsome. And stalking my way.

He set his kids down, and they scurried away to play with Amelia before he greeted me. "Hey, gorgeous."

"Hey, yourself," Jude deadpanned, earning a glower from Dylan.

I flicked my hand between them. "Love this little bromance here."

Dylan shook his head as Jude nodded. "Soul mates."

"You're perfect for each other," I agreed.

Jude held his fist out for his son when Sebastian sulked over. He barely tapped his fist.

"Hey, you did great," Dylan told him. "You got on base, and you had that catch in the third inning."

Sebastian shrugged, clearly unhappy with his performance. "I struck out all the other times."

Dylan huffed. "You know how hard it is to hit a baseball, and you know how much harder it is to get on base and score? Go home and check out some professional stats. It's about two hits for every ten pitches."

"Really?"

"Yeah. Baseball is *hard*." Dylan gripped Sebastian's shoulder. "Don't get down on yourself. It's supposed to be fun, right?"

When Sebastian nodded, Dylan patted his back. "Go home and relax. I'll see you at practice Monday."

Jude held his hand out for Amelia as the trio started away. "See you guys later. Evie, nice to see you again."

Another set of parents with a player approached Dylan to chat, so I mostly hung back, trying to appear inconspicuous. I had no kid on the team and no reason to be there, yet I stayed like some...girlfriend.

Which was totally weird.

As Dylan kept getting pulled into more conversations, I sat down with Scarlett and Tucker in the stands, where she had her little pink backpack stuffed with tiny toys. At least I could make myself useful by keeping an eye on them since some of the people didn't care that Dylan might've had something else to do or another place to be. They kept coming up to talk about fundraising, strength and conditioning camps, and next year's team. Occasionally, he'd slant his gaze to me, though I wasn't sure if it was a silent call for help or to check that I was still there, waiting for him. Each time he looked my way, the corner of his mouth curved, and I smiled back, which seemed to appease him.

And then he did the unthinkable.

He removed his baseball hat, ran his hand through his hair a few times, and stuck it on his head. *Backward.*

I actually craned my neck, peering around to see if any other women in the area were alerted to our homing beacon.

There was only the one who appeared annoyed as her husband—I assumed—talked Dylan's ear off. And I let out a sigh of relief.

Dylan Matthews and his backward cap and dark gaze and rippled abs were mine. All mine.

A minute later, he made his way over to the bleachers, his focus dropping to his kids fooling around with tiny plastic people and animals then lifting back to me.

"You better be careful," I told him, and he propped his hands on his hips, a question in his eyes. "You're wearing your hat backward. That's how you get a girl pregnant."

A beat passed, and he laughed. A big old dimples-carving, head-thrown-back laugh, and my insides turned outside.

He inched toward me, careful not to let his hand linger too long on my waist in front of his kids. "That so?"

"Keep wearing it like that, and see what happens."

His tongue slicked across his lower lip. "Yeah?"

I rubbed at the goose bumps on my arms as I nodded, and with the way he stared at me—not with the slits of the panther or the boyish arch of his brow but with a curious jut of his chin—it almost appeared as if he liked that idea.

I'd meant it as a joke. I was *not* going to get pregnant.

And yet...

I shook myself from my stupor and stood, blurting out an explanation. "I was out for a walk. I didn't know that you'd be here. I mean, I knew you coached baseball, but not that it was—"

"Genevieve."

I lurched back. I loved the way he said my name. "Hm?"

"I'm glad you were here."

"You are?"

He bent to pick up Scarlett's backpack from the ground, a signal for the kids to clean up. "I get to see you do your thing every week. Watch you in your element. 'Bout time I repaid you."

"Quite the payment," I said, looping my arm around him to tug the brim of his hat over the nape of his neck.

Without a blink, he twisted and bared his teeth against the inside of my forearm. A quick tease. Gone before I could take my next breath. Before his kids noticed anything happened.

Meanwhile, I squirmed, my internal temperature topping out at volcanic eruption level.

"Daddy, can we get ice cream?" Scarlett asked.

Tucker whooped. "Ice cream! Ice cream!"

Dylan heaved a sigh at his kids.

"Please!" Scarlett folded her hands. "With sprinkles?"

"Sprinkles!" Tucker repeated.

"From the penguin shop?" Scarlett begged.

"Penguin!" Tucker jumped up and down. "Penguin!"

"Penguin shop?" I asked as Scarlett danced around her father's legs.

"That ice cream place with the penguin statue out front," Dylan explained. "Down on Chestnut Street."

I shrugged. "Right. Obviously. Penguin shop."

"Penguin! Penguin!" Tucker chanted, and I could see Dylan caving as his daughter hung on his forearm.

His muscles flexed as he tensed his biceps, lifting her off the ground like she weighed no more than a grocery bag, and I had a hard time not staring at the veins popping out along his arm.

Or the way he smiled down indulgently at her.

Wrapped around her finger for sure.

"Fine. Let's go to the penguin shop."

Scarlett shrieked in excitement as Tucker headbutted his dad's leg like a puppy. Dylan hauled him up with one arm and hung him upside down.

"Miss Gen, want to come?" Scarlett offered.

"Oh no. That's okay. I—"

"Please!" She folded her hands in front of her, begging me the same way she begged her father.

I set my hands on my hips, trying to look as put out as possible. "I really don't appreciate this. You're too cute for your own good, you know that?"

She nodded. "You coming with us?"

All three of them stared at me. Waiting. Smiling. One with dimples. One upside down. One with her hair bouncing.

"Ugh, fine!"

"Yes!"

As Dylan shepherded us all to his car, I leaned in closer to him. "Are you sure this is okay?"

"What? Getting ice cream?" He spun his keys around his finger. "Are you lactose intolerant or something?"

"No. I mean…" I subtly tipped my head in his kids' direction as they piled into their seats.

"They're not lactose intolerant."

"Dylan."

"Genevieve."

When I scowled at his willful ignorance, he lifted his shoulder. "It's ice cream."

"With your kids."

He ignored the implied meaning as he clicked Tucker into his car seat and then reached over to help Scarlett with hers. It was a repeat of the conversation we'd had at the grocery store, and maybe I was being too sensitive about all this.

But I knew this no-strings-attached fling had the possibility of growing many strings. Besides the two currently strapped in the back seat, there was the one I needed to keep hold of so my heart didn't float away.

Dylan opened the passenger side car door for me. "We'll all go for some ice cream, I'll buy you your favorite flavor, which I know is strawberry, and then I'll take you home. No big deal."

I gave in, since he seemed bound and determined to keep this no big deal, but before I could slide into the car, he caught my elbow. "And when I text you later on tonight after I get them in bed, I expect you to send me a picture of your hand between your legs. Got it?"

I gripped the door tight to keep myself upright when my knees threatened to give out. I cleared my throat. "Got it."

"Good." He closed my door and rounded the hood to hop in his side, tossing his kids a playful nod. "You ready for the penguin shop?"

"Yessssss!"

"Penguin! Penguin! Penguin!"

I shoved my legs together as I offered the saddest excuse for a cheer, "Yay, penguin shop."

Dylan threw me an unimpressed glance as he wrapped his arm around the back of my seat to reverse out of his spot.

He was adorable with his kids, wore his hat backward, *and* did the arm over the back of the seat thing? It was like he was *trying* to kill me.

After spending twenty minutes at the penguin shop, watching Scarlett and Tucker demolish their ice cream, Dylan did exactly as he promised and dropped me off at home with little more than a wave. Inside my apartment, I dove into my drawer for my vibrator and took a *very* long shower. He wasn't sent one picture that night. He was sent multiple.

THIRTEEN
GENEVIEVE

ate Monday morning, I pulled into a spot in front of Matthews Mechanics and checked my lipstick in the rearview mirror before stepping out of my car. I really did need to get my car inspected, as my brother reminded me after noticing the sticker on my windshield, but I thought it was a good excuse to see this hot car guy I knew.

As I entered the shop, I pushed my sunglasses back on my head and crossed the small rectangular waiting room to the counter. When no one seemed to notice or hear me from the garage, I hit the little bell twice. A Black guy with a kind smile appeared. "Hey, how can I help you today?"

"Hi. I need to get my car inspected."

"Do you have an appointment?"

I winced. "I didn't know I needed one."

After wiping his hands off on a cloth, he flipped through a book. "We can maybe fit you in tomorrow or—"

"Today."

I looked up at the same time the man in front of me did. Dylan was there with a baseball cap on his head, a black T-shirt, and coveralls folded down and tied around his waist.

"We can fit her in today," he said to the guy, even though he was staring at me.

"I'm sorry. I didn't know I needed an appointment," I told him.

"You never need an appointment." He rounded the counter, invading my space and snatching my car keys from my hand. He tossed them to the other man. "She's got the gray Acura. Pull it around, and I'll take a look at it."

"I thought you were taking lunch," the guy said.

Dylan sighed with an annoyed breath that had me biting back a laugh. "Just go, Greg."

Greg's gaze flickered between Dylan and me before he got the message, a sly smile on his face as he disappeared. "Sure thing."

Then Dylan's eyes were back on me, glowing panther green under the brim of his hat. "Hey, gorgeous."

"You're kinda hot in that." I waved down the length of his body. "And hearing you be all boss man. That's…" I clucked my tongue, raising my brow, feeling my skin heat.

"You like that, do you?" When I nodded, he kissed me chastely as he eased his hands around my hips. His eyes took me in from the top of my head to my toes. "You paint your clothes on this morning?"

I stepped away from him, looking down at myself in skinny jeans and white bodysuit then smiled back up at him. "You like that, do you?"

"Kitten." He pulled me to him so I could feel exactly how much he liked it. "You have no idea." He combed his fingers into my hair, and there was nothing chaste about this kiss, all tongue and teeth, and after not being with him for a week, I was ready to strip down right here in the middle of his shop. Let him do whatever he wanted to me on the counter.

"All set, boss!" Someone, I assumed Greg, shouted from the garage, and Dylan leaned his forehead against mine, his fingers clutching hard at my waist. He exhaled, and I breathed it in.

"Are you really giving up your lunch to inspect my car?"

"Shouldn't take long. You going to hang around here?"

I motioned to the windows behind me. "There's a pizza place down the street. How about I pick up lunch for both of us? My treat in exchange for you being so nice to me and inspecting my car when I didn't have an appointment."

He squeezed my ass in his big hands. "Sounds good."

He gave me a smack on the way out, and when I turned over my shoulder, he was standing there with his hands on his hips, his mouth tugging up at the corner as I sashayed away. I tamped down the giddy excitement that had me almost dancing down the sidewalk.

After Saturday afternoon, our texts and phone calls had devolved from friendly twenty questions with occasional innuendos to straight-up "I can't wait to fuck you" texts and Face-Time calls.

Not that I minded. It was why I'd decided to drive to his shop. I'd lost my patience.

I only had a few weeks left here, and even though I wasn't sure where I'd end up, I knew I'd regret wasting any time with Dylan. Sure, I was hesitant about his kids discovering the truth, but not enough to make me give up this chance to find any bit of happiness I could. He made me feel good—physically, mentally, and emotionally—and I wasn't about to question it.

After scrolling on my phone for a while at the pizza place, I brought our to-go slices back to the shop, where I lingered in the front. Another man was there, older and gray-haired, reading a Tom Clancy novel, probably waiting on his car.

It wasn't long before Dylan popped around the wall of the garage and gestured for me to follow him. Music blared from the corner, and Greg bopped his head to Billy Joel's "Uptown Girl." Dylan leaned down to a young kid, who looked just out of high school. "Knock on my door if you need something."

The kid nodded, barely taking his eyes off the inside of my car as Dylan ushered me inside an office, closing and locking the door. I set down the pizza and inspected the small space with a desk, computer, and paper calendar hanging on the wall, along with a few framed photos. "Aww." I pointed to one of a little boy in dirty coveralls next to a man who looked like an older version of Dylan. "Is that you?"

"Yep. Me and my dad."

"That's so cute." When I felt him behind me, I spun around and tipped my head back. "So, you pawned my car off on someone else?"

He shook his head, his fingers finding my belt loops. "I checked it out myself. Cory's an apprentice. He's finishing it up. You're getting new windshield wipers and an oil change."

"What—"

He cut me off, hauling me against him. I gave in to his voracious kiss with a laugh and wrapped my arms around his neck, accidentally knocking his hat off in the process. But that only spurred him on more. He pushed me backward until I hit his desk, and then I was lifted up onto it, with him moving between my legs.

"You don't want lunch?"

He shook his head, eyeing me like an untamed animal. His dirty fingers mapped my white top, leaving smudges in their wake, and a low, throaty sound emanated from him. I almost couldn't hear it over Billy Joel's voice filtering in through the walls.

There was something about him in his coveralls with grease on his hands and me in my pristine clothes and hair he mussed with said rough fingers that made me feel like we were living the lyrics of the song.

He must've been thinking it too because as he pressed a soft kiss to my lips, he muttered, "My uptown girl." Then he wrapped his hands around my bare arms. "Don't move."

I didn't dare try as he marched out of the office like a man on a mission. He returned a minute later, still wiping off his now-clean hands, and prowled toward me, tossing the paper towel in the garbage can without even batting an eye in its direction. Then he had one hand in my hair, the other on my breast, swiping his thumb gently over my nipple. Such a stark contrast to the way he sucked at my lips, throat, and jaw. I wrapped my legs around his waist, trying to pull him as close to me as possible, but he skated his hand up to my collarbone, keeping me at a distance as his other hand prodded along my back and waist.

My eyelids were heavy when I peered at him. "What...what are you doing?"

"Trying to figure out how to get you naked. What is this?"

I tried to bite back a smile and failed.

"Genevieve," he growled impatiently, tugging the zipper of my jeans down. "What the fuck are you wearing?"

"A bodysuit," I said, succumbing to giggles.

He was not amused. "A bodysuit?"

"Yes. There are snaps."

His gaze dropped to my crotch. "Snaps? Like a diaper? A onesie?"

"Yeah."

His brow rose as he wiped his hand over his mouth, as if wondering how to handle the situation. Then he backed away and folded his arms. "Well... Lemme see. Come on."

I slipped off the desk, noticing a few more dark smudges on the white material. One, in particular, under my left nipple. When I glowered at him for leaving such obvious marks, he actually smirked at me.

"Proud of yourself?" I asked, and he shrugged.

"A little."

Ignoring him, I dragged my jeans off my legs, and he helped me step out of them before sitting down in the chair in front of me.

"I'm not sure how comfortable this onesie is," he said, tugging at the nylon. "But I do like how easily accessible it is." Then he unsnapped the gusset and blew out a breath. "No underwear."

"No bra either."

I barely had time to register his hands pushing me to lie down on the desk because his mouth was already on me, his tongue licking long strokes into me. I gasped then bit my lip to keep from allowing any more sounds to escape, but with how he grabbed my breast, he wanted me loud.

"You think you're going to prance your little ass in here wearing basically nothing and not expect me to make you moan? I don't think so, kitten."

To prove his point, he slid two fingers into me, and my back bowed as I moaned. I reflexively shot my arms out to grab hold of the sides of the desk, knocking items to the floor in my wake.

"So loud," he said, and I thought I felt him actually smile against my thigh.

"Your fault." I blindly batted at him, though it wasn't much of a scolding since he crooked his fingers at the same time he licked my clit, eliciting a drawn-out sigh. He feasted on me, his fingertips and teeth biting into me, and I was almost positive he was trying to get me to make as much noise as possible. Put on a show.

Even with Greg and Cory mere feet away.

We were separated by the walls of the office, but if I could hear their music, I was sure they could hear me.

Yet I couldn't be quiet even if I wanted to be. My muscles grew taut and the hand he had at my back slid over my hip and stomach to my breast, gripping it with ownership that shouldn't have felt so natural. Yet everything had always been natural between us.

We fell easily into our roles. The panther and his kitten.

He toyed with me, his fingers stroking me to the edge of release then backing off, his tongue taking over with long, lazy licks, and I whined out my frustration.

"Something wrong?" he asked, his lips brushing the crease of my thigh and hip.

"Yes."

"What is it?"

I lifted my head from the hard wooden desk. "You."

"Me?" His eyes flashed, and he tipped his head up so I could see how his mouth and chin were covered in my arousal. He spread it over me with his fingers as if delighting in how wet he could make me. "What did I do? I think I'm being awfully nice."

"You aren't letting me come," I wailed, and he teased at my clit, raking his gaze over me like I was at his mercy.

I was.

Might as well have served myself on a platter.

"Are you gonna say my name?"

"Please, Dylan." I pouted, circling my hips, silently pleading for more.

"You sound so sweet." He placed a chaste kiss at the top of my swollen and deprived sex, barely brushing against where I needed him. "You came in here all shiny and perfect, and now I have you squirming on my desk, your skin flushed and hair a mess. I want to enjoy it a little more."

"Please," I begged, my stomach clenching, my entire body lighting up with the need to release. "Please, please, Dylan."

He teased me for another moment, pushing my thighs wide, the tip of his tongue tracing my opening. When I whimpered, my own hands finding my breasts, he gave in, his gaze fixated on where I pinched my nipples in a poor imitation of him. He muttered something unintelligible, but whatever it was, he liked what I was doing, and he finally gave in to my pleas.

He eased his fingers into me, gently massaging my G-spot until I couldn't take a full breath, riding high on pleasure. He sucked on my clit, and I thrashed against the desk, sparks shooting from my fingertips, nonsensical words leaving my tongue.

Through the white noise and bright light behind my closed eyelids, I could barely make out Dylan's voice, rasping, "That's it. That's what I love."

Then I felt the prickle of his stubbled jaw and chin dragging back and forth between my thighs. A few long moments passed before I pieced reality back together and opened my eyes to find him staring at me through narrowed slits. That was when I felt it, how he was smearing the wet evidence of my orgasm all over my pussy and thighs. Then without taking his gaze from me, he licked it off, cleaning me with his tongue.

"Condom," I told him. "In my purse."

He backed away from me, sucking on each of his fingers in turn, and I was in danger of spontaneously combusting. "You need to hurry up."

"You're right," he said, standing up. "I need to get back to work."

I assumed he meant *work* like me, but when I didn't hear the telltale sound of his zipper, I pushed up onto my elbows. "Wha…what are you doing?"

He fixed my bodysuit and snapped it closed then snagged my jeans from the floor and held them out to me, one leg at a time. "Helping you get dressed."

"Why?"

He nodded toward the digital clock in the corner. "I have a car coming in for a tune-up in five minutes."

"But…"

With a hand on my elbow, he urged me to stand then tugged my denim up to my waist, fastening the button and zipper. Once I was dressed, he reached for the pizza. "Thanks for lunch."

He retrieved a greasy slice from the brown bag, chowing down as I stared in disbelief. "That's it?"

He swallowed his bite of food. "I'm really glad you came."

I rolled my eyes at the innuendo.

"But seriously…" He set down his pizza and wiped his fingers on his shirt. "I'm happy I got to see you today. I mi—"

He stopped himself, and I didn't ask him to fill in the blank. I couldn't even look him in the eye, instead focusing on his throat and how it worked on a swallow.

"What do I owe you?" I asked finally.

"Nothing," he said eventually.

I lifted my chin, meeting his gaze. "Nothing?"

He shook his head. "Just text or call me later."

"Okay." When he bent to kiss my cheek, I tried on a smile. "I guess I'll see you at class tomorrow?"

"Tomorrow." His eyes trailed over me, stopping momentarily at the black smudges he'd left on my white outfit. There was no way Greg and Cory wouldn't know what we'd done, but when Dylan opened his office door, no one was in the garage, and I hoped maybe they'd taken their lunch while I was moaning their boss's name.

"I'll drive your car around to the front."

Outside, Dylan parked it in front of the shop before stepping out, holding the door open for me.

He kissed me once more. "See you later, Gen."

"Bye, Dylan."

Then I dropped down behind the wheel, and he shut the door, knocking on the roof of my car. And for the second time in as many weeks, I had Dylan Matthews in my rearview mirror.

FOURTEEN
GENEVIEVE

"I haven't heard from you in a while."

"Yeah. Sorry." I mindlessly shuffled my foot back and forth as I leaned away from the barre. "I've been busy."

Which was sort of true. I had been relatively busy between teaching classes and working at Walt's. But if I'd wanted to, I could have called my mother back any time. She'd called and texted me for the past few days, and I knew why. My father's birthday was Friday, and unhealthy as they were together, my mother still wanted to know what he was doing every year. Like a scab she had to pick.

I tried not to feed into it, but I figured I had to call her back so she'd stop bothering me. Which was terrible to say—my own mother was bothering me. Although, I'd never had a whole lot in common with her. I was more like my dad, and Nate was like Mom.

"How's everything going?" she asked, and I bent toward the barre, stretching out my heels one at a time.

"Fine."

"Find another job yet?"

"Not yet."

"I'm sure you'll find something soon. Only takes one yes,"

she said in her usual refrain. Both of my parents had been supportive of me in my dance career, and they each showed up to every recital, though they never sat together after the divorce and came at different times or days. Mom was emotional and would cry and tell everyone she knew that I was a dancer. When I became a Rockette, I think she sent out a mass email. I appreciated how happy she was for me, but I didn't know if she ever understood how hard I had to work. If I didn't get an audition, her response was always something like "There will be another. Don't worry." Or, "You know what they say, a door closes but a window opens." When what I wanted to hear was, "I'm sorry. That really sucks."

Especially after my injury. I didn't need platitudes. I needed someone to get it, to get in the *suck* with me.

On the other hand, my dad rarely said anything at all. He checked in occasionally, asking, "Everything okay? Anything I can do for you?"

And that was it. I think I could count on two hands the number of times my father had told me he loved me, and I knew from all of my mother's screaming when I was younger, that was part of the problem. His reluctance to talk.

She was temperamental. He was stoic.

She wanted to fight. He walked away.

"I called to check in and see what you've been up to," Mom said, the leading ellipses nearly audible. "Are you doing anything fun this week?"

Since I knew what she was really asking, I answered, "Nate and I are meeting Dad for dinner for his birthday."

She didn't reply. Merely hummed curiously. Like she wasn't bothered one way or the other.

"What are you doing?" I asked.

"We have plans to go out to dinner with Brenda and her husband. Remember her? I think you met her one time."

I pressed up to relevé, working through my arches. "Not ringing a bell."

"Well, we're going to go out to dinner. They have a son about your age and—"

"No, Mom. I'm gonna stop you right there."

"*What?*"

"I don't want to be set up with another one of your friend's sons." Then I added. "Or with anybody else. I'm not looking for a relationship."

"All right," she said defensively. "I thought it might've been nice for you to meet him, but fine. I won't say anything else about it."

And that tone right there was what I was sure drove my father away. Like she was so hurt by my asking her not to set me up on dates. If she didn't get her way, even if it was something that didn't affect her, she got pissy about it. Nate had more patience for her than I did. Probably because he was "her boy," as she called him. He was spoiled by her. Even now, I had no doubt she'd drive right over from New Jersey and do his laundry if he asked.

"I gotta go, Mom. I have a class starting in a bit."

"Okay, honey. Text or call whenever."

"I will."

"Love you," she said, and I answered with a, "Yeah, you too."

I set my phone on the stereo and reached down to fix my shoe strap. Miss Amy had originally brought me on to take over the kindergarten class, which was an introduction to ballet and tap, learning the positions and how to shuffle step, but I also taught quite a few others too. At first, it was only three classes with the little kids, but as the weeks had gone on and I rehabbed my injury, Miss Amy had started complaining of back pain and asked me to teach more. Now, I was basically teaching everything Shauna, the hip-hop teacher, and Leilani, the ballet and pointe teacher, didn't cover.

I didn't mind, especially since Miss Amy had expressed on multiple occasions that she wanted more of an administrative role, but she knew I wouldn't be able to say no to her. Miss Amy was more than a mentor. She was a second mother to me. If she needed a kidney, I'd gladly hand mine over, but the longer I was here, the more settled I felt.

Which wasn't good. I was leaving, and I didn't want anything holding me back, including thirteen adorable little faces that greeted me with smiles as they entered the studio.

I grinned at each one. "Hi, girls! You ready to dance?"

A chorus of agreements rang out. With only a few classes left to the recital, we dived right into their dance to make sure they could remember it as best they could and clean it up. I'd be there backstage, doing it with them in case they forgot the steps, but I wanted them to try to recall it themselves.

Ignoring the stares of some of the adults in the waiting room, especially a pair of green eyes, I bent at the waist, telling the girls, "We learned the end of our dance last week. Do you all remember it? The poses at the end?"

They nodded giddily, some of them hitting those poses, and I laughed. "Yes, perfect. Why don't you show it to me first, and then we'll go back and review the new steps, okay? Go ahead, show me the end pose."

The girls giggled and bumped into one another as they ran to their spots. Some of them on the floor, others standing with their hands up.

"CiCi, other arm, hon. Good. And Celeste, step out a little bit." I wrapped my hands around her tiny waist and tugged her over so she wasn't blocking Raven. "Beautiful. Now, Scarlett and Lily, lean in toward each other. And smile!"

I pointed to the mirror. "I want everyone to look at themselves and see where you are right now because it's perfect. Now, I want you to go back to your lines—" Of course, they didn't wait for me to finish the directions and started moving. "Walk! You don't need to run, Bella. Is everybody back to their places? Let's practice moving to your last pose. Hands on your hips to march. Ready? And march to your pose."

I backed up to the barre, catching Dylan's gaze on the way. With his arms anchored across his chest, he stood still, watching me, the corner of his mouth tipped up sinfully.

I was sure my cheeks heated, but I did my best not to look at him through the rest of the class. The girls did well, and we performed our usual dance circle. I didn't do it with the older kids, but it was a fun routine for the little ones. A silly little treat after they'd worked so hard. Then I gave each of them a high five and a compliment and opened the door for the special some-ones to make their way inside.

Dylan barely glanced my way as he ambled toward Scarlett. He almost never smiled. Except when he was with his kids. They got his full attention and grins.

And I hated to admit that it was one of the things that attracted me most to him.

I had thirteen girls in this class, and of those thirteen, CiCi had asked her brother who was in high school to dance with her, Naomi had chosen her grandfather, and Quinn had asked one of her moms to dance. The others had all brought their dads, and Dylan, with his worn jeans and plain gray T-shirt, was heads above the rest. If not in physical height, then definitely in rhythm.

Anyone could tell he was an athlete. He moved with ease, each of his actions controlled and precise. He picked up the steps quickly too, though he needed to work on his performance face.

"Let's try that again," I said from the front of the room. "Without the girls dancing with you for this section, your focus will need to be out toward the audience. And I hate to tell you this, but you need to look like you're enjoying yourselves." I broke out my show smile and pointed at my face. "See this? *This* is a performance face." Then I made my expression completely blank. "This is not. Neither is this," I said, looking at the floor. "So." I raised my head and smiled once again. "We're going to try that again, and I want to see you really look like you're having a good time. Right, girls?"

The girls, who were standing off to the side, all cheered.

I met each of the special someones' gaze, Dylan being last since he was in the front row and on the end for this bit. "No grumpy faces."

He only responded with a tip of his baseball cap.

"Okay. Let's take it from the top of the break. Switch lines," I instructed, waiting until they returned to their original places. "Girls, stay where you are. We'll pretend you're running off. Special someones, you're waving at them, waving, waving, waving, and five, six, seven, eight. Walk to the back line," I chanted in time with our steps. I pivoted to my right so I was in profile to the audience, like they were, and then we all clapped four times on beat. "Five, six, seven, eight, and slide step kick ball change, slide step kick ball change. Smile!"

I performed the thirty-counts of choreography inspired by the Temptations with them, all the while reminding them to look up and out. It was slightly better.

I turned to the girls. "What do you think? Did you see smiles?"

"Daddy, you weren't smiling!" Scarlett shouted, pointing her finger at Dylan.

"Tattletale," he mumbled with a shake of his head.

Bella pointed at her dad. "Mine was smiling."

Dylan folded his hand around the bill of his hat as he rolled his eyes, and I bit back a laugh.

"Let's do it again with the music before we bring the girls back on and try it all from the top." I met Dylan's gaze. "I'd like to see everyone smiling this time."

He bared his teeth in a poor imitation of a smile.

"Maybe something a little sweeter, Mr. Matthews," I said, earning a stiff arch of his brow that had me covering my neck to hide the rising blush. "Okay. Let me get the music cued up."

I skirted around the edge of the studio, feeling Dylan's panther gaze on me as I pressed play on my phone and fast-forwarded a minute on the song before making my way to the front and center. "Back to your original places," I directed. "Starting from walking to the back line...and five, six, seven, eight."

Dylan did not smile, but he did watch me in the mirror, his eyes never leaving mine. It was cruel, really. Him forcing me to dance with the weight of his stare. It was truly automatic, how my body could continue on with the steps, while I was mentally stripping him down in my head. And I could only thank all my years of training for not giving myself away.

"That was better. Right, girls?" I asked, although I didn't know if it was or not since I had trouble seeing anything other than Dylan and his fingers absently snapping and gray cotton clinging to his shoulder and pecs.

The girls hooted and clapped for their special someones, and I gestured for them to join us. "We'll take it from the top a few times. Sound good?"

They all agreed with giggles from the girls and a few "Woos!" from the adults, but it was Scarlett's shriek of laughter that had me freezing mid-stride. Because Dylan had her up above his head, joking about her snitching on him for not smiling. His T-shirt had ridden up two inches, revealing golden skin and the indents of muscles, but it was his dimpled grin that captured my attention.

That I was pretty sure split my heart in two.

"Daddy!" she screeched, kicking her feet as he swung her in a circle. "Put me down!"

"If you say so." He somersaulted her in the air, making sure she landed on her feet. She straightened, laughing and brushing loose strands of hair out of her face, and I jumped back into motion. Even as Dylan shot a cocky wink my way.

Like he knew exactly what he was doing to me.

I spent the rest of the class toward the other end of the studio, and when we finished, I clapped a few times. "We have two more classes left. That's it. Next week, we're going to learn the last bit. And then the following Tuesday, we'll review, review,

review. Miss Amy sent you the video a few weeks ago, so you should be practicing at home."

I doubted anyone was rehearsing at home. Although, I knew one person who'd watched the video. Not for the original purpose, but at least he'd opened the link.

"See everyone next week," I said after giving high fives to each of the girls and their special someones.

Dylan and Scarlett were last in line, and he wrapped his fingers around my hand as she scooted out into the waiting room, calling for one of the other girls. Her father didn't miss the opportunity to tug me close. "Am I the MVP?"

"Dancing nine, performance five."

"Kitten," he rasped in warning.

"You need to work on your face."

He aimed one long index finger at his chin. "You mean the one that was buried between your legs yesterday?"

I didn't dignify that with a response, but it was awfully difficult when he was standing so close to me. Close enough that all I had to do was press up to my toes and kiss his mouth that had brought me to a desk-rattling orgasm yesterday.

His eyes flared, and his chest expanded on a deep breath. "I have the kids until Friday. I'll call you when I'm done working."

I nodded with a smile. "Can't wait."

A few of the girls from the next class started to filter into the studio, so Dylan brushed past me with a quiet, "We'll see about that performance score this weekend."

FIFTEEN
GENEVIEVE

"Thanks for giving me a ride," I told Nate as I clicked my seat belt into place.

With one hand on the steering wheel and his other arm bent on the open window, my brother repeatedly combed his fingers through his hair. His nervous tell.

Similar to how my mom and I didn't quite understand each other, my father and Nate didn't either. My brother had always been outgoing and into sports. Dad was introverted and not at all interested in playing catch in the backyard. While I chose a "quiet" extracurricular, in which he didn't have to participate, Nate had football, and Dad was never quite able to fit in with the other fathers at his practices and games. And like my mother's need to hear the words of affirmation, so did my brother, but that wasn't our dad.

"Figured it was better to show up at the same time," Nate said, merging into street traffic. "United front and all."

I agreed with a silent nod, and he turned up the volume on his emo music another notch. Nate and I had argued like all siblings did, but our parents' divorce had brought us close together. We were a team. There was no other way to be when we were spending our time split between houses. Neither one of us wanted to be in a home without the other. Especially when Dad had married his younger secretary, which was the most stereotypical midlife crisis move he could've made. But in a turn of events, Mom had reconnected with her high school sweetheart. She sold the house and packed up, heading to New Jersey with him after I'd graduated high school.

Now, Nate and I would be teammates for a family dinner full of weird tension while everyone pretended there was none.

I mindlessly tapped my feet, my thoughts on the stage, where I didn't have to worry about awkward conversations. I was subconsciously in the middle of a series of triple time steps when my phone buzzed in my purse.

I flipped it up in my palm to see Dylan's name on the screen, indicating he'd dropped his kids off and was free for the weekend. I'd taken to sending him voice notes so he didn't have to read them, and I lifted my phone to my mouth to record another. "I'm on my way to dinner with my dad. I'll call you later."

"Who's that?" Nate asked.

It wasn't like I didn't trust that my brother was looking out for my well-being when he warned me away from Dylan, but he also had nothing to do with my personal life. I made my own decisions, and I decided to be direct when I answered, "Dylan."

Nate took a deep breath as if he was about to lecture me, and I stopped him.

"I know what you think about him, but I don't care. We've been spending time together, having fun and getting to know each other. That's it. I'm still leaving in a few weeks, so no need to get on your high horse about how he's a bad guy or something."

"He's not a bad guy," Nate said as if he hadn't cornered me about Dylan a couple weeks ago. "He's just... I don't want to see you hurt."

"I'm not going to get hurt."

My brother faced me at a red light, and I didn't like the flare of doubt in his eyes.

"It's no big deal," I told him, even as the words were heavy on my tongue.

"So, what? Are you guys dating or something?"

"Or something," I said after a while, and he grimaced.

"Gross, Evie. I don't want to hear about it."

"Again—" I flapped my hand in his direction "—you're the one who brought it up. Besides, you're one to talk. You were the one giving everybody the details about all the sex you had with Denise, even though nobody asked."

He didn't argue with me, so I kept on going. If he thought he could say shit about my personal life, I was going to give it right back. "I don't know why you're so worried about getting back with Denise when Tabitha's right there."

"Tabby?" He shot me a confused look then drove through the green light.

"Yeah. How long have you two been working together?"

"Since I opened Walt's."

"And you've never noticed how good you two are together?"

"We work well together, yeah, but she has that boyfriend."

"They broke up a while ago."

"How do you know that?"

"She told me. You probably would've noticed if you didn't have your head up your ass."

He rolled his eyes. "I'm Tabby's boss. I'm not going to hook up with her."

I nodded. "Because you should date her."

"I'm not going to date her either. She might be hot, but she's got a Maleficent vibe about her."

"Maleficent?" I laughed, but he only nodded. He'd always been afraid of the cartoon witch. Always fought me whenever I'd wanted to watch *Sleeping Beauty*. "I think she's badass," I told him. "She drives a motorcycle and doesn't take any shit from guys at the bar."

"Guys give her shit at the bar?"

"Yeah. I mean, you said it yourself, she's hot."

With her tiny waist and huge boobs, of course guys gave her shit. And she threw it right back in their faces. She'd told me once she was a black belt in karate. So badass.

Nate sighed and brushed his hand through his hair again, and I grinned in satisfaction at the seed I'd planted.

I was pretty positive Tabby was in love with my brother. He was just too dumb to see it.

But I relented. "I'll stay out of your love life if you stay out of mine."

A long moment passed before he glanced my way. "Fine. But Matthews is my friend, so… Don't make it weird."

"Won't make it weird," I promised.

In silent agreement, we spent the rest of the drive to the steak place talking about his anxiety-ridden dog, Lucy. Poor thing couldn't handle thunderstorms, and during the last one, she'd ripped a hole in his couch while he was at work. He'd come home to a living room full of stuffing.

We arrived right on time to the restaurant and were escorted to our table by a handsome host in all black.

Dad lifted his hand in greeting when he saw us, which signaled our stepmom to turn our way. She hopped up. "Hi! I'm so glad you two could make it." She pulled me into her arms. "Evie, you look more beautiful every time I see you."

"So do you." Summer was about fifteen years older than me and had a youthful aura about her. When she and my dad had started dating, she hadn't tried to take on a stepmother role. Instead, she went for a friend, which I appreciated.

Nate had a bit of a harder time accepting them together. I suspected it was because he'd had the hots for her when we were kids. He awkwardly patted her back when she hugged him. "Hey, handsome. How's everything going with the bar?"

"Good. Thanks," my brother said with a tight smile then he shook Dad's hand. I handed him the card Nate and I had both scribbled our names in earlier and bent to kiss his cheek.

"Happy birthday, Dad."

"Thank you. Nice to see you."

Nate and I both greeted our half-siblings with smiles and waves. Addy and Carter were in middle school and reminded me of my brother and me, but opposite. Addy was older and athletic. Summer occasionally sent me texts with her team photos. Carter was quiet and quite an accomplished musician for being twelve. He was in all kinds of piano competitions. Though, neither one of them really wanted anything to do with Nate and me.

Not that we tried all that hard. They had their own lives. We had ours. It was uncomfortable to be with Dad's *new* family. There was nothing much to tie us together. But we sure pretended.

Once the server left the table with our orders, Summer leaned forward, smiling. "I'm so glad you two could come out with us. I love when we're all able to be together. Right, Tim?" She not-so-inconspicuously tilted her head in our direction, clearly urging him to say something.

He cleared his throat and pasted on a smile. "Yeah, this is great. Thank you for coming."

"Why don't you open your card?" Summer suggested, and he obliged, carefully ripping it open. A gift card fell out. It was one of those ones that could be used at multiple restaurants.

I'd volunteered to pick the card if Nate bought the gift certificate, and we both unknowingly had gone as generic as possible.

Dad read the words in gold lettering about fathers working so hard and deserving to enjoy their birthday then tapped the corner of the gift card on the table twice. "Thank you both. Very unnecessary, but thank you anyway."

"You're welcome," Nate and I both said on cue.

Summer slipped the plastic gift card from his hand, slathering it on thicker. "Oh my gosh, that's so thoughtful of you. Gen, Nate, you two are so sweet." She grinned at each of us. "We will put this to good use."

After a few moments of quiet, Summer slid her hand to

Carter's head. "Want to tell your brother and sister where we're going this summer?"

It always struck me as weird whenever I was reminded that Nate and I had two other siblings. Even as they sat right across from us.

Carter, in his crisp short-sleeve button-down with little sailboats all over it, offered us his closed-lip smile, so much like our father's. "North Carolina."

"For two weeks in the Outer Banks," Addy added, her attention finally diverted from her cell phone. "I can't wait. I'm obsessed with that show on Netflix."

"Wow," I said as I felt Nate still next to me. "That'll be fun."

Our parents had taken us for a few weekends to the Jersey Shore, but never for two weeks. Vacations were few and far between because Dad was always too busy.

"You're going for two weeks?" Nate asked Dad, and when he didn't answer right away, Summer filled in the blank.

"We convinced him to. Besides, it's time to take a bit of a step back." She grinned at her kids then at our father. "They're going to be done with school and out of the house in a blink of an eye. We can't miss these years with them, right?"

Dad tugged at the collar of his shirt, his gaze on the table. "Right."

Nate and I stayed silent. Him chugging his water. Me diligently righting my utensils.

When we were Addy's and Carter's ages, our parents were in the midst of a divorce. There was no "stepping back" from work where we were concerned. And I—Nate and I—couldn't pretend it didn't hurt to sit there and listen to their plans for a two-week summer vacation.

Sensing her mistake, Summer dropped her smile, and she moved on to another topic, Addy's eighth-grade graduation, but the damage had been done. No one could turn back the time of the last two minutes to erase the conversation—or the last twenty years, which was where it had all begun.

The stilted conversation continued through dinner and dessert, with Summer valiantly leading the way like some Joan of Arc for a failing blended family, and there was palpable relief when we all stood up from the table.

Nate offered a wave to Summer and a pat on the shoulder to our dad, who repeated his sentiment once again. "Thanks for coming."

"Sure," Nate mumbled, backing away so I could hug him.

"Have fun on your trip."

"Thanks, Evie." He kissed my cheek.

I smiled at Addy and Carter in turn. "Make sure to send me pictures of your graduation, okay? And break a leg in your spring concert."

Both of them nodded but were only half listening, already busy with watching something on Addy's cell phone.

Summer wound her arms around me. "I'm so sorry if I made it uncomfortable."

"Don't worry about it," I murmured. "Dinner was delicious."

She pulled back, her eyes full of disappointment. I was sure she wished we were like the Brady Bunch or something, but that wasn't in the cards for us.

She held me at arm's length. "Make sure you let me know wherever you're headed to next, okay?" When I nodded, she winked at me. "Can't ever keep a bright star like you from shining."

"Thanks, Summer." With one last wave to them, I followed Nate out and took my first deep breath since we'd entered the restaurant.

"Fuck," my brother muttered, scrubbing his hand over his hair and face.

I agreed with a sigh. "Yeah."

We settled back in his car, and I didn't argue when he rolled all the windows down, the wind tangling strands of my hair.

I didn't feel like fixing them. Didn't feel like being the shining version of myself right now. I was too raw.

"I'm gonna go to the bar," Nate said. "You want me to drop you at home or…?"

"The studio's good."

"This late? You don't have your car."

It wasn't that late. Not even nine o'clock yet, and I wasn't worried about not having my car. I could call a rideshare. I just needed to work out the kinks in my neck, the tension in my spine, and the tingling in my arms.

"I'll be fine."

Twenty minutes later, I slipped out of my brother's car with a squeeze to his hand and unlocked the door to the studio.

After flicking on the lights, I kicked off my shoes, tossed my purse to the corner, and plugged my phone into the stereo system. I let it play on random and shook out my arms and legs before launching across the room in a series of turns, skipping a warm-up. I leaped and spun, not caring that they were messy and off-balance. I switched from stomping tap steps to a ballet allegro to modern pliés and robotic movements then eventually transformed into a slightly weird version of the Toy Soldier Dance, which had been a staple in the *Christmas Spectacular* for almost as long as the show had been taking place.

I wasn't precise. I wasn't perfect. I wasn't anything like I was supposed to be, which was exactly what I needed right now.

To let it all go.

The sweat and tears, I gave it all to dance.

And when I collapsed, out of breath and soaked with perspiration, I knew this was my only one true home.

SIXTEEN
DYLAN

Since I hadn't heard from Genevieve last night, I was surprised she called me. Especially so early in the morning. I stepped away from the crowd to answer, though I couldn't help the impatience in my voice. "There you are."

"I know." She sighed. "I'm sorry."

"You don't need to apologize," I said because I shouldn't have been annoyed, and she truly had nothing to be sorry for. We weren't in a relationship. There were no rules to how often we had to communicate, but I'd been frustrated that I didn't get her naked and in bed last night.

"We had dinner with my dad and his family last night. I meant to call you back, but I got in my head about it and spent a long time at the studio."

I absently poked around a couple of bouquets at the flower stand closest to me. "You feel better?"

"I'd feel better if I could treat you to breakfast. Maybe in bed."

I arched a brow. That did sound tempting. "I'm out at the farmers market."

"Really?" She laughed, low and a little gravelly like she wasn't fully awake yet. "It's barely eight o'clock."

"Jude's got a stall here, so I come when I can."

"Huh."

"What?" I stuck my hand in my pocket as I moved out of the way of a woman pushing a stroller.

"Didn't think you were the farmers market type of guy."

I didn't know whether to be offended or chagrined. "It only runs in the spring and summer, down by the library. And I like buying fresh food."

Her tinkling laugh eased the tension in my shoulders. Almost as if she were reaching through the cell phone to massage me. "Can I join you?"

"If you want."

"I'll meet you in a bit. Don't buy anything without me."

"Wouldn't dream of it," I said, fighting a smile.

After I hung up, I headed over to Jude's stall, which he was still organizing.

"Hey. How's it going?"

"Hey." He barely spared me a glance as he worked. "The kids have some kind of stomach bug. It was a mess last night."

I took a giant step back from him, knocking into someone behind me. I spun around to find a familiar woman carrying two coffees. "I'm sorry. Didn't mean to—"

"It's okay, Dylan. No harm done."

I racked my brain for her name. She was Jude's friend and fellow farmers market vendor.

"Brooke," she reminded me, still smiling kindly.

"Sorry."

"Don't worry about it." She shrugged and stepped around me to give Jude a coffee. "Here. Your favorite."

He accepted it with one hand, gripping her arm with his other. "You're a goddess."

"Well..." She swept her loose braid over her shoulder dramatically. "If you say so."

Jude closed his eyes, sighing in relief after he swallowed a sip of the coffee. "That's so good."

"Donna makes the best," she said, and Jude gestured to me.

"Have you ever tried it?"

I shook my head. "Don't like all that fancy shit."

Jude rolled his eyes. "Plebeian."

I didn't know what that word meant, but I was sure it was an insult. I knocked his shoulder, jostling him and his precious coffee. "Dick."

Brooke snickered and snagged a rope of licorice. "Mm. Green apple, fancy."

Jude threw his head back to laugh.

"I gotta get back to my stall. Dylan, it was nice seeing you again."

I tipped my chin to her. "You too."

As she sauntered off in the other direction, I couldn't help but notice how Jude's gaze followed. Though, I didn't bring it up. If he wanted to talk about…whatever that was, he would.

"Who's with the kids?" I asked once he got back to work, playing around with an iPad stand.

"Youmna and George came over."

Youmna and George were Jude's mother- and father-in-law —at least, that was how he still referred to them. "That's good."

"This damn credit card scanner," he muttered to himself and then, "So, obviously, Seb won't be at the game today."

"Don't worry about it. I hope he's feeling better."

Jude plopped down in a chair, still fiddling with his equipment. Exhaustion was clear on his face.

"Do you need help with something?" I offered.

He scrubbed his hand over his beard before meeting my gaze. "Unless you know how to fix this, no."

I shrugged. "I feel like that would be more Liam's department."

"Oh yeah?"

At hearing the voice of our friend, Jude and I both turned to spot Liam and Finn.

"Hey, man." Jude stood up to clap him on the back. "What're you doing here?"

"We're meeting Tess for lunch later. Said she had something important to discuss."

Jude and I both waited for what Finn's mom might have had to say, but Liam only shook his head. "No idea what it's about, but Finn'll never be able to sit still if I don't run him."

Finn, though highly uncoordinated, was like a pony. He was in constant motion, even if most of it was lost to gravity. I bent down to offer my hand for a high five. Finn slapped my palm, but I didn't let go, instead twirling him up in my arm, so he couldn't get away. He shrieked with laughter when I hauled him up as I stood.

"And what was that about my department?" Liam asked, one hand in his pocket, the other catching Finn's glasses when they fell off his head, without really looking. Helluva dad move right there.

"I'm having trouble with the credit card scanner connecting to the iPad again." Jude moved it all to the end of his table so Liam could take a look as I hefted Finn onto my shoulders. "If I can't get it to work, I'll only be able to take cash, and I didn't bring enough for change."

Though Liam taught history...or something, he was pretty knowledgeable when it came to tech issues. Always good to have a nerd on the squad.

"We're gonna take a lap," I said, and Liam absently waved in my direction. I looped around to the start of the market. It was small, only the length of two blocks. The stalls and tents were set up in the middle of the street, with traffic being redirected around it. Most of the vendors sold produce and homemade products like honeys, jams, and baked goods, with the occasional gourmet something or other like Jude and his candy or the fancy coffee.

"See anything you like?" I asked Finn, jostling his legs around my neck.

"Tow!"

"Tow? What's that?"

"Tow! Tow!" He wiggled around my shoulders. "Tow!"

Finn didn't talk a whole lot, and when he did, it was usually hard to understand him. He'd gotten hooked up with speech therapy recently, but I felt a special kindred spirit with him. I couldn't quite make sense of letters, and he couldn't quite make sense of his words.

I spun in a slow circle, repeating his word over to myself. "Tow… Tow…"

"Toooooowwwww! Moooooo!"

That was when I understood and walked him over to the table with a gray-haired man in a white shirt behind it.

"Tow!" Finn shouted, hopping his little butt up and down on me. "Tow!"

I chucked him over my shoulder, so he didn't fall off in his zeal to get to the giant picture of the cow on the signage for grass-fed beef and artisanal cheese.

"How can I help you today?" the man asked as I set Finn down. He attempted to get away, but he wasn't going anywhere with my firm grip on the back of his shirt.

"We're just looking," I said and pointed to Finn, who was running in place. "Big fan of the cow."

The man chuckled and offered Finn a small plate with samples. "Would you like to try some gouda cheese?"

I doubted Finn cared what kind of cheese it was. He ate all of it. Kid liked his cheese. He stopped moving and inspected the plate, so I snagged one and handed him the chunk of pale orange cheese. He shoved it into his mouth happily then immediately took off.

"Hey, whoa!" I waved my thanks to the cow guy and rushed after Finn. I caught him around the waist and lifted him to my side. "Don't run with food in your mouth. You'll choke."

"Solid advice."

I whipped my head around to Genevieve.

She grinned with her red lips, sapphire eyes sparkling in the morning sun. "Hi."

I caught myself smiling too and bent to kiss her. "Hi."

"Who's this?"

"Liam's kid, Finn."

She leaned toward the toddler in my arm. "Hi, Finn. I like your glasses."

He made a sound of acknowledgment but was already waving his arms to go.

"I'm taking you back to your dad now," I told him. "Can't be on babysitting duty all day."

"I don't mind."

I stepped back from her, permitting my gaze to slowly wander down the length of her. She wore sneakers, pink spandex shorts that hit mid-thigh, and an oversized white T-shirt which was basically see-through, revealing a sports bra that matched her shorts.

"I do," I said. I minded that this fuckhot woman was next to me, and I had a squirming two-year-old in my arms instead of her. Genevieve only laughed softly as she followed me back to Jude's stand.

I passed Finn off to his father, saying, "Harassed the cheese guy for a while."

"Shoulda known." Liam took hold of Finn's hand, even as his attention was on the woman at my side, while Jude smiled like an absolute idiot.

"Nice to see you again," he said, and at Liam's confused expression, Jude went on, "Evie happened to be at the baseball game last weekend."

"Oh really?" Liam asked, his own idiot smile growing to match Jude's.

I ignored it. "You remember Genevieve?"

"Yeah, of course," Liam said. "How are you?"

"Good." She gestured to Finn. "I met your little guy. He's really cute."

"A cute little terror," he corrected, and she laughed.

I unconsciously settled my hand at the base of her spine as I tipped my chin to my friends. "I met these two because of our kids." When she quirked her brow, I explained, "We kept seeing one another at this play place, and we kinda became friends."

"Kinda? No." Jude waved me off. "We're friends."

"*Best* friends," Liam added because my supposed best friends were clearly trying to make this as uncomfortable as possible.

Genevieve didn't seem to mind, though, tucking in closer to my side. "So…this is, like, a dads' support group or something?"

I shrugged as Liam said, "Exactly," while Jude added, "Club. We're a club."

She giggled, shaking her head like we were doing a bit. "Where does my brother fit in?"

"He doesn't," I said, and she snickered.

"He'll be devastated to hear."

Jude and Liam both chuckled, and I skimmed a proprietary hand up to the back of her neck. Some instinctual need to piss a circle around her.

Before I could dig myself into a deeper hole, I led her away with a nod to my smirking friends. "See you guys later."

"Lemme know how the game goes," Jude said, but I barely acknowledged him, already too lost to Genevieve and her laughing mouth. I kissed it.

"Miss me?"

"Too much." I released her neck to take her hand, lacing our fingers together. It was bad, this longing between days I got to see her. I wasn't supposed to want her this much. But I didn't know how to stop it. The floodgates had opened, and I didn't know if I could close them again.

If I wanted to.

And that was a big fucking problem.

"So, this must have started up after I moved away," she said, referring to the farmers market, taking in all of the different tents. "Oh, pie!"

She tugged me to a stand with fruit pies and loaves of banana bread.

"Mmm. Strawberry rhubarb," she mumbled to herself.

"You want it?"

"I can't eat that whole thing by myself."

"Do you have any smaller ones?" I asked the young girl behind the table, who shook her head.

Genevieve sulked momentarily before she spotted the coffee. "I'm gonna need some of that."

"You drink this fancy shit too?"

She hopped in the short line. "And I guess that means you don't?"

"Coffee is supposed to taste like coffee. That's the point."

"Is it, though?" She nudged the brim of my baseball cap.

I bit at her hand and narrowly missed her wrist.

"Be nice," she warned, though it was more an invitation, and I slipped my palm to her ass for a quick squeeze. She was so perfect. Every inch of her.

When it was her turn, she ordered her coffee then angled her body toward me while they made it. "Jude said to let him know how the game went. Isn't he going to be there?"

"Seb's sick." When I handed over my credit card to pay for her drink, she pulled a face. "*What*?"

"It's becoming a real problem," she said.

"What is?"

"You." She smiled. "You're becoming a real problem for me."

I nodded in agreement. If she only knew.

Once she had her fancy coffee with syrup and cream and drizzle, we meandered around, checking out every stand. She bought a bouquet of flowers, along with raspberry jam and a loaf of bread. I purchased string beans, sweet potatoes, and zucchini from Brooke before swinging back around to Jude for some of his chocolate since Gen loved her sweets.

"What time's your game?" she asked me while peering down

at her hand, where a bit of melted chocolate was smeared on her index finger and thumb.

"Noon."

"So, you need to go soon?"

I nodded, lifting her index finger to my mouth, licking off the chocolate.

"I thought you didn't like sweets," she purred, closing her other hand around my forearm.

"You're sweet," I murmured, moving on to her thumb, stroking my tongue along the pad.

Her eyes sparked with heat, and pink bloomed on her cheeks. I bent down to take her mouth, but she let out a breath and glanced over her shoulder.

"What? What's wrong?"

"Nothing."

"What're you doing?" I asked when she yanked on my wrist, dragging me behind her while swiveling her head back and forth like we were being followed. "You okay?"

"Yeah." She suddenly switched direction, heading toward the park across the street. "I just…"

"What?"

"Come here." She pulled me into the gazebo with chipped white paint. It faced a stage that was equally as old and unkempt as the gazebo. Using the term "park" was rather generous, but the flat and green block had been named a century ago after some president when it'd been used for town gatherings and… concerts, I supposed. Now, people mostly let their kids run around in the open space while they walked their dogs.

I stared at Genevieve for a hint at what we were doing here, in this structure that felt like it could fall apart at any moment. She set down her bags then took mine from my hand to do the same and reached for my belt buckle.

"What—"

"Let me do this." She knelt on the dirty wooden planks. "I want to do this."

"Out here?" I wheezed, my muscles tight as her lithe fingers undid my button and zipper.

"Why not?"

I glanced around. Sure, we'd taken chances before, but this… this was wild. "Gen."

"Please. No one's around." She gazed up at me with her wide blue eyes, and I couldn't deny her anything. Especially when my cock was hard and already weeping for her. "I can't wait. I need to taste you."

I peered outside. We were completely encased except for the side facing the stage, and she was right, no one was around. But still, it was a big risk.

"We can't get caught," I told her, and she nodded.

"I'll be quick." She took my length in her hand, swiping her thumb over the head and a bead of clear liquid gathered there. I puffed out a harsh breath and slapped my hand on the wall closest to me, squeezing my eyes shut for a few moments, until I could control myself.

"Thing is, Dylan," she started, and I nearly collapsed with my weak knees once I dragged my lids back open to see her running her tongue over her bottom lip. "You like me to be loud so people will know what you do to me, and even though I like that, I don't want anyone to hear you." Then she licked me from root to tip.

With her soft voice that wrapped around me like a vise and her eyes pulling me under, I didn't stand a chance.

"I don't want anyone else to hear you," she told me and curled one hand around my denim-clad thigh, the other around my aching balls.

"You're killing me, kitten."

She smiled, a sinfully evil smile, then surrounded my cock with her perfect mouth. She hummed, sending a shock wave of pleasure up my spine, and I rolled my lips over my teeth, trapping a groan.

I balled my hand into a fist against the wood, allowing my

other to sink into her hair, though I refused to be as rough as I wanted to be. She swirled her tongue around the tip a few times, and I dropped my head back on my shoulders even as I thrust my hips forward. I couldn't watch her sucking me off and not want to tell her what a hot mouth she had, that I wanted to smear her lipstick, fuck her throat raw.

I couldn't say any of that.

My girl wanted me quiet. So I'd be a goddamn stone.

Even as my pulse pounded in my ears and my muscles ached. I muffled a moan when she worked her tongue along the underside, gently scraping her teeth, and I gripped her hair a little tighter as I brought my gaze back to her face.

She was flushed and blinking at me with glassy eyes. So innocent yet so shameless.

"I'm not sure how much more I can take," I rasped, my voice barely a whisper above the sound of people laughing in the not so far distance. "You gonna let me come in that pretty mouth of yours?"

She nodded, pursing the lips I'd become obsessed with around the head of my cock as she stroked the length. Friction and heat and nothing but visceral need boiled my blood, and I cupped her face between both of my hands, my fingertips in the shiny strands of her hair, my thumbs bracketing either side of her mouth as I thrust once, twice, three times before my orgasm barreled out of me.

I hunched my shoulders, crowding her space, as if I could shield her from the rest of the world while she swallowed down every drop I had to give her. I couldn't move away even after my dick hung limp and she tipped her chin, delicately swiping her fingers along her lower lip.

I pushed down the lump of possession in my throat, the same reflex that had me claiming her in front of my friends. After getting on her knees in public—for all intents and purposes— there was no way I could let her go now.

She thought I was an animal? Well, this was what we did. We claimed what was ours.

"Come on up off the floor." I helped her to stand and put myself back together. Once I had my jeans zipped, I sank down to my haunches and wrapped my hands around her legs. "You shouldn't have done that. Your knees..."

"Are fine," she finished, combing her fingers into my hair.

I brushed dirt off her kneecaps, rubbed my thumb over a red spot that looked sore, and then kissed each of her thighs in turn. When I straightened, I held the back of her head in my hands and stared into her eyes, her pupils less dilated than they were a minute ago. "You shouldn't have done that, but I love that you did."

She pressed up onto her toes and kissed her grin into my mouth.

And I had a real big fucking problem.

SEVENTEEN
GENEVIEVE

Even though we'd just seen each other yesterday, when Dylan called to ask if I wanted to come to his house for dinner, I answered immediately. There was no pause or hesitation. Only a *yes*.

I'd told him that he was becoming a problem for me, but he already was a problem.

This was supposed to be casual. No strings attached, no hurt feelings at the end, and yet I was a magnet, unable to fight the pull to him.

I didn't know what had come over me at the farmers market—actually, that was a lie. I knew what had come over me; it was the security of Dylan's fingers laced with mine. It was the play-fulness he'd displayed with his friends. The gentle yet very real possession of me.

It had felt like a date yesterday, like we were together, and a wave of gratitude crashed over me. I'd needed to express what I felt for him, but I damn sure couldn't say it out loud. So I showed him on my knees.

And now I was standing at the door of his townhome in a maxi dress that had taken me way too long to pick out and meticulous makeup that I'd spent half an hour applying. I tried to remind myself that I'd made my decision long before I'd met Dylan Matthews. I was going to dance again. I couldn't stay.

I wouldn't.

Even for a grumpy yet charming single dad who saved his smiles for his children…and me.

Before I could raise my hand to ring the bell, the door flung open, and there he was, mouth quirked up at the corner.

"Hey, gorgeous."

I stepped through the doorframe and kissed his cheek. "Thanks for inviting me over."

He curved his hand around my hip, scrunching the cotton material of my dress. "You smell good."

"So do you." I ducked my head into his collar, and his warning throaty growl did nothing to dissuade me.

"I'm making you dinner, Genevieve. Don't sidetrack me."

I gave in with a peck to his jaw and took his hand when he offered it, adding a petulant, "Fine."

The neighborhood seemed like a relatively new construction of homes, and though Dylan's house was small, it was cozy and clean. He led me through the tidy living room, with colorful bins of toys slotted into a cabinet under the flat-screen mounted on the wall. Everything was gray or brown, interspersed with pops of color from the kids. Pink sneakers, a bright-yellow umbrella with frogs, a miscellaneous sippy cup, which he snagged on the way to the kitchen. He tossed it into the sink then opened the refrigerator. "What do you want to drink? I have beer, soda, water… I doubt you want a Capri Sun."

"What flavor?"

He met my eyes from his bent position. "Fruit Punch."

I sucked air through my teeth and shook my head. "Maybe if it was Pacific Cooler."

He straightened and let the fridge door shut. "A woman of refined taste. I like that."

He was full-on panther tonight, and my skin prickled with goose bumps at what awaited me later. "I'll have water."

He filled a glass then led me outside, and I caught a glimpse of the dining room on the other side of the kitchen with a blown-up picture on the wall of Scarlett and Tucker, their faces dripping with ice cream. I smiled to myself as Dylan ushered me through the sliding screen door and out to a small patio, where a table and matching chairs were set up underneath an umbrella. It was almost June and unseasonably warm. Or it could've just been me. I couldn't tell.

He pulled out a chair for me like a gentleman and tucked me in with my glass of water, already sweating in the heat.

"Food'll be ready in a few minutes." He motioned to the chips and corn salsa on the table. "Help yourself."

"Look at you, Chef."

He lifted the hood of the grill, heat and spices wafting toward me as he picked up tongs. "Hardly. But I try my best."

I stuffed a chip with some salsa into my mouth as I watched Dylan in his pristine chino shorts and snug polo. With his stubbled chin, slightly messy black hair, and roped muscles in his arms and legs, he didn't quite fit the pretty boy look. But it was *real* nice. My belly fluttered at the obvious energy and detail he'd put into this night with the clothes and food and lights strung around the patio.

"It's cute out here," I said, noting the small playhouse by the tree and the handful of sparkly windmills and decorative plastic animals stuck in the ground.

He spared me a glance while he piled our food onto platters. "Thanks. I spend most of my time outside with the kids, so..."

"I like your pool. Is it hard to take care of?"

I could tell he was fighting a laugh as he shut off the grill. "We could skinny-dip later."

The plastic kiddie pool with sea creatures decorating it would not hold two fully grown adults, but I shrugged anyway. "I might be convinced."

He set down the food between us and settled into his chair across from me. "Careful what you wish for."

I gave in to a smile as I gulped my water and took in the platters in front of me. The shrimp skewers—slices of lime included—were perfectly grilled, and the peppers and onions smelled wonderful. "Mmm. Looks delicious."

"The shrimp are a tad spicy," he told me. "Got some cumin, chili powder, and cilantro on there."

We dug in, quiet for a few minutes as we ate. I finished my water pretty quickly, and he offered me his beer.

"You like IPAs?"

I lifted my shoulder as I sipped the bitter ale. "I don't really drink a lot of beer. I don't drink a lot, period."

"And you work at a bar," he said, forking veggies into his mouth.

"Ironic, I know. When I was in the city, I went out with friends, but I only drank on weekends for brunch. I think I could count on one hand the number of times I've gotten drunk. I didn't do the whole young girl in the city thing."

"Because you were too busy making people fall in love with you on the stage."

We both stiffened at that, and I took a big swig of his beer before setting it back down on the table in front of him. He clearly didn't mean *he* was falling in love with me, but now that the word was out there in the atmosphere, it was impossible to ignore how we were sitting here on a quaint and quiet date, cozy in our own bubble.

There was nowhere else I'd rather be. No one else I'd rather be with.

Dylan cleared his throat and drank about half his beer, his eyes downcast. "Have you figured out where you're headed yet?"

I crossed my legs under the table, my sandal slipping off my foot. I didn't bother to put it back on. "I sent in a bunch of audition tapes, and my friend Josie reached out to a choreographer in LA."

He dragged his gaze up to mine and tipped his head to the side. "That's where you want to go, Los Angeles?"

I toyed with my fork. "I'll go wherever I get a gig."

"It's like you're waiting on draft day."

"Exactly."

That was why I liked Dylan so much. He understood exactly what I was going through, and it was one of the reasons I knew I was going to have a hard time pulling myself away in a few weeks.

When we went quiet again, he scooched the plate of shrimp toward me, but I shook my head. "I'm full."

"I hope not." He leaned back in his chair. "I got you strawberry rhubarb pie."

I let out a tiny, surprised gasp. "You got it?"

"I did," he said, lounging like a proud jungle cat. "So you better have some room."

Emotion lodged in my chest, and that same urge to *show* him since I couldn't *tell* him came over me. I hopped out of my chair and threw myself into his lap. He caught me with an arm around my waist as I flung my arms around my neck, kissing my appreciation into his mouth. His tongue tasted like his beer, and I raked my fingers into his hair, angling my head to kiss him deeper.

His chest vibrated with one of his low groans. "Kitten."

I barely pulled back. "Hm?"

"I bought the pie. You're eating the pie."

I was confused until I felt the hard length of him under my butt.

"I don't want to skip any steps," he said, and the camp of emotions in my chest expanded, ready to stay forever. For the last month, all we'd done was skip steps. We'd begun with a one-night stand and had been working our way backward ever since.

Now, we were back at the beginning, where we were

supposed to have started. With a date. And he didn't want to skip any steps.

So, I wouldn't either.

"Dance with me?" I asked, and he angled his head, brow raised. "Come on." I kicked off my other sandal and hauled him up with me, pointing to his cell phone. "You listen to anything else besides country?"

"Not really."

"Okay, well, turn it up, at least."

He poked at the screen of his cell phone, the volume of the music rising. The singer crooned in a twang about God making the good stuff, like a woman who was five foot nine. I smiled and reached for his hand. "Five foot eight and three-quarters, but close enough."

"Five foot eight and three-quarters is exactly right."

He curled his hand around mine and twirled me in a circle, eliciting a laugh from me. Then he took both of my hands and lifted them over my head as he twisted me underneath him. "You've been holding out on me. Where'd you learn to dance like this?"

"My parents are big into country line dancing."

I grinned as he two-stepped me around. "Tell me about your parents. About Arizona."

He pulled me in close to him, his eyes settled somewhere over my shoulder. "You know my dad's a mechanic. I think I told you my mom's a teacher, right? They met when she was on a road trip with some friends and their car broke down. She's originally from the Phoenix area and is part of the Ak-Chin Indian Community."

"She's Native American?"

He nodded, pressing his hand into my back to guide me into a series of spins. "She's mixed race but was raised in the community. We all used to go down on the weekends. She wanted me and my sister to know her family, her traditions, and I do, but..." He brought me back into his chest. "I started getting into baseball, and it took up all my time. I used to feel bad because I wanted to take part in all their celebrations, but I wanted base-ball more." He shrugged, though he was still looking out past the backyard. "She understood, but I always felt like I was disap-pointing her a little bit. Like I had to make a choice about who I was, and I chose wrong."

I smoothed my hand up his neck when the song changed to a slower number, and he held on to me with his hands around my waist. I was a full-blooded white girl, so I couldn't relate, but I could empathize. "I'd imagine that she and the rest of your family are really proud of you. You might feel like you made the wrong choice, but you used your talents in a different way. I'm sure they were very proud of you."

"They were," he said, dipping his chin to meet my gaze. "Just one of those things, you know? Those things that you think about at night before you close your eyes. All the mistakes you've made."

That I could relate to, but I didn't want to admit he was the thing that kept me up at night lately. I couldn't regret agreeing to our one-foot-in, one-foot-out relationship because I wouldn't have been here, slow dancing with him. But the way my heart misunderstood, I knew it was a mistake.

Dylan went on, "And whenever I take the kids home, we always visit the tribal community centers and drive down to hang out with family."

I toyed with the hair at the nape of his neck. "Do you miss Arizona?"

"I miss the mountains and the sky. The East Coast is kinda flat, with buildings everywhere."

I dropped my head to his shoulder. "We have mountains."

"We have snowcapped mountains in Flagstaff."

"We're not far from the ocean."

"If you don't mind driving two hours through traffic."

I huffed a laugh. "You make it sound like it's a chore to live here."

He skated his palms over me, one to my lower back, the other between my shoulder blades. "Nah. It's no chore. This is my home now."

He meant West Chester, Pennsylvania, was his home, and yet my idiot heart flip-flopped.

"Wherever my kids are, that's where my home is," he said, and I tipped my head up, seeking a kiss.

"They're lucky to have you."

He didn't answer, and I knew he struggled with his confidence as a father, but any stranger could see he loved his kids more than life itself.

"You ready for pie?" he asked, and at my excited nod, he gave my ass a playful smack and trotted inside. He returned less than a minute later with a pie, two forks, and my water refilled.

He directed me to the pool, where he moved two chairs so we could stick our feet in while we shared the dessert, straight from the tin.

"I've actually never had rhubarb before," he said, munching on a bite.

"No? What do you think?"

"I'm not sure exactly what it tastes like." He swallowed down another big bite. "But whatever it is, it's delicious."

I swiped my thumb over the bright-red filling at the corner of his mouth and licked it off, just like he'd done with the chocolate on my fingers yesterday, and his eyes darkened. Without saying a word, he stole the fork from my hand and placed it with his in the pie tin and dropped it on the ground next to his chair before tugging me into his lap.

Then his hands were in my hair, and his mouth was on my throat.

I tried to settle my knees on either side of him, but the length of my dress was in the way, and I struggled to yank it up. "Put your hands on my shoulders," he instructed, and I did, lifting one leg at a time as he untangled my skirt from my legs. "Better?"

I sank my weight down onto him. "Better."

Especially when he skimmed his hands up my thighs, underneath the cotton fabric gathered at my hips. My underwear was thin and seamless, and his fingertips glided right underneath it, squeezing my cheeks.

"I'm finally going to get you in a bed again." A predatory smile graced his lips, and his fingers gripped me tighter, drawing me flush against him to scrape his teeth over the shell of my ear. "I'm going to bite you. Suck bruises into your skin. Mark you."

I moaned, rubbing myself on his bulge, aching for friction.

"I'm going to strip you naked and lick you until you're begging for me to fuck you."

My eyes were closed, drunk on his voice, and I lolled my head back. He wrapped his hand around the bottom of my throat, his palm on my collarbone, his thumb and index finger digging into me, urging me to meet his gaze.

"What do you think of that?" he asked when I finally forced my eyes open.

"Yes. Yes, to all of it."

He grunted in satisfaction as he slid his other hand over my hip, teasing at the quickly dampening material between my legs. "But first, I want to feel you come on my fingers."

"Out here?"

He nodded.

"But…" I peeked behind me. He had no fence or anything around his yard. "Someone might see."

"So? You like people watching you. Let them watch."

My argument died on my tongue when I sucked in a breath, unable to tear my gaze away from his as he nudged my panties out of the way, sinking two fingers into me.

"You're wet already," he whispered, and I bit into my bottom lip, rocking my hips, unbalanced over him on this tiny chair, and he slipped his hand at my throat to the back of my neck, holding me, steadying me. He gave one slow nod as if letting me know he had me and I could let go.

So I did.

I rolled my hips, found the rhythm I needed, while he scratched his stubble along my throat, leaving openmouthed kisses under my jaw, helping me to climb higher and higher. My nipples puckered under my dress, and he sucked on one, right through the cotton. I panted, rising up so he could shift his hand, circling his fingers over my clit, and I was close, so close.

I tilted my head back to the sky, pink and purple with the sunset, but my skin was scorching as if I were under the midday sun, and without thinking, I slid the straps of my dress down and off my arms. The top drooped forward to my waist, baring my breasts to Dylan, to his neighbors if anyone was watching, but I was too lost to care.

He immediately took one of my nipples into his mouth while plunging his fingers back into me, crooking them until I was moaning my pleasure to the sky, completely abandoning any reservations.

"Going to scare the neighbors," he said, amusement dripping from his voice, his head still at my breasts, licking his way over to the other side, not caring about X-rated cries or my peep show. "Let 'em see how gorgeous you are."

He gently pulled at my nipple with his teeth at the same time as he circled my clit, and that was it. That was all I needed. I dug my fingers into his hair, pressing the side of my face against his as I rode his hand over the edge, breathless and shaking.

Dylan dropped chaste kisses on my shoulders and neck, waiting until I caught my breath. Then he slid the straps of my dress into place and set me on my feet, careful to make sure I was stable before he let go to take the pie and our dishes inside.

I was still coming down to earth when he stepped back outside and scooped me up in his arms. "Time to follow through on the rest of those promises, kitten."

EIGHTEEN
DYLAN

As I carried Genevieve through my house and up the stairs, she licked at my Adam's apple, snuggled up against my chest like an actual kitten, warm and soft and practically purring. Meanwhile, I was coiled so tight I felt like my muscles might burst out of my skin the moment she touched me. I'd been waiting to get her back in a bed, and now that the moment was finally here, I was losing my cool.

Worse than our first night together.

Maybe because there had been no pressure then. I'd gone home with her expecting some fun and to never see her again.

Now…

Now, I wanted it to be perfect.

I set her down at the foot of the bed and stood back, my hands on my hips, sucking in lungfuls of air to calm down. But all I inhaled was her innate flowery scent and strawberry pie. Honeyed springtime air, that's what Genevieve was.

She raised her hands, heading for my belt buckle, but I shook my head. "I'm the one in charge tonight, and I told you…" My stomach churned like before a baseball game, and the electricity in my chest hummed. I shucked off my shirt, relieved to feel the cool air on my skin. It was thin cotton, but it was much too tight with how my skin was tingling. I kicked off my shoes, followed by my shorts, and her gaze was a languid stroke down my abdomen, settling below my hips. I palmed my aching cock over my boxer briefs, forcing her eyes up to mine. "I'm going to bite you and suck you and mark your skin. So, be a good little kitten and take your dress off."

Her cheeks flamed as she froze momentarily, her eyes wide, hands in midair, and then after one breath, she stood and lifted her dress over her head. The flush from her cheeks trekked down her throat and onto her chest. And that was where I started.

I wound one arm around her back and cupped her breast with the other, her nipple puckered under my palm. I'd get there eventually, but first, I wanted a taste of her throat. I skipped right over the gentle kisses and licks and bit the curve where her shoulder and neck met, and her answering hiccup of a breath was enough to make me do it again on the other side.

It was almost summer, and in the back of my mind, I was conscious that she'd be wearing tank tops and skimpy little outfits that no doubt would show off her body, but I had trouble reining in my need to stake my claim. She arched her back, offering more of herself up to me, and I nibbled her collarbone. I bent, taking both of her breasts in my hands, pushing them together to lick along the gentle but lush slope of the valley between them. I rubbed my jaw there too, satisfied at the red marks, and I opened my mouth to one nipple and then the other, teething the tight peaks, pulling them until she was shuddering in my hold.

Her skin shone from my treatment of them, and I smiled against her sternum as I lowered myself to the floor, kneeling in front of her. I gripped her hips, staring up at her. At the way the tip of her tongue wetted her parted lips, at how her middle expanded with every breath, and how her belly was quivering. I kissed her there.

I'd already felt her orgasm on my fingers, but now I wanted it on my tongue, and I slipped her beige panties off her legs, tossing them carelessly to the side before hauling her to me, my fingers digging into her ass cheeks, my face pressing into the slight curve above her pubic bone. She squeaked out a surprised sound, a bit unsteady on her feet, and I loosened my grip, easing her down to the bed.

"Lie back," I told her, my voice reverberating in my own ears, and I briefly wondered if it was too much with how the whites of her eyes were more prominent, but then she extended her hands to me, a silent plea to come closer, and I didn't care what I sounded like anymore.

I placed her heels up on the edge of the bed, and her knees fell to the sides, allowing me full access to her pussy. Her dark curls were trimmed to a strip, her skin was pink and glistening with her arousal, and I curved my hands around her thighs, holding her open. She whimpered when I didn't immediately kiss her there, but I wasn't finished leaving evidence of our time together on her skin yet.

I bent over her, ignoring how my dick strained at her musky scent, and dragged my teeth over her hip bone. She canted up off the bed, trying in vain to drag my mouth where she wanted it, but I was going to take my time, enjoy snacking on every inch of her. With my arm banded across her lower stomach, I held her down while kissing my way across to her other hip then the crease of her thigh, sucking red marks there. She wiggled back and forth, her arms aimlessly swishing up and down on the sheets, her quiet moans like those of a satisfied house cat.

I rubbed her stomach as I trailed my mouth down her leg, scratching my teeth and chin in my wake, making sure she'd feel it tomorrow. I placed my hand around her knee and kissed the underside.

She snapped her legs closed. "I'm ticklish there!"

But I wasn't fazed. In fact, I liked her long legs caging me in. I scooted her toward me, right to the edge of the bed, and urged her to wrap her legs more fully around me, so all I could see was her creamy skin, all I could smell was her need. "That's it," I murmured, clutching her hips tightly. "Hold on to me."

Then I finally gave her what she wanted and licked my tongue through her slit. Her answering moan of my name was a call to my soul. I'd hear it in a natural disaster, through hurricanes and tornadoes. I'd brave fire and ice for it. And somewhere in the back of my sex-addled brain, I knew that quiet, breathy plea would haunt me for the rest of my days.

For now, I closed my eyes and surrendered to it. I buried my face between her thighs and wrapped my right arm around her hip so I could splay my hand over her lower stomach, using my thumb and forefinger to hold open her soft flesh. I teased at her clit, drove my tongue into her heat, licked up every bit of her slickness until she was writhing and panting under me.

Her legs tensed, her feet twitched reflexively, her fingers uncontrollably bunching and releasing the bedsheet, all signs she was close to coming, so I broke the hold of her thighs around me and tunneled two then three fingers into her. She cried out, lost to her own pleasure.

I worked her over with my hand and mouth, and the more she gasped my name, the more my spine curved, my natural instinct to fuck her almost unbearable. My abs and thighs were tight, my ass clenched, but I wasn't going to give in until I brought her over the edge.

I focused my tongue on the bud of her sex and rubbed at the spot inside her that sent her back arching, her neck flushing, and I felt her inner walls contract around me. "That's it," I rasped, my voice nearly lost with need. "Good girl."

I hadn't turned on the lights when we'd first entered my bedroom, and now that the sun had almost completely set outside, we were bathed in shades of blue and gray from the fading light through the windows. Enough we could still see each other.

I stood, yanking off my boxer briefs to fist my hand around my cock. My fingers were wet with Genevieve's orgasm, and I smeared it over my length as she came down from her high. She appeared wrung out, but I wasn't close to being done with her, and I snagged the box of condoms I'd tossed on my nightstand earlier in the day.

Her eyes followed me, openly staring as I rolled on the condom, her hands lazily roaming her sides and breasts and neck as I palmed my cock over the condom. She swept her tongue along her red lips again, her throat lifting on a swallow, and I didn't know how many seconds and minutes we spent watching each other. But I couldn't stop. Having this beautiful woman luxuriate on my bed was natural. It was right, exactly where she was supposed to be.

Even before I prowled over her, urging her to wrap her legs around my waist, I knew this time was different. The electricity in my chest that had been a constant hum ratcheted up, and I leaned down, placing her hand on my breastbone. I wanted her to feel it. To know this steady yet completely new rhythm beating under my ribs was because of her.

Then she took my hand and settled it between her breasts, right over her own heart.

And I felt it.

The echo of my own.

The corner of her lips tipped up in what I could only describe as a contented smile, and I notched myself at her entrance, slowly pushing inside. We didn't take our eyes off each other, her hand on my chest, mine on hers.

When I was fully seated in her, she sighed. I did too. And then we moved together. I rocked my hips, ground down on her clit before pulling out a little and thrusting back in. She drew me closer with those strong legs around me as I held myself over her with one hand next to her head, refusing to move the other from her chest.

We were both breathing hard, and I lowered my forehead to hers so her every exhale was my inhale, and at some point, I lost myself to what we were doing, like an out-of-body experience.

I was both wholly aware and still experiencing it on another level. I felt the pull of my orgasm deep in my gut, felt the tingle in my spine and the growing burn of release in my balls, yet I was watching it happen.

Watching her eyes go from deep blue to a puddle of near black.

Watching the tips of my fingers curl against her skin between her breasts.

Watching the pulse in her neck, the bead of sweat on my temple drop to her shoulder, the ripple of my abs when I looked down the length of our bodies to where we were joined.

And then I watched both of us find our home.

I buried my face in her neck as I shuddered and pulsed with one last thrust, and she wrapped her arms around me, trembling.

"So good," she groaned against my ear, and when I finally managed to back away, both of our skin damp from exertion, I could only nod. I placed a chaste kiss on her mouth then forced myself to stand up straight, and she winced when I pulled out of her.

I immediately lowered myself over her again, combing hair away from her forehead and temples. "Are you hurt?"

"No." Her smile was sleepy. "Not at all. It just feels… It's silly to say."

I skimmed the tip of my nose against hers. "Tell me."

"I feel empty now, is all. I like feeling your skin on mine, feeling you inside me. It's like…" Her teeth sawed into her lower lip, and I tugged it free, forcing her to finish her thought. "It feels right, you know?"

"Yeah," I breathed. "I know."

After more pecks of my lips to her jaw and throat, I stood up and dragged my hand down my stomach. Even though I loved the smell of Genevieve and sex on my skin, I needed a shower, and I told her so. "Do you want to take one with me?"

She held out her hand for me to tow her up and off the bed. I dealt with the condom and led her into my adjoining bathroom, where I started the shower, checking the temperature of the water before guiding her inside with a hand on her elbow.

She held her hands up under her chin, groaning happily when the spray hit her, and I huffed at how my blood surged at the sound. I was like a dog with a bone.

But I was an old goddamn dog, and I needed some time to recover first before I could fuck her again.

I passed her the loofah and soap, and we took turns lathering it over each other. I was gentle with her, careful of the tender skin between her legs, and only permitted myself one light squeeze of her ass. I could tell she was tired, and I snatched a fresh towel from the closet to wrap around her when we stepped back out of the shower. I dried off with another and hung it up before tending to her again, holding her against me.

"Give me a few minutes," she said with drowsy eyes. "Then I'll go."

"No." I picked her up, carrying her to the bed. "You're not going anywhere."

"You want me to sleep here?"

I nodded even as I knew it was a bad idea and set her on the bed to find one of my shirts. It was one of my old baseball tees, and I couldn't help but grin as I dragged it down her body, my last name on her back. I didn't bother with clothes, merely put on a clean pair of underwear and hopped into bed, tucking her into my side.

She hummed, her hand on my pec, her cheek on my shoulder, and I let out a breath that I thought I'd been holding for the last few years.

I was in deep. So fucking deep with this girl, and I had no desire to crawl out. Not when she was yawning so cutely and hunkering down like she belonged here.

With me.

NINETEEN
DYLAN

My internal clock was set permanently for 6:30 in the morning, about the time Scarlett woke up every day. Whether she was sleeping in her room down the hall or not, I woke up anyway.

But this time, instead of my daughter begging me to put on *Peppa Pig* while she ate her cereal, it was Genevieve silently begging for my hands on her with how she was burrowing into my side.

"Kitten," I rasped, my voice hoarse with sleep.

She wrapped one of her legs around my thigh, rubbing her pussy against me.

"What are you doing?"

"Nothing." She curled her fingers around my dick, already hard, and kissed my shoulder.

"Doesn't feel like nothing."

"Okay," she murmured. "It's something." Then she pushed the thin sheet off us and bent to lick up my length.

"I have to pick the kids up at eight," I told her, already picturing how I could lose myself in her for another few hours. Even after exhausting ourselves last night.

"This won't take long," she said and swirled her tongue around the tip of my cock.

I blew out a big breath. "I don't want to rush."

It was a common theme with us.

Before, it was an endgame, to get off as quickly as possible. But I didn't want to do that with her. I wanted to be present in the moment, slow down, and enjoy the ride.

Especially when she reached out her long arm to the box of condoms and extracted one. Her fine, elegant fingers ripped open the foil, and she straddled my legs to carefully roll it down my length. Then she leaned forward, placing her hand on my chest as she slid herself back and forth over me, drenching me in her slick heat, warming and waking both of us up like the first sip of coffee on a cold morning.

I lifted my head, sucking her nipple into my mouth. With a slight tilt of her hips, she rubbed her clit with every pass, gradually becoming wetter and wetter, and even as I knew I wouldn't have hours with her like I wanted, I wasn't pushing to slip inside her. I could stay in this in-between place—with her undulating over me and her sweet sighs and soft eyes —forever.

But, of course, we didn't.

Keeping one hand on my shoulder, Genevieve reached behind her to hold my erection up. And then she was sliding down. So fucking achingly slowly.

She moaned quietly and eventually straightened up.

"Feel good?"

She didn't verbally answer, only bent back, anchoring her hands on my thighs.

"You feel like heaven. Every time I'm inside you, it's like seeing God."

"It's…" She breathed heavily. "It's so good."

I skated my hands from her waist up over her breasts and back. "Feels so good, you fucking me like this. I can feel you squeezing me." I licked the pad of my thumb and circled her clit, earning a surprised gasp. "Use me, kitten. Fuck me however you need to. I want to feel you soak my cock."

She rocked her hips in lazy figure eights, and I cupped her breasts in my hands, admiring her body, the slight lines of muscle running along either side of her abdomen, the perfect pink pebbles of her nipples, the way her neck arched and her short hair swayed around her face.

This slow and lazy sex was better than any cup of coffee. I wasn't tired anymore. I was wide awake, my heart racing, my skin tingling.

"I'm gonna come already," I told her. "Watching you on top of me is so hot, feeling how tight your pussy is, you're killing me."

She peeled her eyelids open and met my gaze, her mouth parting to swipe her tongue over her lips. "I...I..."

"Get there, kitten." I pinched her nipple in one hand, keeping my attention on her clit with the other until I felt her squeezing me as her skin flushed red. I hummed in pleasure. "My favorite thing."

She sank her weight down on me, and I wrapped my arms tight around her, holding her to me, and allowing me to pump into her, finding my own release while she sucked and nibbled on my throat.

Skimming my fingers along her spine, I kissed her head over and over, giving myself time to calm down and for her to sit up. With me still inside her, she grinned down at me. "Good morning."

"Morning."

"Can I borrow a toothbrush?"

I gave in to a smile and patted her thigh. "You can borrow whatever you want."

Then I helped her off me, watching as she sashayed into the bathroom. I stayed in bed another few minutes, my eyes closed as I breathed deeply, satisfied.

I got rid of the condom and stepped into a pair of shorts just as Genevieve walked back out of the bathroom in her dress from last night.

"Gorgeous," I said, pulling her into me for a hug, tucking her face against my throat.

"Thank you," she murmured, and I left kisses along her neck and shoulder. "For last night and this morning."

I huffed, my breath blowing a few strands of her hair into the air. I combed my fingers through it and held her face away from me, forcing her to look into my eyes. "Don't ever thank me for things I'm supposed to be doing."

It was a trigger for me. She didn't say it condescendingly or mean it that way, but I couldn't help my automatic reaction or how the skin at the back of my neck prickled.

She took it in stride. "So, you're supposed to be giving me orgasms morning, noon, and night?"

"Fuck yes."

She laughed, and I gave her one quick kiss then linked my fingers with hers to lead her downstairs and outside to her car. I held her door open and waited until she was settled inside with her seat belt on to bend down, popping one more kiss on her mouth. "See you in class tomorrow, kitten."

I closed the door and knocked twice on the roof of her car before she drove away, leaving me with about thirty minutes to shower, dress, and pick up my children.

But it was well worth it.

Since all the kids had Monday off for Memorial Day weekend, the boys and I decided to get together for a playdate.

"Walk!" I reminded Scarlett, who was too elated about handing out her birthday party invitations to her friends to care about cars in the parking lot of Imagination Station. I'd already talked to Jude and Liam about the party and knew they were coming, but she still insisted on handing them invitations.

Tucker yanked on my hand since I was clearly moving too slow for him. "You too. Slow down."

Scarlett exaggeratedly looked both ways before crossing the

open lot to the sidewalk, and I let go of Tucker's hand. "All right. Go ahead."

The two sprinted inside, while I was in no rush since visions of naked Genevieve were swimming in my head.

I swung open the door, earsplitting screams of joy hitting me in the face, and I helped myself to another big gulp of my coffee. I ambled over to the bench. Jude was already there, holding Scarlett's party invite, glittery cutouts of a ballerina for Amelia and Sebastian with her name messily scrawled on the back as well as the time and address of Paige's house.

Jude greeted me with chocolate chip cookies. "Morning."

I helped myself to one. "How's it going?"

He nodded toward where Sebastian was engrossed with a Switch. "He decided he wants to go to a baseball game."

I unconsciously tugged on the bill of my cap. "In Philly?"

"Yep."

"I'm occasionally in touch with some players and front office people. I could see about getting you tickets." I still hadn't been able to go back to the field since I was let go, but I was cool with reaching back out for my friends. They probably wouldn't be very good seats, but they'd be free.

"No, that's okay. Amelia's got no interest, so I'm not even sure when we'll go. Maybe an afternoon game. I just gotta see what grandparents are available to take her for the day."

I shrugged. "Offer stands, but besides that, if it's a day I've got the kids, you can always drop her with me."

We both turned to look at where Amelia, Scarlett, and Tucker were all playing in the salon together. The girls were applying "makeup" to his face. He was loving it.

"Yeah, thanks. I'll see. We're goin—"

"Hey." Liam appeared next to us and set down a wiggling Finn. He ran right over to the plastic tree in the center of the room that had rungs to climb. "Careful!"

Finn didn't acknowledge him, and Liam plopped down next to me.

"All right?" I asked from behind my coffee.

He extended his legs out in front of him and crossed his arms over his chest. Liam was tall, though not quite as tall as me, and lean. He was usually pretty put together with his clothes, but he looked genuinely haggard today. Even wore his glasses.

"I love my child," he said quietly. "I love him. I love him. I love him."

Jude and I chuckled.

"What happened?" Jude offered him the container of cookies, but he passed with a wave.

"What didn't happen is really the question." He huffed. "I needed to get some work done for my book, so I thought I could give Finn an iPad for a bit. For just, like, half an hour. That's all I needed this morning. But I couldn't even fuckin' get that," he said, his South Boston accent coming out, a sure sign he was pissed. "I was working in the dining room, and I had him in the living room. I should've known it was too quiet."

I sucked air through my teeth while Jude nodded. "Yep."

Liam threw his hand out toward Finn, who was still struggling to make it up the tree. "This guy had taken every goddamn cushion off every piece of furniture and built a tower for him to jump on. I didn't realize until I heard him hitting the floor and the subsequent crying. I ran out to go get him and stepped on a fucking Lego. I think I have permanent nerve damage in my foot now."

"How was Finn?" I asked, and Liam motioned to his son, who had given up on the tree and was moving toward the grocery store, obviously unhurt and unaware of the literal pain he'd put his father in this morning.

"I don't know how he hasn't had any real serious injuries yet," Liam said and rapped his knuckles on our wooden bench.

"You need a break?" Jude asked. "Should we head to Walt's?"

"I've got the kids until Wednesday night." I shrugged. "But I could do later. This weekend is pretty much out with the party."

Jude waited for Liam to answer, but he was already shaking his head. "I don't know."

He had a good relationship with Finn's mother, and it was highly unusual that he couldn't make plans.

I furrowed my brow at him in silent question.

He answered with an exhausted groan. "When I saw you guys on Saturday, I said we were meeting Tess for lunch."

Jude and I nodded.

"It was to inform me that her grant finally came through, and that she's taking a sabbatical."

Like Liam, Tess was also a professor at the university here but was in a different department. Something with science.

"What's that mean?" I asked.

"She's taking a year off to go to Antarctica."

I stared, confused.

"Wait..." Jude blinked a bunch of times. "What?"

"She's been applying to this program for so many years, and she finally got in. She's been awarded a grant to live there for a year to study climate change. She leaves next month."

Making sure I understood, I asked, "Leaves for Antarctica? Like, where penguins live?"

"Yeah." He sat forward, his elbows on his knees. "She's wanted this for so long, and she wasn't sure what she was going to do because of Finn. She didn't want to leave him."

"But she is," Jude said then winced. "That came out wrong. I didn't mean it to sound like that."

"I said the same thing," Liam told us with a pained expression, "and she didn't take it well." He scrubbed at his face, his Southie accent easing away. "If I said I was taking a sabbatical for a year, I don't think anyone would bat an eye. But because she's the mother, everyone is going to think she's abandoning Finn. And that's not right."

I didn't think myself to be of below average intelligence, but my mind was still stuck on penguins while Liam continued on this feminist kick. I was having trouble computing it all.

"My first reaction was no, absolutely you cannot go, but that's…" He shook his head. "This has, literally, been her dream for I don't know how long."

That sounded familiar to me. Something I could actually understand.

He went on. "I couldn't say *no, you can't go*. Plus, we're not married. She doesn't owe me anything."

"But what about Finn?" Jude interjected.

"She cried about it," Liam said. "She really was on the fence. A year is a long time to be away from your kid."

I nodded. I wasn't sure I could do it. Then again, I didn't have any big dreams anymore. My dreams lived in the two dark-haired hooligans currently riding the cars.

"I told her it was fine," Liam continued. "I could handle it. Because if it were reversed, that's what she would say."

"So…" I started, scratching at my jaw. "It's you and Finn alone for a year."

Liam slouched back against the bench. "Yep."

Jude and I exchanged a look.

"We'll help you out," Jude said.

"Yeah," I added. "Whatever you need."

"But what about day care?" Jude suggested, and Liam shook his head.

"Tess hates day cares. Her family's got some trauma about it because her niece rolled off a changing table while at one and cracked her skull. The workers never told Tess's sister, and they didn't realize until the next day when the baby wouldn't stop wailing and had a giant bruise. CPS got involved. It was ugly."

"Damn," I muttered. "What're you gonna do?"

Liam combed his hand through his hair. "This summer will be fine, but I'll have to try to get my schedule fixed up for next semester so I can teach as many classes as possible while he's at preschool, and…" He shrugged. "I'll figure it out. People do it all the time."

It was true. There were single parents out there, who did it completely solo with no support. I didn't know how, but I heard stories."

The three of us stayed quiet for a while, soaking in this information. Sebastian stowed his game away to join the other kids, all five of them playing with the rope ladder. I was sure it would be difficult for Liam, but we'd help him through it.

I gave him a few pats on the back.

Scarlett flew over then and snatched the last party invitation from me to hand to Liam, who smiled down at her.

"This is for my birthday party," she explained seriously, pointing to the name on it. "See this? It's for Finn, but I thought he would lose it or something."

Liam turned it over in his hands. "He probably would. I will hold on to it for him."

"Can he come? It's at my mommy's house, and we're gonna have a ballerina cake that's chocolate."

"Chocolate's my favorite."

She grinned, rocking back and forth. "Me too!"

"You can put us down in the yes column. Finn will be there."

She twirled away. "Okay!"

Liam tucked the invitation away then regarded me, all evidence of his earlier frustration gone.

"What?"

He only tipped his chin in Jude's direction on the other side of me, so I turned to him.

"*What?*"

He shrugged.

And I had one guess what it was about, but I waited for one of these two assholes to spit it out.

"How's your ballerina doing?" Liam finally asked.

I hitched my right foot up on my left knee and slurped down the rest of my coffee. "First of all, she's not a ballerina. She was a Rockette."

He lifted his hands in apology. "Sorry."

"Second of all, she's not mine."

Jude toggled his head back and forth. "Could've fooled me with the way you were at the farmers market."

I huffed, completely unable to argue otherwise.

"Looked like you two were pretty…" Liam stopped, squinting like he did whenever he was thinking. "Together."

I rubbed at my shoulder, an old ache. "I guess. We are together for now. That was the agreement. No-strings-attached fucking."

Jude sent me a bland look. "Hate to break it to you, but it seemed like there were plenty of strings attached."

I shook my head. "There aren't."

"But you really like her," Liam pointed out.

I didn't answer.

"And I'm pretty positive she likes you," Jude said.

I rolled my eyes. "Did you guys rehearse this? Jesus."

Jude bit into another cookie. "No, but it's obvious how you feel about each other."

"It doesn't matter how we feel about each other. She's leaving soon, and I'm not getting into another relationship. What we have is short-term. Always was. There is no changing that."

The guys stayed mercifully quiet. I didn't know if I had another denial in me.

I couldn't speak out loud what I felt for her. I couldn't make it real, because I knew if I did, I wouldn't be able to let her go. But like Liam with Tess, I wasn't going to hold Genevieve back from her dream.

I would say goodbye when the time came. Like I'd planned to from the beginning.

TWENTY
GENEVIEVE

Tuesday, I stood at the studio door as the girls pranced in, a blur of pastel colors and giggles. I did a mental head count, noticing Scarlett wasn't there. Ever since I'd re-met Dylan at the first special someones rehearsal, he had made it a point to watch every single class, so it was unusual they were late.

Especially when he'd tucked me into my car yesterday morning with a "See you at class, kitten."

I waited another minute, making small talk with the adults in the waiting room, but I couldn't hold class any longer and started by turning on our "warm-up," which was a cute little song about bunny rabbits sleeping, waking up, and jumping around the room.

I was in the middle of a hop, arms tucked at my sides, paws out, nose scrunched when the door to the studio swung open and Scarlett ran in to squeeze in a few hops before the bunnies went back to sleep. Dylan poked his head in, an apologetic slant to his mouth. I grinned.

Then he grinned too. Dimples and all.

And my stomach somersaulted.

When the song ended, I faced the girls and held up my index and middle fingers. "The recital is in less than two weeks. Can you believe it?"

They all tittered in delight.

"I'm so proud of everything you girls have accomplished this year, and you should be proud of yourselves too."

Scarlett raised her hand. "Miss Gen, I want to be a dancer like you when I grow up."

My nose and eyes suddenly burned with emotion. I pressed my hand to my heart. "You can be if you work really hard, practice every day."

Scarlett smiled. She had the dimpled smile of her father, even though it was rare to be blessed with one from him. I was so lucky.

"I will," she said. "I'll practice all the time. You'll help me, right?"

I couldn't lie to her, but I also couldn't say no. Not to any of these girls, but especially not to Dylan's daughter. I managed a nod as I cleared my throat of what felt like a tap shoe lodged there.

"Okay, girls. Let's stand up and go to your places."

After we rehearsed their recital number three times then performed our ritual dance circle, I called in all the special someones. Dylan entered with a sly pat to my thigh as he leaned in close. "Sorry we were late. She spilled juice on her favorite leotard, and it was a whole thing."

"I know how that is. Every dancer has a favorite leotard, and it messes with our headspace when we can't wear it. Totally get it."

"I like this one," he murmured, dragging his fingers up my rib cage, over the cobalt-blue spandex of my own leotard. "Matches your eyes."

It was officially my new favorite.

"Come on, Daddy!" Scarlett wailed, and both Dylan and I

snapped our attention out to the class. We'd clearly spent a little more time whispering together than we thought because everyone was staring at us.

I dropped my chin, letting my hair fall to cover my cheeks, hoping my blush didn't spread everywhere else as Dylan hustled over to Scarlett. I took a breath then lifted my attention to the class.

"Let's take it from the top, shall we?"

We ran the dance twice before I finished teaching the very end and put everyone in their final poses, with the special some-ones on one knee and the girls sitting on them. "Make sure your arms are out straight. I don't want to see any floppy fishes." I flapped my arm, loose at the elbow and wrist, and all the girls laughed. "No floppy fishes" was one of my common refrains. I gestured to Juan, grinning with his sister, CiCi. "That's perfect. I want to see everyone smiling." I pointed to my own face. "Smile, Dylan."

He bared his teeth at me, and I snorted a laugh. "Close enough. All right, let's do it one more time."

At the back of the room, I waited until everyone cleared the floor for their entrance then pressed play, watching as they walked on, some performing more than others. Dylan kept his focus on Scarlett while they swung their hands back and forth. It was adorable, but I couldn't stare at them the whole time and, instead, moved to the front corner to perform the dance with the class.

Although, it was impossible for my gaze not to wander back to my favorite duo. He might not have smiled out to the "audi-ence," but he certainly didn't have any problem smiling at his daughter, and maybe that was even better.

Scarlett would remember this forever. Twenty years from now, when most of her memories from childhood would be like sand, individually indecipherable but together painted a picture, she would recall moments like these. That her dad had danced for her. That her father had smiled for her. That she was loved like he loved no one else.

And it was my downfall.

As the song ended and everyone hit their poses, I forced a smile, ignoring the goose bumps along my spine. Then I crossed my arms, hiding how my nipples pebbled too. I couldn't ignore them.

"Next week is our last class before the recital, so I hope you're practicing at home." I earned some mumbles with that. "We'll be going over the whole number a few times, but the mirror will be covered with paper, so you won't be able to watch yourselves. It'll be a test to see who can remember the steps." That got me even more grumbles. This time, they sounded worried.

"Does anyone have any questions about next week?"

Scarlett popped her head up. "Miss Gen, it's my birthday soon!"

I laughed, remembering how her friend Amelia had told me all about her birthday in December. "Is it? That's so exciting."

"Are you gonna come to my party?"

"I, uh, well, it's *your* birthday party. It's for kids." I knew she'd invited all the girls in class since she'd handed out the little cards two weeks ago.

"You can come too," she said, and the rest of the class nodded excitedly.

I smiled at them but lifted my attention, briefly meeting Dylan's gaze before slipping away. "Any questions about rehearsal or the recital?"

"Yeah, I have one." Bernie, Naomi's gray-haired grandfather, raised his hand. "Do we need to wear our suits to dress rehearsal?"

"Yes. Wear whatever you're planning on wearing the day of the recital. I'd advise you to scuff up the bottom of your dress shoes a little bit if you've never worn them before."

There was no costume for the special someones, but they

were asked to dress as if attending a special event. Suits for men and black cocktail dresses for women. The girls would be wearing their dance costumes. It was always a cute juxtaposition.

"Do we have to stay for the whole rehearsal?" Juan asked.

"No, you don't. In fact, we'll be moving a bit out of order, and you guys will be the second number in the rehearsal, even though your dance won't be until after intermission in the show. You're more than welcome to stay after you're finished rehearsing, and, of course, you'll need to if you're the one driving your student home." I counted off my fingers. "We're going to practice the finale first and then your dance, but their recital number won't be until a bit later. After their rehearsal, they'll be permitted to leave."

At their nods of understanding, I folded my hands together. "Any other questions or comments?"

Matt, Hannah's handsome dad, stepped closer to me to take his daughter's hand. "Yeah, thanks for all your help. I didn't think I'd like being here so much, but you made it real enjoyable."

I didn't miss the way his eyes momentarily sank below my neck, and I certainly didn't miss the grunt from the other side of the room. No one else acknowledged it, so maybe they didn't hear it. Perhaps my ears were specially tuned to Dylan because it was loud and clear to me. And he wasn't happy.

"Well, thank you. I appreciate that, and I appreciate you all for sharing your girls with me. It's been my absolute pleasure being with them this year." I gestured toward the door. "So, I guess I will see everyone next week for our last dance class."

I let out a tiny shriek and shot up jazz hands by my head, earning grins from all the girls.

I moved to the door to offer high fives on the way out, and since Dylan and Scarlett were on the other side of the room, they were always the last ones out. But even if he weren't, I had no doubt he would figure out a way to be.

"Go get your bag," he told Scarlett, and she skipped away, leaving me alone with her dad. And he definitely noticed my nipples.

"You're staring," I informed him, but it was a long time until he dragged his eyes up to my face, unrepentant.

"Hard not to."

"You didn't get enough this weekend?"

He licked his bottom lip. "Nope."

I was kept from fisting my fingers into his T-shirt and dragging his mouth to mine by Scarlett darting between us.

"Miss Gen." She tugged at my hand so I'd bend down to her.

"Yes?"

"You have to come to my party."

"Aw, hon, I don't think—"

"You have to!"

I looked to Dylan for help, but he only shrugged. "You should come."

"Really?" I sank to my knees in front of Scarlett. "You really want me there?"

Her ponytail bobbed as she nodded, her little hands on my shoulders. "Yeah. It's at my mommy's house, and Daddy's getting me chocolate cake, and everyone's gonna be there! You hafta come!"

Once again, I checked with Dylan, and at his subtle smile, I agreed. "Okay. I'll be there."

Scarlett threw herself at me, flinging her arms around my neck. "Yay! Yay! Yay! It's gonna be so good."

As she babbled on about the party, I looked up at her father, and behind the wicked promises swirling in his gaze, there was also something soft. Something warm and welcoming that settled deep in my chest.

"All right, sweetheart, you're choking your favorite teacher," he told Scarlett, gently disentangling her from around me so I could stand up.

With the girls in the next class parading in, he couldn't touch me, but he mouthed, "Talk later."

I acknowledged him with a tip of my chin and waved at Scarlett before pivoting to my older girls. "Okay! Quick warm-up and then you're going to hammer your dance over and over. Gia, spit your gum out. Come on!"

TWENTY-ONE
GENEVIEVE

I opened my legs, pointing my toes, and rolled to the top of my sitz bones while holding my cell phone to my ear, listening as Josie explained that Jeremy, her choreographer friend, didn't have any openings right now.

"Well, that's okay." I sat up tall, staring at myself in the studio mirror. "I figured it was a long shot anyway."

"So, that means you're taking the cruise ship job?"

I'd received an email from the producer earlier, informing me I was invited to audition in person. It was why I'd called my best friend. "I didn't make it yet. It's only the callback."

She snorted. "You'll make it."

There was no change in my reflection. No smile or even embarrassed blush at Josie's faith in me. I had no physical reaction whatsoever, and I wasn't sure what that meant.

"Where do you have to go?" she asked.

"Fort Lauderdale. It's next week."

"But isn't your recital next week?"

"Yeah. I'll get there Wednesday morning, spend the day at the audition, and then return Thursday. Dress rehearsal is Friday with two shows Saturday."

"Woof."

The schedule was a nightmare, but that was the life of gigging. You had to take what you could get, and right now, I could get an audition with a cruise ship.

And then we were quiet. I didn't want to admit I knew why, so I changed topics. "How's everything going with you?"

"Same old stuff, you know. Getting ready for the summer intensive."

"How'd your date go?" I asked.

"*Pfft.* Total bust. Cute but no personality."

I swung my legs together and bent over them, reaching for my flexed feet. "That sucks."

"Online dating is a swamp. I need to do what you did and find myself a daddy."

"Jos," I whined.

"What? You hit the jackpot with that one. A hot single dad who doesn't want to be tied down? He's perfect."

That was the thing; he was perfect. Yet, it didn't *feel* perfect.

It felt wrong. Not that Dylan was wrong, but the very wrong feelings brewing inside me. I wasn't even supposed to have feelings.

Because I was auditioning for a cruise next week and most likely setting sail on the high seas after that.

I rolled to my back with an ungraceful thump. "Yeah. He's pretty perfect."

"She said so enthusiastically."

"Well, I mean, what's there to be enthusiastic about?"

Her answering sympathetic sigh had me pinching my nose at the burn growing there, and I squeezed my eyes shut. "I'm sorry, honey. I know this… Well, it just fucking sucks. I miss you. I wish you were here with me."

My chin wobbled, and I bit into my lower lip.

"I love you so much, and I want you to be happy," she said.

I nodded even though she couldn't see it.

"Are you happy?"

I blinked my eyes open and looked up at the tiles of the ceiling. Was I happy? "Not at the moment."

"You have to figure out what's going to make you happy and then do that. Don't say yes to a job just because it's a job."

"Yeah, but I can't stay here," I said weakly.

"Why not?"

"Because…" I forced myself up to a sitting position and crossed my legs. "I don't have anything here."

"What do you have anywhere else?" she asked, and I could imagine her hand flailing over her head, like she always did when she was animated about something. I remembered when we'd first made it to the kickline, she had to work hard to control her arms. She naturally swung them freely about when she tapped, and our director used to joke that she'd tie them to Josie's sides.

"Home is wherever you make it," she sang, and I sputtered a laugh.

"That sounds like a wall sign."

"It is. My mom owns it. From Target."

I pushed up to standing. "How is your mom?"

"She's good. Coming to visit next month."

I absently brushed my foot along the floor, thinking about my mom and then my dad and how society raised us to believe home was wherever our parents lived, but it wasn't true. I'd learned that lesson the hard way.

As trite as it sounded, home was wherever you made it, and my home had always been this studio. I held on to the ballet barre, the wood as familiar to me as my own reflection. But if I stayed here, I would never dance professionally again, and that thought alone had my chest tightening. I'd never be able to let loose and be free, fly above all the crap of everyday life that I'd leave behind. I'd never feel those jitters of excitement about taking the first step out onstage again.

Would it be worth giving all that up for my home here?

I didn't know.

My cell phone buzzed with a text alert, and I pulled it away to find a misspelled text from Dylan, informing me he was dropping his kids off after baseball practice and asking if I could come to his house for dinner. When I told Josie, she laughed.

"You got nothing there, huh?"

I refused to answer and, instead, checked the time on the clock in the corner, the one with a ballerina whose legs moved to the minute and hour. "I gotta go. My class is going to start in a few minutes."

"Uh-huh. You enjoy your dinner with your *daddy* tonight."

I hung up on her giggles and prepared for class.

By the time I parked in front of Dylan's house, I was exhausted and emotional. I wasn't due for my period for a few days, but I swore I was getting PMS earlier and earlier lately. Is that what your thirties were? Worse periods and creaky joints?

I hated it already.

I also hated the pit in my stomach, the same one that had been there since I'd opened the email about the audition. The same one that had grown since talking to Josie.

Heaving a sigh, I opened the door, finding Dylan tossing toys into bins. He stopped and glanced over his shoulder, his mouth quirking up like *Welcome home.*

And suddenly the pit was gone, broken into a million pieces which sprouted wings.

Because he gave me those same preshow jitters I craved. He gave me freedom to let loose and forget all the bullshit. He was becoming more familiar to me than the scuffs on the studio's floor.

So familiar, I knew that as soon as I kicked off my shoes and threw myself onto the couch, he'd follow.

He sat on the edge of the sofa, gliding his hand up and down my side. "Tired?"

"And hungry and emotional."

He tweaked the strap of my leotard. "Emotional about what?"

"It's…" I had to tell him about the audition. I *wanted* to. He understood the life of an athlete. And yet…

"It's weird to think someone else will be teaching my classes next year, and Cynthia, this girl in one of the older classes, asked if I could help her with an audition piece for a summer intensive at the community college, and I was—I got emotional. And yesterday!" I slapped my hand on his sturdy shoulder. "Your daughter inviting me to her birthday party! It makes a girl feel really wanted."

He combed his fingers through my hair, tucking it around my ear, thumbing my earring. "You are wanted. By everybody." Then grumpily, he added, "Including that motherfucker Matt."

"You jealous?"

"I don't like the way he looks at you."

I sat up, wrapping my arm around his neck. "What way is that?"

He nipped at my neck. "Like he wants to eat you."

"Mm, but you're the only one who can."

"Don't tempt me, kitten. Dinner's ready in a few minutes. How do you like your steak?"

"Medium well," I said as he laced his fingers with mine to tow me off the couch. "Would you mind if I took a shower?"

"Of course not." He kissed the side of my head and smacked my ass. "You know where everything is. Come outside when you're done."

I made my way upstairs and through his room to the en suite bathroom. Like the rest of his house, his bathroom wasn't *clean*, but it wasn't dirty either. The fixtures and mirrors hadn't seen a rag in a while, and the counter was littered with a few Hot Wheels and pastel-colored hair ties among his deodorant, hand soap, and razor. But he did have matching mats on the floor and lots of clean towels in the linen closet.

I stripped off my clothes and left them in a pile next to the laundry basket in the corner then turned on the shower. It didn't take long to heat up, and I stepped inside, closing the opaque glass door behind me. Dylan kept his bottles of shower gel and shampoos on the floor, and I clucked my tongue, thinking that I needed to buy him a basket for them until I remembered I couldn't because I was leaving. It would be weird to give him something like that.

That was what a girlfriend would do, and I most certainly was not his girlfriend.

I squeezed some of his body wash out onto the black loofah hanging around the faucet and lathered it in my hands, closing my eyes at the familiar scent, before running it over every part of my body. I didn't bother washing my hair, but I did rest my hands on the wall as the water pounded against my back, loosening the muscles there. And while I would've liked to stay in there for another few minutes, I couldn't keep indulging in the fabulous water pressure. Dylan had said dinner would be ready soon.

After drying off, I searched through drawers until I found a tee, a soft Matthews Mechanics shirt that fell halfway down my butt. Even though I was positive he wouldn't mind my being half naked while we ate, I slipped into a pair of his compression shorts.

Downstairs, I helped myself to a glass of water and slid open the back door.

"Right on time," he said, his back to me as he shut off the grill. With a plate in each hand, he pivoted to me, his face going completely slack when he spotted me.

I fidgeted, my big toes rubbing against each other. "I stole some of your clothes. Hope that's okay."

He blinked, a lewd smirk crawling across his mouth. "Only if I can steal them back." He nodded to the table. "Come on. Get some protein and iron in you, and you'll feel better."

He set my plate in front of me with a juicy steak and baked sweet potato with a bit of butter and cinnamon. In between us was a small platter with a few slices of grilled pineapple.

"My compliments to the chef."

Underneath the table, he leaned his leg against mine. "Gotta get your energy back up. I have plans for you later."

I smiled and cut into the meat. It was cooked perfectly, and we ate for a few minutes in quiet, his usual playlist of country music as our soundtrack.

"Are you sure it's okay if I go to Scarlett's party?" I asked eventually.

"Of course. Why?"

"I don't want it to be a *thing*."

"A thing?"

"It's your ex-wife's house, and I'm your current…whatever."

He set his fork down and wiped at his mouth with his napkin before taking a swig of his beer. Then he handed it to me to do the same. "I would want you there even if we weren't…doing what we're doing, because that's what Scarlett wants."

Both of us being unable to define what we were doing reminded me of the sex talk my mother had with me when I was in high school. "If you're embarrassed to talk about it, that means you're not mature enough to be doing it."

Ignoring the alarm bells ringing in the back of my head, I swallowed another bite of sweet potato and asked, "Is it hard for you and Paige to do things together? Like having a birthday party?"

My parents did nothing together after the divorce. It might've been easier for them that way, but it was more difficult for Nate and me. I assumed it was hard for Dylan, but in the long run, it would be better for Scarlett and Tucker.

As I suspected, he nodded. "The divorce was… It was the worst thing I've ever gone through. We're both happier now, but yeah, sometimes it's really hard to do the co-parenting thing, especially when there's still a lot of anger and hurt."

We shared another sip of beer, and my curiosity won out when I asked, "She's remarried, right? I think I've seen him once or twice."

Dylan cleared his throat and sat back in his chair while he

skimmed his hand down my leg, urging me to place both of my feet in his lap. "Neil, yeah. She got remarried pretty quick."

"How quick?" I blurted then aimed for an explanation. "It's only, my dad remarried really fast too. It was weird for Nate and me. She was his administrative assistant, and suddenly, she was our new stepmom."

He pressed his thumbs into the arches of my feet, his gaze down as he worked. It felt glorious. "Paige marrying Neil wasn't a surprise."

"Were they—" I stopped myself from speaking it out loud.

"They were having an emotional affair," he finished for me, and I winced.

I had been devastated when my high school boyfriend cheated on me, so I could somewhat imagine the pain of a spouse having an affair, and I'd guess an emotional one might feel just as bad.

"I'm sorry," I said, and he dragged his focus up to my face.

"When she first told me, I was furious. We'd been in couples counseling. I'd still thought there was a chance for us. She'd just gotten pregnant, and we were working through it. But then she told me about Neil in one of our sessions, and I lost my fucking mind." He started playing with my toes, pinching and tugging on each one. "I filed for divorce the next day. Although if I hadn't, she would've. I was really angry for a long time, but eventually, I recognized that if I'd been a better partner to her, she wouldn't have needed to look elsewhere for support."

"Yeah, but still. It sucks she did that."

"Yep," he murmured, gaze back down on my feet as he curved his palms around the bottom of them, rubbing up and down my ankles and shins. "Sometimes it feels like she thinks of me as a glorified babysitter instead of Scarlett and Tucker's dad."

I stayed quiet, not knowing what to say to make him feel better. But I suspected he didn't need me to say anything; he simply needed an ear to listen.

"I wasn't a good husband or father, and even though she

made the decision to have a relationship with Neil, I still pushed her to do it."

Regret roughened his voice. His pain was palpable, especially in how he gripped my legs, his fingertips pressing into my skin like he needed a lifeline.

"You're an amazing father," I told him, and he barely nodded. "And I know you've grown as a person. I can tell how much work you've done with therapy and everything. I didn't know you before, but I know you now, and you are..." I let out a wisp of a breath. "You're perfect."

He huffed, his eyes fixing me in place when I reached across the table to touch him. "I'm not perfect."

"Well, no one is *perfect*, but you're—"

He shook his head and let go of my feet to cross his arms. "The kids are much happier now, and that's all that matters. They're my number one priority, and I won't ever put them in the middle of a shitstorm again. I can't get into a relationship and have it turn out the same way. I can't do that to them again. I won't."

His words were both an explanation and a warning. He didn't want to hurt his kids by entering into another relationship that didn't work. Though less obvious was the undercurrent of pain and possible real reason he kept his feelings out of his love life. He didn't want to get hurt again.

By now, I'd learned the difference between his scowls and stares, how his dry humor was the way he showed his love, and that his so-called grumpy personality was all a mask. This man felt things deeply, loved widely, and he hid it from the world, scared of messing up again.

It was heartbreaking. For him. For his kids.

For me.

Until he saw himself as good enough, he'd never be able to go all in.

Silently, I stood up and collected our plates to take inside.

Dylan followed with our drinks, and we set everything on the counter then wordlessly headed upstairs.

We kept the light on as we peeled off each other's shirts. I roamed my hands over the plane of his back as he placed hot and wet kisses across my shoulder and breasts, and before I knew it, I was naked and lying on the bed, his mouth mapping my stomach and hips.

I curled my fingers into his hair, wanting to tell him something, anything, to express what I felt for him, but with his tongue exploring the hottest part of me, I couldn't think. Couldn't grasp the words circling in my mind.

But he had to know. He had to know what a good man he was. "Dylan, I…"

He slid two fingers into me, not bothering to tease me into a slow state of delirious pleasure. Instead, he skipped straight to the end, to my back arching off the mattress, my legs clenching his shoulders as he forced an orgasm. I had trouble catching my breath, my lips and tongue dry from my restless panting, but he didn't slow down.

It was as if he didn't want to.

Didn't want to give me a chance to confess any of the number of things I wanted to.

That I didn't think I'd ever find someone like him again.

That he wasn't perfect, but he was perfect for me.

That I wasn't sure about this audition next week.

Seconds later, he had a condom on and was rolling me to my stomach, pushing my legs wide as he guided me to my hands and knees. He thrust into me at the same time he pulled me onto his lap, so I was draped over his thighs, almost sitting on him. He was so deep like this that it took a few seconds for me to adjust, and he slid his palms over my rib cage to my breasts, palming and pinching them.

"Feel that?" he asked, his voice a knife's edge.

I didn't know if he meant the warmth of his hands, the gust

of his breath on my neck, or the stretch of fullness from his cock, but I nodded anyway. I felt it all.

I felt everything.

His thrusts were shallow but powerful, and all I could do was fist the sheet and take everything he had to give me. So much and not enough.

"Genevieve, I need you to come with me. Come with me," he ordered, and I bore down, spreading my knees wider, white spots edging into my vision, and I closed my eyes. He sank his hand between my legs, circling my clit, and it was all I needed to send me flying. "That's it. That's it. I love to feel you gripping me so tight."

He hissed and wrapped himself around me, though he didn't pull out, and I ended up flat on the mattress, breathing hard against a pillow. He kissed my spine, squeezed my waist and ass, possessive and heartrending, whispering words about how good it was between us, how beautiful I was, how he could stay inside me forever.

If only he knew I was already so gone for him, I would only need one word to never leave this bed.

If only he knew I would stay.

TWENTY-TWO
DYLAN

I arrived at Paige and Neil's house about twenty minutes before the party with the cake and trays of catered sand-wiches, chicken fingers, and pretzel bites. Tucker was waiting at the door for me, a carrot stick in one hand and a piece of peanut butter bread in the other.

"Daddy!"

"Hey, buddy." I balanced all of the trays in one arm to open the door and nudged him out of the way. "You need to watch what you're doing with that carrot. No eating while running around. You're gonna choke on it."

He waved it at me. "No choking!"

"Yeah. No choking. Where's your sister?"

"Back-y yard."

He ran ahead of me to the kitchen, where Paige was cutting up strawberries. I placed all the food on the table. "How's it going?"

"You're late."

"I know. It took a while to get checked out. The store was jammed."

She didn't acknowledge my excuse. "I'm gonna need you to deal with the food. I need to finish putting the decorations up."

"Where—"

"Your daughter's been a menace today. She changed into another outfit because she spilled juice all over her last one. It's her third for the day."

"I thought she wanted to wear that dress you bought her."

"She did, and it's in the laundry. It was the *first* tantrum of the day." She turned over her shoulder, eyeing me like this was my fault.

Scarlett had been looking forward to her party for a while, so she was probably twirling around like a tornado. I held up my hands, a gesture to calm Paige, but it only riled her up more.

"You were supposed to be here at 1:30. I really wish you could follow directions for once."

I wrenched my head back. "Wow. Okay. Starting early with this, huh?"

The knife she'd been using clattered on the counter when she smacked her hand on it, and she took a deep breath. "I'm sorry, but I need your help."

Paige, though highly organized, always got huffy whenever she put a party together. It was like she went into hyperdrive, stressed about every little thing. As if people would care about the napkins and paper plates matching.

And she wondered why our daughter had trouble cooling off.

"That's why I'm here," I grated out. "So, do you want my help, or are you gonna bitch at me about being ten minutes late some more?"

I knew it was unhelpful, but if she was coming in hot, I wasn't about to back down.

After a moment, she turned, pinning me with a glower. "Put the cake in the fridge for now." She tossed her knife into the sink and dried her hands. "They're two kids coming with allergies, so I got pink and blue platters and bowls." She tipped her chin to them. "The blue ballerinas get nut- and berry-free food. Pink gets everything else."

"Fine."

"Bring it all out when you're done," she directed and marched out the back door. "Tucker! Get that out of your mouth!"

I gave myself a minute for my ire to cool before I got to work. This was my daughter's sixth birthday party, and I wanted it to be fun for her, but I also didn't know what the big goddamn deal was. There was no reason for Paige to be so uptight about it. The kids would be happy with pizza and a *Blippi* soundtrack. It wasn't like they were real discerning creatures.

But that was Paige, a perfectionist.

And I was sure she would hate how I piled the food on the plates instead of making it like a Pinterest board, but it'd have to do.

Outside, a line of cutout ballerinas hung on the laundry line, while pink and white balloons floated above every table, tied down with plastic dancers, of course. Confetti and glitter were *everywhere*.

Neil offered me a nod. I gave him one back then scooped up Scarlett. "I need you to take it down a few notches. I know you're excited, but you're at a twenty-five when we need you at an eight. Can you do that, or do I need to take your batteries out?"

She pulled a face, and I scratched at her back, pretending to take out her batteries. "Okay. One out and…" I lightly smacked her a few times like a stuck remote control. She giggled. "Second battery out."

Then she went limp in my arms, and I set her on the ground, talking to no one in particular. "Always a good idea to turn it off and on."

She giggled again, her face smooshed in the grass.

"I'm going to make one more trip for food, and then I can put the tornado's batteries back in."

"Ballerina!" she corrected, flopping onto her back.

"Sorry. Ballerina." I stepped over her to head back to the

kitchen, but Paige cut me off, throwing her hand out toward Scarlett.

"What're you doing? Get up off the ground. Your friends are going to be here soon, and you are *not* changing again. I don't want to hear it if you get grass stains on your skirt."

"Daddy took my batteries out," Scarlett said, and Paige did her best to hide her eye roll from our daughter but not from me.

"She needed a little rest," I said.

"*I* need a rest," Paige snapped. "And I still haven't changed yet." She motioned to her cutoff shorts and Carrie Underwood tour T-shirt.

"Then go change."

"I still have to bring out the games."

"Where are they? I'll go get them."

She started to tell me then let out a frustrated growl. "Never mind. I had to hide them in the basement. You'll never find it. Just take care of the kids, will you? Neil!"

She spun away from me, wound up in her own tornado, and stomped into the house. Presumably to change and find whatever games she had planned. Neil followed, snagging a pretzel bite on the way.

"All right, kiddo." I squatted down to Scarlett, still on the ground, and whacked her back twice. "Batteries back in." Then I pressed my finger into her nose. "Power on."

She stood and jumped at me for a hug. I lifted her into my arms and held her as I crossed the yard to the swing set, where Tucker was laid over on on his belly, swinging back and forth by running as far forward as he could then lifting his legs in the air.

"Tuck, stop for a minute. I need to talk to you both."

I set Scarlett down but kept her close as I kneeled on the grass and held on to one of the metal chains so Tucker couldn't go anywhere. "I know parties are exciting. You're super excited, I'm super excited, everyone's super excited, *but* we also have to be cool and calm about it." I looked both of my kids in the eyes, holding up my fingers as I counted off how to do it.

"That means still following directions, being good hosts to your friends and sharing your food and toys. and not screaming and crying or throwing tantrums if you're upset. Got it?"

I waited until each one answered.

"Got it."

"Got it!" Though Tucker just wanted to be able to swing again.

I rubbed the back of his head and patted Scarlett on the bum. Not even thirty seconds later, the first guests trickled in. Scarlett hugged each of her friends, while their parents huddled together chatting.

I mostly kept to myself in the corner by the food as more and more people streamed in until, finally, Liam showed up with Finn, who ran off with Tucker. A few minutes later, Jude arrived with Amelia and Sebastian in tow.

While Amelia folded right in with all the other girls, Sebastian stayed with Liam, Jude, and me.

"You pumped for the game tomorrow?" I asked him.

"Yeah. Dad bought me a tee to practice my swing."

"Good for you. The more you practice mechanics, the better you'll get."

He stood a bit taller, and pride swelled in my chest because I had a hand in helping him be confident in himself. I hadn't known Jude and his family before his wife passed away, but from my understanding, Sebastian had had an understandably hard time. He'd struggled to connect with people and open himself up to new things. But baseball seemed to be something he was enjoying, and I was grateful to be a part of that.

I wondered if that was how Genevieve felt with her dancers, and as if I'd imagined her into reality, she floated through the back door in another one-piece contraption. This one was loose-fitting shorts, dark blue with little buttons down the front. It appeared to have less easy access than the skintight number she'd worn to my shop. But I'd need a closer look to be sure.

She made her way over to me with a radiant smile, and our hands briefly tangled together.

I pulled at one of the straps on her shoulder. "You look cute."

"Thanks. Quite the shindig you got here," she said then greeted my friends. "Hey, nice to see everyone again."

They all responded with the usual chatter, and she held up a small gift bag. "Where are the presents going?" When I tipped my chin toward the table on the other side of the yard, she held up a finger. "Be right back."

I watched as she sashayed to the gift table, only to be intercepted by Scarlett and all of the other girls from dance class.

"Are you going out with her?" Sebastian asked, and I shot him a frown. *"What?"* He shrugged. "You're like that emoji with heart eyes. I figured..."

Jude threw his arm around his son. "You figured right."

I glared at my friend.

Liam chuckled into his pink plastic cup of soda.

I glared at him too.

I was about to reiterate what was going on between Genevieve and me, but Paige called everyone's attention to her with a few claps. She was smiling as her gaze made a circuit of the party until it landed on the group of giggling girls with Genevieve in the middle of them. I was positive no one else noticed the momentary slip of Paige's grin, but I did.

"Hi, everybody. If you don't know me, I'm Scarlett's mom, and we're so glad you could be here. We're going to start with a game. Who wants to play ballet bingo?"

The eager squeals were answer enough, and Paige motioned to the tables.

"Everybody sit down, and I'll hand out the cards."

Genevieve got up from her squatted position and shook out her legs as she made her way back over to me. "A dozen six-year-olds is a lot of pressure on the knees."

I smoothed my palm up and down her back. "You want a drink or anything?"

She shook her head. "I'm okay for now."

"I'm gonna help out with the game," I said and, without thinking, brushed my lips over her temple.

Everyone stiffened. My friends, Sebastian, Genevieve, me—hell, even the birds went still.

Though insignificant, the kiss was a public display of affection in front of all the people who mattered in my life. It might not have meant anything, yet it meant everything. And when I pivoted, Paige's eyes were glued to me.

Because, of course, she'd seen it too.

"What do you want me to do?" I asked once I crossed the yard, and she shoved the container of colorful bingo chips at me.

Paige kept her voice low and quiet, but her irritation came through loud and clear. "Why is Scarlett's dance teacher here?"

"Because Scarlett invited her."

"Why didn't I know?"

"What do you mean why—"

"Lemme take some of these," Neil said, interrupting us as he stuck his hand into the bowl for a handful of chips. "Got some excited little girls ready to play bingo."

It was an obvious reminder that we couldn't get into an argument in the middle of our daughter's birthday party, and even though I moved away from my ex, dumping a bunch of chips in front of every kid, I knew Paige wouldn't let the subject drop.

She cornered me in the hall after I'd gone in search of a first aid kit for Finn. He needed a Band-Aid for a scrape.

"I can't believe you didn't tell me you're dating Scarlett's dance teacher," she said without preamble, shaking a box of candles in one hand and a cake server in the other.

"We're not dating."

She did the annoying headshake, shoulder-shrug combination that never failed to rub me the wrong way. Like she was *confused* by it all.

"I saw you touching her back. You kissed her."

I didn't appreciate her accusatory tone. "Am I not allowed to kiss other people? We're divorced. I can do whatever I want."

"Oh," she huffed, flinging her arms up, that cake server perilously close to denting the wall. "I know you do whatever you want. It's why we divorced."

I sighed and removed my baseball hat, scrubbing my hands over my face then leaned against the wall. "What do you want? What is this actually about?"

"First of all, you can't bring your girlfriend to our daughter's party without telling me. Did you even tell the kids? Do they know?"

"There's nothing to tell. We're not dating."

Her face flushed, jaw tight, left eye twitching. "And you thought it would be appropriate to bring her here? What the hell, Dylan?"

"I didn't bring her. Scarlett invited her." I pointed toward the windows. "You see how she is with Genevieve. Scarlett loves her. All the girls do. I don't understand what the problem is."

"My problem is no one told me she was coming. If you knew, you should have."

"Does it matter?" I had trouble keeping my voice down now. "It's one person. It's not like you need to do anything extra."

"It's the principle of it, but that's what you never understood. You've always done whatever you wanted. It didn't matter what I wanted or what I asked you to do. It was always on your time and your schedule." She flicked her hand, the candles rattling. "You bring your girlfriend or fuck buddy or whatever the hell you call her to our daughter's party and just expect everyone to accept it."

I slapped my hat back on my head and pushed off the wall. She had no right to be affronted that I was or was not dating or fucking Genevieve. "So what? I can't be with anyone else? Is that it?"

She held the cake server between us. "We agreed we would talk to each other about introducing the kids to our significant others and only when it was serious. You don't get to be pissed at me about this. *You're* the one who isn't holding up your end—surprise, surprise."

"Oh, come off it, Paige. You've known Genevieve longer than I have. Scarlett spent a whole year in her class. Her being here has nothing to do with me. You can't hold it over my head that she's here and I—god forbid—touched her back."

Paige only rolled her eyes and crossed her arms, but I wasn't done.

"And I don't want to hear any of your shit about what we agreed to. Because I never agreed to you going behind my back with Neil—" I ignored her sucked in breath "—but I didn't hold him over your head. So don't you dare think about holding Genevieve over mine."

Her eyes shifted away briefly, her lips pursed, fists at her side before she straightened up and met my gaze once again. "You don't think Scarlett notices what's going on between you and her dance teacher, who, as you keep saying, she loves? Of course she notices. Don't treat me or our kids like we're stupid."

"I don't—"

"No." She stepped into my space. She was full-on mama bear when it came to the kids, but I wasn't doing anything to hurt them. In fact, I was doing everything in my power *not* to hurt them. "Your problem is you don't see how your choices affect other people. You don't *think*. You only *do*. And damn the consequences."

"What are you even talking about? What consequences?"

"I don't care what you have going on with Genevieve, but you can't bring her to our daughter's birthday party," she hissed.

I was so done with this conversation and just wanted it to end. I propped my hands on my hips. "There's nothing going on between Genevieve and me."

The lie tasted like ash on my tongue, but it drained the fight from Paige. "All the more reason she shouldn't have been here."

Before I could respond that she had every right to be here, the floor creaked, and Paige and I both swiveled our heads to the sound.

There was Genevieve, shoulders hunched, eyes wide and pained. "I, uh, was looking for the bathroom."

I swallowed down my mortification at being caught in the middle of an argument with my ex-wife *about* her, but I still couldn't answer.

Paige cleared her throat and spoke instead, voice wiped clean of all frustration, though she was noticeably embarrassed, her body plastered against the wall. "Sure. It's right here."

I shuffled away from the door, and Genevieve kept her focus down as she closed it, the lock clicking in place. I sighed, dropping my head back against the wall while Paige slipped outside without another word.

When the bathroom door opened a few minutes later, I caught Genevieve's hand, cool and damp from washing it. I laced my fingers with hers. "How much of that did you hear?"

She shrugged, and I grimaced, thinking of everything Paige had said about how she shouldn't have been here, and then when I claimed there was nothing going on between us. That wasn't true.

None of it was true.

"I'm sorry."

"There's nothing for you to be sorry about."

"I'm sorry," I said again.

Her smile was so tender, and I didn't deserve it. I didn't deserve the way her hand cupped my jaw as she placed a sweet kiss to my cheek. "I'm going to head out."

"What? No." I gripped her hips. "You can't. We're about to have cake."

"I know, but I think it would be best if I go."

"But Scarlett—"

"Is fine." She glanced over her shoulder to the window, where the herd of girls was running in circles outside. "She won't even notice I'm gone."

"I doubt that." Besides, even if she didn't, I would. I wanted Genevieve here as much as Scarlett did. That fight with Paige had made those feelings quite evident. As much as I'd wanted to shut her up with all that talk about Scarlett inviting Genevieve, the truth was *I* wanted her here. Scarlett was just my excuse.

"You've got your hands full here," Genevieve went on. "Call me later, okay?"

When I nodded, she tipped the bill of my cap back and kissed my lips but didn't linger. It didn't feel like *see you later*. Felt more like *goodbye*.

Then she strode right out the door.

I pressed my hand to the sudden pain beneath my ribs. Watching her mask the hurt that flashed over her features was as painful to me as if I'd been cut with a knife. And I didn't know how to stem the flow. It felt as if my own blood was trailing behind her.

TWENTY-THREE
GENEVIEVE

The days leading up to the audition had moved in double time, but now that I was hours away from boarding my flight, the minutes were yearslong. Especially as I stood at the front of the studio, watching the special someones and their girls rehearse the dance for the final time in class.

Dylan had called me Saturday night after he had returned home from the party, and he'd apologized multiple times, though I didn't know why he thought he needed to. He'd done nothing wrong. Neither had Paige. Sure, it wasn't great walking in on a heated argument about my being at the party, but I understood why Paige would be upset. She knew me but didn't really *know* me, and when Dylan told me he hadn't informed her that I was coming, I heaved out such a sigh that he apologized again.

"You should've told her," I'd said, to which he had answered, "I didn't think it was that big of a deal."

And I understood that too. It was what'd had me biting the inside of my cheek, so I didn't cry while we were on the phone. When he'd asked to come over, I'd told him I was on my period, which was the truth, but then he'd said, "I don't care about sex. I just want to see you."

I'd made up an excuse about not feeling well, when the reality was I couldn't face him. Not after hearing him tell his ex-wife nothing was going on between us, on top of him repeating that my being at the party wasn't a big deal while we were on the phone. What he meant was *we* were no big deal.

From the beginning, I'd known that was how he felt. It was what he'd always said. "No big deal."

And I got it. Had it explained in simple terms like a kinder-garten teacher and the alphabet. Dylan Matthews did not want to be in a relationship. A, B, C...

Yet, my heart didn't want to believe it. She was an idiot.

Always flopping about, never in rhythm, completely out of sync with reality.

And she was making it impossible to even glance in his direction today. I couldn't meet his eyes, could scarcely fake a grin in Scarlett's direction. Because overhearing Dylan and Paige's argument made me realize exactly how much I didn't want to be the source of disruption between them. I didn't want to be an unexpected guest.

What I did want was to be invited from the beginning, completely expected to be there. I wanted to be the woman Dylan talked to Paige about introducing their kids to as someone serious in their life. I wanted to *be* there.

With him.

With them.

But what Dylan and I had was no big deal. It would never be anything more, and I had to focus on what was ahead of me, which was my audition in Florida.

And definitely not on the last few weeks with a grumpy dad who insisted on stealing all my concentration.

I pushed off the ballet barre as the last notes of the song plunked into silence. "Great! That was really great. Almost everyone was on the correct foot for kicks that time."

As everyone stood up from their final pose, I swept my gaze over the ragtag group of adults and kids, who had learned and could *almost* remember their dance in only six weeks. It was amazing to see how far they'd come.

Especially the girls. Being a teacher might not have been in my immediate plans when I'd busted my ankle, but watching them light up had brought me so much unexpected joy. For that, I was eternally grateful.

I waved all the girls closer to me. "This was our last class together. Our last time dancing. Can you believe it?" When Bella pouted, I said, "You still have dress rehearsal and the recital, but then no more dance until next year."

As the girls crowded in closer to me so I could give them all a group hug, I pasted on a smile for the adults. "I appreciate all your hard work. It's been an honor to teach your girls this year. I thank you for trusting me with them."

"Miss Gen, you're leaving?" Amaya held on to my hand.

I straightened and nodded, not quite sure my voice would be steady.

"Where're you going?" Priya asked.

Even as I felt hot pressure on the side of my face from where Dylan stood, I kept my attention on Priya's sweet smile. "Well, I have an audition tomorrow, and it's in Florida."

"Florida!" Kayleigh piped up. "Did you know Minnie Mouse lives there? I saw her last year."

"I heard she lives there. You're so lucky to have met her, but I'm not going to meet her. I'm going to a different city."

"Where?" CiCi asked, and all their earnest questions had my mouth pulling up even as my heart was by my feet.

"I'm going to a place called Fort Lauderdale."

"What's in Fort Lo...Lotterale?" Scarlett asked, and Dylan was the one to come to my rescue.

He took her by the hand as he motioned to the door. "All right, I think we're keeping Miss Gen from her next class."

The special someones all murmured their thanks to me, but as they filed out, I remembered one last thing. "Make sure their names are on everything! Shoes, headband, tights, everything. You can write it on the tag of the costume and tights."

"Got it," someone hollered, and my heart actually sank at the thought that I wouldn't be returning to the studio to see these girls next week. I wouldn't be surrounded by their giggles and shrieks. I wouldn't hear their random thoughts about TV shows or favorite snacks or how their baby brother threw his puffs on the floor and the dog ate them all, so he cried.

I'd never imagined I'd miss that. Yet somehow I already did.

I spun to find Scarlett and Dylan in front of me. She swung his arm back and forth, his big hand engulfing hers, and I knew that feeling. The callused fingertips, the warmth of his palm, the strength of his hold.

"Miss Gen, what's your audition for?" she asked.

This time, I couldn't help but tip my head up to Dylan. He was staring at me, eyes unreadable.

"It's, uh, for a show on a cruise ship."

"A cruise ship?" Scarlett and Dylan both repeated, though she was much more curious than his flat echo.

"It's a really big boat that can take people to different locations and is basically like a hotel on water," I explained to Scarlett. And then to her father, I added, "It's for a couple of variety shows and a tribute to Tina Turner. Nutbush city limits," I sang badly, and when he made no move or sound, I rambled. "Anyway. If I get it, rehearsals will start at the end of the month, and it's about four weeks before the ship leaves."

He nodded, his lips pursed as his eyes flattened to slits, but I went cold all over. This wasn't Dylan the panther. This was some other side of him I'd never met.

Dylan was the type of person who took a while to open up but was pretty easy to read once he finally did.

Except for right now. He might as well have been a complete stranger.

"I'm flying down tomorrow morning and coming back Thursday night," I said.

He licked his lips then smoothed his palm over his mouth before nodding a few times, his focus on the floor. "Well, I've got the kids until Friday, so…"

"So I guess I'll see you at dress rehearsal," I finished for him.

"Yeah." His shoulders rose on an inhale, and he dragged his gaze up the length of me. Not in the way he usually did, like he couldn't wait to strip me bare, but like he was trying to memorize me. And the goose bumps on my arms weren't because I was excited, but because I was scared of what I'd see in his eyes when they finally met mine.

I was right to be afraid. Because they were empty. No glowing danger or spark of dry humor in sight. No heat of desire or ember of memories. There was nothing.

And I absently folded my arms behind my back, reaching for the door, using it to hold me up.

"I won't say good luck," he told me. "You don't need it. I know you're gonna kill it."

"Thanks," I managed to say to his back as he tugged Scarlett away.

It wasn't until I was home packing my bag, while I sat on my bed in my sparsely decorated room that I thought about what made me happy. *If* I could be happy here.

Growing up, dance was my escape, but I didn't need that anymore. I needed a home. I needed what made me happy.

And that was all here. Working with my brother. Teaching my classes. Being with Dylan.

I was happy. The only question was if he was happy too.

TWENTY-FOUR
DYLAN

"Hello, dancers!" Miss Amy, the short but mighty owner of Rhythm Nova Dance Studio, waved from the stage to the audience of dancers, decked out in bows and tulle, the chemically sweet smell of hair spray permeating every corner of the auditorium. "We're going to start in five minutes," she overenunciated, one hand spread wide in the air, while the other gripped a microphone. "If you're in more than one number, you should be in your first costume, and if you aren't sure what that is, you can check the list on the stage doors or ask one of our volunteers. We also emailed it to all of the adults, so if you're here with one, you can also ask them. Mmkay? Five minutes, then we're beginning with the finale."

She turned off the mic and made her way off the stage, and I checked the time on my cell phone, my patience wearing thin even though I would be here for another forty-five minutes or so. Scarlett danced around with her friends, all of them in matching purple-and-black costumes with sequins on the straps and around the skirt. I'd struggled to get her hair in a slicked back ponytail, and I hadn't even attempted to put makeup on her, so when I'd dropped Tucker off, Paige fixed her up quick before we left.

Paige and I barely exchanged more than ten words. Ever since the party, I'd kept my communication to the absolute minimum with her. I knew my anger was irrational. It wasn't her fault I was pissed off.

Really, it was my fault. I'd put myself in this position. I was the one who'd pursued Genevieve. I was the one who'd said we were no big deal. I was the one who couldn't face what I felt for her. And blaming Paige was easier than swallowing the harsh fucking pill that was my own deficiencies.

Genevieve swore up and down that she wasn't hurt by what she'd overheard. In fact, when I'd asked her to tell me exactly how much she had heard, she'd refused, saying, "Not much. It's fine."

But it wasn't fucking fine.

She didn't deserve to be caught in the middle of all my bullshit.

My therapist would be getting an earful at my next appointment.

"Daddy, is it time to dance yet?"

"Almost." I eased myself back against the wall, taking in the rows of dancers, all of them grouped in their classes. Volunteers scattered throughout, making sure everyone knew what they were doing. Miss Amy was still onstage, speaking to one of the other teachers. But I had yet to spot Genevieve.

I hadn't spoken to her since our phone call Tuesday night. Hadn't seen her since the few hours before that, when I'd put on the performance of a lifetime as she'd informed me of her audition.

We'd had so many conversations about our careers in the last few weeks, and I knew how much being onstage meant to her. As much as being on the field had meant to me.

I was happy for her. Truly, I was. She was getting another shot at the big time.

What I wouldn't have given for one more chance.

So I wasn't going to shit on it just because I was drowning in my emotions.

Even though I felt more for her than I wanted to admit, I would never ask her not to audition or go after her dreams. I wouldn't ask her to give that up for me, especially since I wasn't worth it.

I'd fucked up my marriage to Paige and was still paying the price. I wouldn't risk failing at a relationship with Genevieve.

"All right! Dancers!" Miss Amy was back on the mic. "I'm going to call out everyone's names or classes, and you'll need to meet Miss Shauna or Miss Leilani at the side door, and they'll walk you backstage. Miss Gen will tell you where to go. We're going to run through the finale two times, okay?"

A few dancers responded, but she went on as if they were all pumped up.

"Great! First up, I need all the graduating seniors up onstage with Miss Gen, please."

Genevieve popped out from the side, a clipboard in her hands and a headset on her ears. She was speaking to someone —I assumed whoever was in the tech booth—as she waved to the girls making their way to her.

I couldn't tear my eyes away from her even as Scarlett pulled on my arms, squealing about the "finally."

"Finale," I corrected her absently while Genevieve spoke to the graduating seniors for a moment and then gave a thumbs-up to Miss Amy, who called other classes, instructing them to meet Miss Shauna or Miss Leilani.

Gen directed every new group of students to a certain spot where they were supposed to bow and then clap along to whatever song would play. Eventually, Miss Amy called for Scarlett's class to go to the side door, and I slipped into a seat to watch.

I had precious seconds to drink my fill of Genevieve. I wasn't about to waste any of them.

She was wearing sneakers, black leggings, and a recital T-shirt, the same one the other teachers wore.

But she might as well have been wearing nothing for how my focus never left her ass any time she turned around.

Once all the dancers were onstage, Miss Amy had them all walk off, and Genevieve said something into her headset. A moment later, the lights dropped down and the music turned up. "Shut Up and Dance" blared through the speakers, and the seniors began clapping on beat as the other classes filed in to bow and join in the clapping and dancing, which I supposed was to involve the audience. As the younger classes entered, it became more chaotic. Only some of them were able to find the beat; almost none of them remembered to bow.

But Scarlett took her place in the front, kneeling and waving like Genevieve had told her to do, and I found myself grinning up at her even though I knew she couldn't see me.

"Okay. One more time," Miss Amy said through her microphone. "This time with feeling!"

All the dancers exited, only to return on their cue, but Miss Amy was satisfied enough to move on. "Next up, we'll have our special someones dance, and then after that, we'll go back to the beginning and start with the opening and continue on. Our younger ones, the mini-movers and kindergarteners, you can leave after your number, but for everyone else, you'll need to stay until you've rehearsed all of your numbers, but you don't have to stay until the end. Mmkay? Special someones onstage, please."

Scarlett and I made our way backstage, where Genevieve pointed out how those of us on the other side of the stage had to sneak behind the curtain to get there for our entrance. I shouldn't have been surprised that she didn't pay me extra special attention; she was in pro-mode. Yet, I wanted something.

Anything.

Why? I don't know. I didn't deserve it.

Still, I needed it.

Scarlett and I held hands, ready for our entrance, and I could see Genevieve, on the other side of the stage, put her clipboard down along with her headset then face forward. She'd said she'd do the dance in the wings in case anyone forgot the steps, and I was certain motherfucking Matt would.

The Temptations started playing, and we all shuffled out to the stage. I was shocked to be so nervous with the stage lights shining and the suit and tie making me hot, but I remembered every single step, not needing to look over at Genevieve for what came next, though my gaze still slanted her way occasionally because I liked to look at her, even in the shadows.

On the final note, Scarlett sat on my knee as we posed with our opposing arms out. The audience of dancers and volunteers clapped for us, and we walked off the stage in our two lines. Since I was last, I ducked down to Genevieve's ear. "How'd I do?"

She was slow to meet my eyes. "Dance ten, performance six."

"I'll take it."

"You need to smile, Mr. Matthews."

I offered her one, and she dropped her gaze from mine, although I could tell she was fighting a smile of her own.

Before I could get another word in, I was ushered out of the backstage area. I took a seat in the audience and since my job for the night was over, I removed my coat and tie, hanging them over the seat in front of me while Scarlett whispered and giggled with the girls around her.

It was another minute before the lights fully dimmed in the auditorium, with only a single blue spotlight onstage. Then the familiar opening of Whitney Houston's, "I Wanna Dance with Somebody" began, and one by one, all of the studio's teachers danced onstage—Shauna, then Leilani, Genevieve, and Miss Amy. The four performed together through the second round of the chorus. Or, I was guessing the other three did. I couldn't be sure since I was focused solely on the woman with red lips, shiny hair, and pearl earrings, who literally took my breath away. Sometimes they all did the same choreography, sometimes they split apart, but at one point, they each had a solo.

Genevieve spun across the stage in her heeled dance shoes, graceful and unearthly beautiful. She was at once a blur and clear as day as she stopped on a dime and flicked her leg out to the side, doing some little come-hither move with her hands. Her mouth was stretched wide, her smile never fading, and the hairs on the back of my neck and arms stood on end. Her endlessly long legs kicked high into the air, which delighted the crowd. They whooped and hollered for her, and she smiled even brighter as she stretched her arm out to the side then kicked and leaped and spun in the other direction, allowing another teacher to take center stage.

Still, I couldn't stop watching her.

I didn't know a jazz square from a pirouette, but she was a star.

Mind-blowing.

Perfection.

As the song faded away, the teachers left the stage, and a class of girls and one boy took their places, but I'd lost any interest in watching anyone who wasn't Genevieve or my daughter.

It was about a half an hour before a volunteer appeared to take Scarlett's class backstage for their number, and all the girls scooted out of their seats.

Although I'd watched the class practice their "Little Bitty Pretty One" routine for the last few weeks, I couldn't stop the grin spreading across my face at my little girl, tapping her foot and swinging her arms perfectly in sync with the music. She loved being onstage, I could tell. She radiated joy, from the top of her bouncing ponytail to her pointed toes. She sashayed and turned and step-ball-changed wonderfully, and my heart about burst with pride.

When they all hit their final pose, I stood up, whistling like I was at a ballpark. "Way to go, Scarlett!"

A mom a few rows down shot me a nasty look, but I didn't care. I was going to cheer for my little girl whether that lady liked it or not. A minute later, Scarlett came careening down the aisle, jumping into my arms when I bent to her.

"Did you see me? Did you see me, Daddy?"

"I did. You were great. I'm so proud of you."

She hugged me, smearing glitter and a bit of pink lipstick on my white shirt, but I didn't give a shit right now. I was flying high.

It wasn't until Scarlett slipped away from me that I crashed back down to earth because I had to get her back to her mom's, and I hadn't been able to talk to Genevieve at all.

Once I had Scarlett's dance shoes off and her sneakers on, I slung her bag over my shoulder and took her hand in mine. "Ready to get out of here?"

"Yeah. I'm hungry for a snack."

"I've got Pirate's Booty in the car."

She shot her fist in the air and hopped along beside me as we made our way out of the auditorium.

After I dropped Scarlett off, I didn't even pretend I had any plans other than to see Genevieve.

I waited in the parking lot of her apartment building until she came home, over two hours later. As soon as she parked, I was out of my car, and she wasn't at all surprised to see me, even as she asked, "What're you doing here?"

I shoved my hands into my pockets to keep from touching her, but I couldn't resist stepping into her space. My head tipped down, hers tilted up, and our eyes clashed while unspoken words wound around us like a hangman's noose.

"Dylan..."

That cracked voice, delicate and breathy, broke through my resistance, and I let my forehead fall forward, resting on hers. Her breath smelled sweet, like a lollipop or some other candy.

"Did you eat dinner?" I asked because it was easier than anything else.

"A few snacks backstage. Brielle, one of the seniors, had some gummi worms that I stole."

"You're not hungry?"

She shook her head, forcing me to straighten, but I felt unmoored without any part of me touching some part of her, so I wrapped my hand around one of her elbows.

"Don't really feel like eating," she said, and neither did I.

My dinner had been a protein shake before I'd left the house with Tucker and Scarlett in tow a few hours ago. Normally, I'd need something, but right now, all I wanted was Genevieve.

So, I got on with it. "You hear back about the audition yet?"

My attention snagged on her throat when she swallowed. "I was offered the job while I was there."

I knew it. I knew she'd get it, but hearing the words was a punch in the gut.

I tugged her to me, closing the last few inches of space between us. "I'm so proud of you."

She bit into her bottom lip, her gaze tripping over my mouth and my jaw to my chest, where she pressed her hands against my pecs.

"You were amazing onstage," I told her as a slight breeze caught pieces of her hair, sending a few against her cheek. I tucked them behind her ear. "I couldn't take my eyes off you."

Still, she was quiet, her fingertips dug into my dress shirt.

"I knew you'd get the job, and I'm so goddamn proud of you, Gen." When her breath hitched, I snuck my hand around her neck, nudging her head back. "I was watching Scarlett up there, doing her thing, thinking I'd never seen her so full of life, and it's because of you." I spoke my next words against her mouth. "*You* gave her that, and I don't know how I can thank you."

And I couldn't ever thank her, so I kissed her instead.

I kissed her because it was my favorite thing to do, tasting those red lips of hers.

I kissed her because I'd learned exactly how she liked it these last six weeks.

I kissed her for all the ones I'd miss when she left, and we only pulled away once we were both breathless, lips swollen, eyes dazed.

"You have lipstick on you," she murmured, and I rubbed my thumb over my mouth, but she shook her head. "On your shirt."

"Oh." I plucked at it. "Yeah. I guess I'll have to—"

"Come on inside. I'll get it out."

TWENTY-FIVE
GENEVIEVE

Dylan followed me inside my apartment, and I dropped my bag and keys on the kitchen table, much like the first night we'd been together. And like that night, I didn't expect to see him again.

After tomorrow, this fling was officially over.

As we'd always meant it to be.

No matter how apprehensive I was about dancing on a cruise ship, it felt good to be auditioning again, to be *really* dancing and not just teaching the difference between a shuffle and a flap. The contract had arrived via email this morning while I'd waited for my flight home.

All I had to do was sign on the dotted line and return it for a six-month stint on the *Explorer's Oasis*. Pay wasn't great, but it did come with insurance and free room and board on the ship.

Plus, it felt damn good to be chosen. To know I still had it.

Proof I wasn't past my prime, like the fears in the back of my mind had almost convinced me.

But I still hadn't sent the contract back in. Not that I'd had all that much time. I was too busy with dress rehearsal and now getting lipstick out of a dress shirt.

"If it sets too long, it'll stain," I said and waved him into my bathroom. He leaned against the sink as I dug through my cabinet for cotton balls and rubbing alcohol. When I found them, I spun around, realizing it would be better for him to take his shirt off, but at this point, I didn't know if my body, brain, or heart could handle it.

She was still holding out hope. For what, I didn't know. Not even ten minutes ago, Dylan had told me how proud he was of me for getting the job and said how he'd never be able to thank me for teaching his daughter. If that wasn't a send-off, I didn't know what was.

"Can you…?" I tipped my chin, gesturing for him to remove his shirt, and he tugged it out from his black dress pants like some kind of slo-mo porno, hinting at golden skin before starting in on the buttons, undoing one at a time, revealing the ladder of muscles along his abdomen.

I smacked the bottle of alcohol down on the sink next to him. "Aren't you supposed to have a dad bod?"

He had the audacity to smirk as he slid the shirt off his shoulders and down his arms. "I am a dad, and I have a bod." He handed over his shirt. "Would you prefer me to put on another shirt? Maybe find one of your little tops. Think you might be into that?"

"I'd prefer you to sit right there." I pointed to the closed toilet lid. "And let me get to work."

He sank down, watching as I poured the alcohol onto the cotton and dabbed at the smear of hot pink. "This from Scarlett?"

"There's certainly no other woman in my life."

The reply was in his usual dry humor, but I couldn't find it in me to laugh. I couldn't pretend to ignore that in a perfect world, I'd be a woman in his life.

He curled his hand around my thigh the same way he'd done so many times since the night we'd met and I'd brought him back here. When he'd treated my body as if he'd known it intimately already, as if he'd owned it.

Of course, it hadn't been true then. But it was now.

He knew me inside and out. He owned me inside and out.

It took a minute or so of carefully wiping at the lipstick to remove it. "When you get home, you'll need to wash this in cool water."

He stood and hauled me up into his arms, and I automatically dropped his shirt to skim my hands around his bare shoulders, warm and smooth under my fingers.

"One last time." His words were barely audible, caught between our mouths. "I need one last time."

I answered by crossing my ankles at his waist, and he pressed me against the wall. When I dropped my head back, I winced at the fluorescent lights of my bathroom, though they weren't as harsh as our ragged breaths.

It was too real, too intense, the way my blood thundered in my ears and the pressure of his fingers against my ribs, my hips, my thighs. Anywhere he could touch, his hands wandered like he was learning my topography for later. But there was no later.

This was it.

His teeth scraped my jaw, and I snuck my hand between us to fiddle with his belt, but I was clumsy and couldn't get it undone.

"Here," he rasped and tapped the side of my leg so I'd unwind from around him. With my feet settled on the floor, he dropped to his knees, pulling my leggings and thong down and off. Then he threw one leg over his shoulder, kissing the needy place between my thighs.

He kept his gaze on me, and I refused to break eye contact with him, wanting to memorize everything about these moments. The same way I supposed he was.

I combed my fingers into his hair. He squeezed my hips and waist. I traced my thumbs along his brow. He coasted his hand up my stomach, spreading his fingers wide. I panted his name, and his eyes blazed.

I wouldn't ever forget the way he looked at me. Like I was his.

That was when I had to close my eyes. To him and to the pleasure rippling through me as he slid his fingers inside me.

I was burning up, my standing leg shaking, and it only took one tiny movement of his fingers and kiss of his lips to send me tumbling into an orgasm. I slumped forward, but he caught me and stood up, dragging his tongue over my throat, his mouth and chin still wet from me.

His teeth teased along the curve of my ear. "You still with me?"

A sob bubbled at the back of my throat, and I clamped my lips shut to keep it from escaping and nodded. I wrapped my arms tight around his neck, crushing my chest to his as he opened his pants, the quiet clink of his belt and crinkle of his zipper sending goose bumps racing over my skin. I ducked my face against the side of his neck, trying to catch my breath, shoving the building emotions back down.

"Kitten," he murmured, one hand on my naked backside, the other around his length, resting against my lower stomach. "I forgot to grab a condom from my car. Do you have any?"

I forced myself to push away from him, realizing I didn't have any. I shook my head, teeth buried in my lower lip.

He blew out a breath, and we both lowered our attention to where he dragged the broad tip of himself between my legs. This was our one last time. I needed it. Needed him.

"I'm on birth control. It's okay."

"Is it?" he croaked.

I hitched my leg over his hip. "Yeah."

"Gen, I—"

Quieting him with a kiss, I forced him to catch me when I hopped up, draping myself around him. I couldn't bear to hear whatever it was he was about to say.

"One last time," I said.

"One last time," he agreed.

And then he drove inside me, wrenching the air from my lungs and the sob from my throat that I'd contained until now. I clung to him, my arms over his shoulders, my legs around his waist, and he held me up, his hands tight on my thighs, my back against the wall, hips meeting with brutal slaps.

It wasn't romantic or soft, but I didn't want it to be. I didn't think I would have survived if he were sweet with me. I needed teeth and bruising grips and hard thrusts.

He grunted over and over, his skin damp beneath my fingers, and right when I thought he'd come, he stopped and lifted my T-shirt as he bent, sucking my nipple into his mouth.

"No, Dylan," I whined, wanting him to finish already. I needed this one last time, and then I needed him to leave. Let me start the grieving process. But he didn't listen, didn't pull away.

He only held my other breast in his hand and licked the tip until I was rolling my hips, silently begging him to move, to give me more.

"I think I'll dream of this." He lifted his head, and his hair was a mess from my hands, his cheeks ruddy, his eyes wild and wide open as if he was intentionally allowing me to see inside him.

"I think I'll dream of your sounds, your gasps," he said, and I could picture all the memories of our times together in his gaze.

"Of your skin and how pink it gets when I suck on it." Then he sucked on a spot below my collarbone as if to prove it. Once he was satisfied, he met my eyes again, and I saw all his contented possession. *That*, I'd never forget.

"And maybe when I can't sleep, I'll think of all my favorite places." He traced my lips with his index finger. "Here." He slipped his hand between us and circled my clit. "Here." Then he pressed his palm between my breasts. "Here."

My stupid heart clanged around under his hand, wanting out.

Wanting him.

And this was exactly what I was afraid of.

I folded my arms tight around him so he couldn't see the well of tears in my eyes as I urged him to move again. "Please..."

He steadied himself with one hand on the wall next to my head and looped his other arm around my waist, holding my hips up and away from the wall as he started plunging in and out of me again. "Okay, kitten. Okay." He latched his mouth onto the side of my neck, and my vision blurred. "You can let go now," he whispered against my throat, and I wasn't sure what hurt more, knowing we'd never do this again, or that he was the one letting me go. "Give it to me."

The first tear rolled down my cheek, and I surrendered to a cry, the agonized sound of my sob masked by the mutual crashing of our orgasms. His movements eventually stuttered then stilled, his breath hot on my neck, and I wiped my face before he might see how destroyed I was.

"You all right?" he asked, his voice sounding as ragged as I felt.

I nodded and blinked, making sure my eyes were clear, cheeks dry before I placed my feet on the floor. He kept his hands on me, waiting until I was steady to step away. "Genevieve."

I cleared my throat and forced a semblance of a smile. "I'm fine."

"You sure?"

"Of course." I brushed by him to snag a washcloth, which I wetted for him, then sat on the toilet, wiping away the evidence of our sex. We both cleaned ourselves up in silence, his back to me as he zippered his pants and buckled his belt. He passed me my underwear and leggings, and I slipped into them, having a hard time meeting his stare.

But once we were both fully dressed again, we couldn't avoid it.

"Thanks," he started, vaguely motioning to the spot I'd cleaned off his shirt.

"Mm-hmm. No problem."

"I'm sorry about…" This time, he gestured to the wall, and I wasn't sure if he was apologizing for not having a condom or for the hard way he'd taken me or that what we had was finished. Maybe all of it.

I shook my head, making sure I looked him in the eyes when I said, "I'm not."

He held out his hand to me, and I laced my fingers with his as we made our way down the hall.

"What's your favorite season?" I asked, and he sniffed a laugh.

"I don't know." He opened the door, leaning against the jamb, facing me, our linked hands against his chest. "Maybe summer." He squinted for a moment then asked, "What's your favorite color?"

I pressed up onto my toes and gave him one last kiss on his mouth. "Green." I cupped his jaw, my thumb stroking under his eye. "Obviously."

An echo of our first night together.

He smiled.

I smiled.

And I tried not to crack again.

"See you, Genevieve."

"See you, Dylan."

He squeezed my fingers, lifted my palm to his mouth for a kiss, then dropped my hand. He turned and crossed to the steps, but this time, he didn't double back or pause. He kept on going, walking out of my apartment and out of my life.

TWENTY-SIX
GENEVIEVE

The recital was a blur of lights and sounds, missing tap shoes and too much hair spray.

Despite my goodbye with Dylan last night, I still had two shows where I had to watch him, in his black suit and tie, dance with his daughter and smile down at her like she was his whole world. I smiled too, though my gut felt like someone was drilling into me.

I wasn't so much empty as I was filled too much, and the hole was an attempt to let some of the pressure out. But now it felt like I was leaking all the good stuff, and I pressed my hand to my middle, like I could actually stop it.

I'd been too busy during the first show to speak to Dylan backstage, but as I was trudging across the lobby to the bathroom, our gazes met over the heads of strangers, and I swore the hole got bigger.

Scarlett's mom, brother, and stepdad were there, and I forced myself to face forward, keeping one foot in front of the other, even as Tucker swung himself up onto Dylan's shoulder and reached his hand out to me, waving hello.

I offered the little boy a quick wave then sped away.

During the two hours between shows, I munched on a granola bar. It might as well have been a bar of sand.

"Are you so excited?" Shauna asked me. Her bright-red hair was pulled back in a high ponytail, and it bounced when she spoke, never actually giving me a chance to answer her question. Shauna was a college student, twenty-one with stars in her eyes. "I'd love to get a job on a cruise and go exploring the world. You're living the dream! Twice! First a Rockette and now dancing on a ship. Amazing!"

I nodded and washed down the sand bar with a few swigs of water. "Yeah, it's pretty amazing."

Even though I still wasn't sure about the whole life-at-sea aspect, it was exciting to know I'd be visiting so many places. It would be like being on vacation for a few months.

At least, that was what I hoped for. Forget about everything I was leaving behind.

"Your life…" Shauna sighed. "You're so lucky."

"Not luck," Miss Amy butted in. "That's hard work."

"Right. Of course!" Shauna laughed, though slightly chastened. "It's just that you're lucky you're still doing it. You know?"

So few dancers were able to dance professionally. Even fewer did it for as long as I had. Shauna's eyes cut to Leilani, who'd been quiet this whole time, playing on her cell phone. Leilani had attended a conservatory for college, where the competition had gotten to her, and she'd ended up being hospitalized for an eating disorder after passing out at a rehearsal. She was now twenty-three years old and teaching ballet classes for Miss Amy while attending community college for a business degree.

I was lucky.

I was still in relatively good health and about to start a job that would allow me to travel the globe while doing what I loved. I was so incredibly lucky.

It might not have been my first choice or the perfect timing, but my worst day dancing was still better than most of my days not dancing.

It was the dream. Not just mine, but so many people's. I couldn't thumb my nose up at it because I'd let my heart run away with wild ideas about a man with a backward baseball cap and two kids slung over his shoulders.

No. I had to remember I was lucky. So, so lucky.

"You feeling okay?" Miss Amy asked, tapping my knee.

"Yeah. I'm a bit cold, though. I might step outside for a few minutes and warm up."

I could tell Miss Amy didn't believe a word out of my mouth. "They do always keep it so cold in here, huh? I'll go ask Johnny to turn the air up a tad."

We walked in step, out of the auditorium and into the lobby, where the cafeteria directly across from us was decorated with end-of-school posters. I guessed the kids only had a few days left. We sat on one of the benches.

"Don't worry about what Shauna said."

"I'm not," I said, shoving my hands under my thighs to keep from giving myself away by touching my earrings.

"Shauna's a good dancer. You're a *great* dancer. She probably could be too, if she actually put in the work."

"And yet you hired her."

Miss Amy waved her hand in the direction of the auditorium. "Like I said, she's a good dancer, but she's got no drive. Not like you." When I stayed quiet, she shifted closer to me, leaning her shoulder against mine. "But I hope you know it's okay to choose something else."

"You mean choosing to stay here and take over for you?"

She nodded. "There's nothing wrong with wanting that either."

"But I don't."

She eyed me.

"I don't," I said defensively. "I feel like I'm not done. I still have more in me to leave on the stage. Besides, I couldn't stay here."

"Why not?"

I hadn't told her about Dylan. I didn't want her to think I wasn't taking my job at her studio seriously or that I was being at all inappropriate by having a relationship with a parent.

"Is it because of Dylan Matthews?"

I whipped my head around to her. "You… You know?"

She huffed a laugh. "Honey, everybody knows."

"Oh my god!" I dropped my head into my hands, feeling nauseated.

Miss Amy only laughed some more and smoothed her hand up and down my back. "Anyone with even half-good eyesight could see how it was between you two. Like sparklers on the Fourth of July."

I sat up. "Everyone knows?"

She shrugged. "The other girls do," she said, meaning Shauna and Leilani. "And some of the parents. You two are good gossip."

"And you don't care?"

"Of course not. I want you to be happy, and if he makes you happy, then good."

"Well, what we were…we're not anymore."

"Why not?"

I tugged at my hair, feeling like we were talking in circles. "Because I'm leaving."

"But what if you don't have to?"

"I have to. I signed the contract. I have my flight booked, my housing arranged."

She wrapped her arm around my shoulders, towing me into her like a mother, humming in my ear like she was helping me solve a problem. But there was no problem to solve. There was no *if*. Only when.

And when was in a couple of days.

"Did you ever tell him how you feel?"

I backed away from her. "There's nothing to tell him."

"You love him, don't you?" she asked like she was asking *you know two plus two equals four, don't you?*

I didn't know, but I guessed that made sense.

With this hole I'd been walking around with all day.

"No." I shook my head, sniffling. "I never told him."

"Well, I think you owe yourself at least that much before you leave, hm?" Then she stood and kissed the top of my head. "Why don't you go for a little walk? I really do want to see what I can do about the air conditioning in there."

I stood, and she squeezed my hand before I turned toward the main doors. Balloons and streamers in the studio's colors decorated the front, and a few older girls were giggling about a video on one of their cell phones as they split a pizza between them.

"Hey, Miss Gen! Want a piece?" one of them offered, and I shook my head.

"You guys eat up. You need your energy. And Becca, I know you aren't eating in your tights. I *know* you aren't."

Becca froze, her hand in midair with a slice of pepperoni, then bent her legs underneath her, hiding them.

They all giggled harder, and a genuine smile spread across my face for the first time today.

I made three laps around the school as more of the dancers arrived for the second performance, parents and kids waving at me, and I could see myself doing this, staying here and taking over. It wouldn't be so bad. In fact, I think I would love it—but not without Dylan.

I would be heartbroken to live here and teach at the studio without being with him. I couldn't look at his daughter and know what I'd had, what I'd lost. It would be way too hard to do that. And no amount of dancing would let me escape it.

Though, Miss Amy was right. I owed myself that much, at least. To find out if it was a choice. If staying here with Dylan had ever been a real option.

The second show, much like the first, was over before I knew it, and suddenly the seniors were crying in my arms, and I was blinking away tears in my own eyes. Flowers were thrust into my arms, and by the time I made my way out from backstage, the auditorium and lobby were mostly clear. I searched for Dylan, and when I didn't find him, I held my cell phone in my palm. What I planned on saying over a phone call—I didn't know—but I dialed his number anyway, and when he didn't answer, I tucked my phone away. Like I tucked away my relief at not having to face him, while still disappointed we'd never talk again.

The studio was responsible for cleaning up the auditorium and spaces we used as dressing rooms, so I got to work picking up. It was easy not to think about Dylan during the shows, but now that I had time and quiet, it was impossible not to.

His eyes and his sense of humor and the way he looked at me like I was the only thing in the world. I hadn't thought I could fall in love with someone in six weeks, but I knew better now. I learned you could fall for someone in as much time as it took for them to learn how to do a jazz square.

"Go," I told Miss Amy, collecting the signs and balloons from her arms. "I'll take care of this."

"Are you sure?"

I tipped my chin to where her husband was waiting for her by the front doors. He was the one who worked the tech booth for all the recitals. Their two sons were about my age, and while they didn't dance, they'd always been around the studio at recital time, helping out when needed. It was a family affair. That was one of things I loved about it.

"Yeah. Go ahead. I know Bill's taking you out for something to eat," I said.

"Tradition." She grinned and curved her soft hand around my jaw. "You can drop everything at the studio. I'll take care of it next week." When I nodded, she gave me a hug. "Thank you for everything you did for me this year. I love you so much."

"Love you too."

With a kiss to my cheek, she met her husband at the doors. I watched as he swept her up in a bear hug, saying something that had her cackling in delight as they made their way outside. I performed one more sweep of the auditorium for anything left, then thanked Johnny for his help and took one last look at the stage, said a silent goodbye, and hopped in my car.

I dropped everything off at the studio and slipped off my shoes to feel the scuffed floors under my toes. I smiled at my reflection in the mirror and hit the classic Rockette pose, arms strong at my sides, beveled foot. Then, with the music in my head, I counted off and completed a few waist-high kicks before preparing for a pencil turn and struck another pose. This time, when I popped my foot out, someone clapped, and I gasped.

"What are you doing here?"

Dylan stepped into the studio. "I took Scarlett out for ice cream and was on my way home from dropping her off at Paige's. I saw the lights on and..." He shrugged and closed the distance between us in only three strides. He was so tall, and here barefoot, I felt so small. "I saw you called me."

I nodded, all cottonmouthed.

Like last night, he had lost his suit coat and tie but still wore the dress pants and shirt, sleeves rolled up to his elbows. He tugged a folded piece of construction paper from his pocket. "Scarlett made you a card. She was upset when she couldn't find you afterward."

"It was really hectic," I said, accepting the light-pink card. She'd drawn a person with long brown hair in a black-and-purple dress, which I assumed was her dance costume. There was another figure next to her, taller with short brown hair in black pants and a tank top and red lips. It was me. I unfolded it from the small square to the full rectangular paper. The inside was covered in stickers and hearts drawn in markers, along with a few sentences, written in all capital letters, without any punctuation or spaces. It read, THANKY-

OUFORTEACHINGMEHOWTODANCEY-
OUARETHEBESTILOVEYOU!!!!

I didn't realize I was crying until a tear darkened the paper.

"Tell her…" I sniffled and attempted to clear my eyes. "I love it, and I'm going to keep it forever."

Dylan caught my chin between his thumb and forefinger, tipping it up to him. He wiped at my cheeks. "When you called me earlier, what did you want to say?"

I tried to move my head, but he wouldn't let me. He forced me to hold his gaze, forced me to ask the question and get the answer I deserved to know.

At the very least.

"When I met you, I didn't think…" My voice cracked, and he wiped his thumb under my eye. I swallowed thickly, clearing my throat. "I didn't expect you, is what I'm trying to say."

"Ah, Genevieve," he grated, "no amount of time could have prepared me for you."

Like with my tears, I hadn't realized I'd clutched his shirt in my fists until his hands curled around mine, loosening my grip to hold on to them.

"I wanted to know if… What would you say if I weren't leaving?"

"What do you mean?"

"If I weren't leaving, if I were staying here instead, what would you say?"

His brows furrowed, thumbs paused in their passes over my knuckles. "Are you staying?"

I licked my dry lips, lifting a single shoulder.

"Genevieve." This time, my name wasn't a promise. It was a dismissal.

I panicked and blurted out what I knew to be true. "I love you, Dylan."

"No." He shook his head, dropped my hands, rubbed his palm over his mouth. "Don't tell me that."

There was no hope now. I knew that. "Why not?"

"Because." He squeezed his eyes shut tight and tunneled his hands through his hair, and after I swiped the backs of my hands over my eyes, he met my gaze. It was as tortured as I felt. "I don't… I can't love you."

Don't. Can't. There was a distinction. Though, I couldn't find it at the moment. Dylan didn't love me.

I hiccupped through a sob, and when he reached for me again, I backed away from him. "Please don't. I don't think I could handle it."

"I'm sorry," he said, holding his palms up in apology. "I'm so sorry. But it's for the best. I don't want to hurt you."

I heard the words, yet I couldn't understand them.

"You need to go out into the world. You need to dance. That's what you were meant to do, and I would never ever take that away from you. Do you understand?"

I didn't, but I nodded anyway, a headache forming behind my eyes, my jaw sore from so much crying.

"I can't be the guy who holds you back. If you stayed, I'd only fuck it up."

I was having trouble breathing, and I twisted away from him, stretching my arms up, pushing my rib cage to expand, my lungs to work.

"I haven't been able to take my eyes off you from the moment I first saw you. You shine so bright, there is no one else in the room for me. I don't want to be responsible for dimming your light."

Even though I couldn't see him to know for sure, I felt him right behind me, his heat and smell enveloping me. "Don't cry over me. I'm not worth it."

I wiped uselessly at my face and nodded, but he was wrong. He was worth it. He was worth everything.

"I'm sorry," he said once again, and a moment later, his scent and warmth were gone. I listened for the sound of the door closing, and I could barely hear it over my heaving breaths.

As soon as it clicked, I sank to the floor. I didn't know how long I was there, but at some point, my brother stalked inside.

"Wh-what are you do-doing here?"

"Dylan called me. Told me to come get you."

That sent me into another tailspin.

"I'm going to kill that motherfucker," Nate grumbled, and a hysterical giggle bubbled up out of my crying. "*What*?" He was so offended. "I am."

"Okay, big brother."

"You're such an asshole." He used the bottom of his T-shirt to dry my face and hauled me up to my feet. "You're lucky I love you."

I was.

It was a good reminder. I was so lucky.

TWENTY-SEVEN
DYLAN

I sent out a group text message to Jude and Liam. I had an emergency and needed a goddamn drink. I'd spent Sunday in a stupor, my sleep-deprived brain wondering if I'd made the right decision.

I knew I'd hurt Genevieve. Each one of her tears was a slap to my face, but even if she hadn't been crying, I'd felt her pain as strongly as my own. Which was exactly why she needed to leave.

Besides the job waiting for her, she was meant for bigger and better things than me, a failed baseball player and divorced single dad.

I screwed stuff up. That was what I did. I was trying to be better for my kids, but I knew I wouldn't be good for Genevieve. That was why I'd said we had to be short-term. Why we had to keep our feelings out of it.

But now that I had the distance of two whole days, I was having trouble remembering exactly why I'd thought it was a good idea.

I pulled up to Walt's and tucked my keys into my pocket, fixing my hat on my head as I trudged through the door to the bar. Jude was there already, and seeing him made it all clear. *He was the reason I'd let Genevieve go.*

If I'd thought my breakup with Paige was bad, I couldn't imagine what it would be like if Genevieve and I ever got together and then split up. It would shatter me completely.

Just looking at Jude told me so. He still grieved Mira. He'd told me once that he simply hadn't felt like taking much interest in what he looked like anymore since Mira had passed. That was why he'd put on weight, wore his hair up in a bun most days, and didn't bother with shaving. He didn't care.

And Jesus, I didn't want that to be me.

I had to cut my losses now rather than deal with the fallout later. Let her move on. Let me work on my relationship with my kids. That was my priority anyway.

"Hey, man," I said, sliding onto the stool next to his.

He glanced my way then did a double take. "You sick or something?"

I huffed. "Perfectly fine."

He nodded sarcastically, and I ordered a beer from a female bartender, but it wasn't Gen, so she might as well have been a stick figure. I took my first sip as Liam dropped onto a seat on my other side. "You look like hell. You sure you want to be drinking on a Monday?"

Before I could answer, a commotion stirred in the kitchen area. Glasses clanked, and then Nate was charging toward us.

Right at me.

"Motherfucker!" He yanked me away from the bar by the collar of my shirt, and I let it happen, his fist meeting my face.

Liam and Jude jumped back, people stood and gasped, the bartenders all froze.

But when Nate raised his hand again, Liam caught it and pinned his arm behind his back, steering him a few feet away. Nobody would know by looking at the lanky professor, but Liam was a trained boxer, and he kept Nate separated from me.

"What the hell is going on?" Jude shouted between us, and

after a few seconds, the fight drained out of Nate, some of the red fading from his face.

"Ask that asshole," Nate snapped, pushing away from Liam to stomp behind the bar. He waved to the patrons. "Sorry for the interruption, folks. Your next drink is on the house. Tabitha will take care of it."

Tabitha, the bartender, shot a murderous glance at Nate. He only lifted his hands in a gesture like what else was he supposed to do. Then he grabbed a towel, filled it with ice, and handed it to me.

I accepted it and took my seat. Jude's eyes were huge. "I ask again, what the hell is going on?"

"Genevieve," I answered, and Jude and Liam both nodded in understanding.

"I'm gonna need a beer for this," Liam said to Nate, and he filled up two pints, passing one to Liam and downing about half of the other.

Nate set his glass on the bar and stood right in front of me. "You look like shit."

"I feel like shit." I pointed to my cheek. "Thanks for that, by the way."

"You deserved it."

I couldn't argue otherwise, so I pressed the ice to my face and lifted my beer to my mouth.

"I told her not to get involved with you," he went on. Indifferent to the punch already thrown, he kept coming at me. "Told her you'd hurt her."

I would've preferred another punch instead of what he said next.

"You *wrecked* her."

I thumped the ice on the bar and hung my head. "I didn't mean to."

"But you did. Fuck, man, *you* were the one who called to tell me I had to get her last night. You made her cry, and then you fucking left her there."

From either side of me, Liam and Jude both admonished me quietly.

"You made her cry?"

"You left her?"

I sat back in my seat, scrubbing my hands over my face until I hit the sore spot. Then I grunted with impatience and frustration. I hadn't come here to rehash Saturday night. I'd come here to do anything that wasn't think about her. "She didn't want me to touch her. She was crying, and I knew she needed somebody. The last thing I wanted to do was leave her."

"Then why did you?" Nate asked, throwing his arms out to the sides.

"Because…" I shook my head.

"You're a dick," Nate supplied.

"Ungentlemanly," Jude said.

"Wrong," Liam added, and Nate snapped, pointing at him like he was the winner.

I rolled my eyes. "I really don't need this shit from you guys, okay? I never wanted to hurt her. That's why we agreed to—"

Nate sighed and leaned his elbows on the bar. "I don't need the details."

"Short-term."

"Thought you were supposed to be good at that," Liam said, all astutely.

I pressed my fingers against my cheek and jaw, gauging if it would be bruised tomorrow. Most likely. "I was. Not anymore, I guess."

Jude lifted his beer to his mouth. "So, what are you going to do?"

"Nothing."

"What do you mean, nothing?" When I shrugged at Nate, he gestured to the door like she was standing there. I peeked over my shoulder to make sure she wasn't. "I'm taking her to the airport tomorrow morning."

I nodded. "Good."

"Good?" Liam repeated.

Nice guy Jude actually looked disgusted with me. "You're not going to do anything?"

Nate folded his tattooed arms over his chest. "No big, grand gesture?"

"No." I took a sip of my beer and focused on the baseball game on the television across from me. Philadelphia was playing. "This is what she deserves. Better than me."

Nate made an indignant sound and slapped his hand on the towel of ice, swiping it from the bar with as much force as his fist on my jaw. He threw the ice into the sink with a loud clank, earning another eye from the bartender. He tossed the towel on his shoulder and placed his hand on her shoulder, leaning in to whisper something to her. She nodded, and then they both got to work taking care of customers.

I supposed he was done with me for the night.

On my left, Liam tapped his glass of beer against mine. "For what it's worth, I think you're wrong."

"Yeah. Got that. You already said so."

"Wrong about thinking there's nothing you can do. There's always something."

"Well, I don't know what that is," I mumbled.

On my right, Jude patted my back. "But you are right about one thing."

I turned, optimistic.

"You don't deserve her."

I sighed. Not what I wanted to hear.

"But that's the beauty of love. We're all a little bit undeserving of it. Doesn't mean we shouldn't have it."

Well, fuck.

TWENTY-EIGHT
GENEVIEVE

"You don't have to park. Just drop me off at the curb," I told Nate as he drove around the circle of Philadelphia's airport.

"It's fine," he said and turned into the short-term parking lot, rolling his window down for a ticket. He tossed it on the front of his dash and found a spot to park.

"You got everything?" he asked over the roof of his car once we were both out.

"Yeah."

"Wallet?"

"Yep."

"ID?"

"Yes, Nate."

"You checked in already?"

I looped my crossbody bag over me. "You ever see those TikToks with the airport dads?"

"Yeah."

I lifted my hands at his blank stare. "That's you."

He snorted and popped the trunk. "I'm not an airport dad. I'm not any kind of dad."

I took the rolling suitcase from him. "You're an airport dad."

"I'd be a terrible dad." He held my oversized duffel in his hand as he shut the trunk and locked his car, gesturing for me to keep up with him. He was the one who'd insisted I arrive at the airport three hours ahead of time. I should've just taken a rideshare.

I thought he'd be a great father, but I was sure he didn't want to hear that. Especially since his own relationship with our own wasn't great. Probably why Nate didn't recognize he was such a *dad*.

He hummed some snappy tune as he strode across the concourse, and I butted into his foot with my luggage. He swung the duffel at me. Then we both laughed, and he threw his arm around my shoulders. "You talked to your new roommate?"

"Yeah. Her name's Ingrid. She sounded young."

"You'll be the old lady there, eh?"

I nodded. "You think that means they'll put me on the lifeboat first?"

"I don't know, but don't let anybody give you shit about sharing a door. Two people can definitely fit on one. I saw it on some science show."

"Since when do you watch science shows?"

"Tabby got me into them." When I raised my eyebrows pointedly, he shoved me away. "She started dating some guy."

"Interesting how you felt you needed to tell me that."

"It's interesting how you can never mind your own business."

"*Me*? You gossip worse than high school girls."

"I guess that's why I was so popular back then."

I rammed my suitcase into him again, this time much harder, and he hissed out a curse. "Goddamn it, Evie."

"Oops."

"You're such a little shit, you know that?" he groused, rubbing at his ankle once we were on the sidewalk in front of Southwest Airlines. He passed me the duffel bag so I could load it on top of the suitcase. "You sure you want to do this?"

"What? Fly Southwest? Of course not, but the other tickets were so expensive and—"

"Don't be dense. You know what I mean."

"Yes. I'm sure I want to do this."

He scratched at his beard. "Why?"

"There's nothing left for me here."

He motioned to himself, playing at being offended.

"I meant besides you."

"Is there anything left on the stage for you?"

I crossed my arms, focusing on some point in the distance. "It's not about what's left for me. It's about what I'm leaving there."

"So what is this, then? Some farewell tour? You know Elton John was on his farewell tour for years."

"Yeah, maybe I will too."

He pulled me into a begrudging hug while people streamed by all around us.

"I got used to you being around," he said, patting my back. "I liked it."

"Yeah, same."

He let go of me. "You better not make it another ten years before you're home again."

I shook my head, and he stuck his hands in his pockets, stepping away from me. With his tats and beard, I guessed he did look a bit intimidating, but he was a big teddy bear underneath.

"I'll miss you," I said, and he offered me a half smile.

"Miss you too."

With a smile and a wave, I made my way through the doors. As I waited in line to check in, my phone buzzed with a text. It was Nate telling me to let him know when I arrived.

He was *such* a dad.

I responded with the salute emoji and typed in my information at the kiosk for my ticket when someone caught my attention out of the corner of my eye. My breath seized, and I whirled toward the tall figure with the backward hat coming toward me and then immediately deflated.

It wasn't Dylan.

Of course it wasn't. He'd told me to go. That he didn't love me. He couldn't.

So I checked my luggage, waited forever in the security line while they yelled about removing laptops from their carriers and taking everything out of our pockets, only to momentarily lose my mind and think about exiting the line because a man with a fitted gray T-shirt lifted his hand in the air.

I realized with one step toward him that he wasn't Dylan either and I seriously needed to get my eyesight checked.

An hour later, I was boarding the plane when I froze mid-step at a head of dark almost-black hair. Wasn't Dylan. Obviously.

I sank into the tiny seat on the aisle and kicked my bag under the seat in front of me.

"Excuse me."

I whipped my head around at the voice. Not Dylan's.

I stood up to allow him to take the window seat before sitting back down, my brain filled with fog and my heart filled with cement.

I had to get over this ridiculous hope that he was coming for me.

But it wasn't until I landed in Fort Lauderdale a little under three hours later that I knew for sure. There would be no more chances to spot familiar hair or clothes, no more *maybe that's him*.

I collected my luggage and slogged through the swampy weather to my rideshare.

Dylan Matthews and I were well and truly over.

TWENTY-NINE
DYLAN

The kids were outside drawing on the sidewalk with chalk when I parked in front of Paige's place.

"Daddy!" Scarlett ran over to me, her hands covered in pink and purple dust. "Look! I drawed a rainbow!"

I sank to my haunches. "Very nice. What about you, Tuck? What'd you draw?"

He barely spared me a glance as he attacked the sidewalk with the thick squares of chalk in each hand. He banged them over and over, making messy dots of green and white.

"Noooo! Tucker! Ugghhh!" Scarlett stomped her foot. "You're ruining my heart!" She pushed Tucker over, and he immediately started to wail even though he was perfectly fine. Brick shithouse.

"Hey. Hey. No way." I helped Tucker to stand, and he wrapped his arms around me. "Is there ever a reason to push people?" I asked Scarlett, and she shook her head even as she drilled her little brother with evil eyes. "Scar, look at me. Even when you're angry, you can never push people. Do you understand?"

"Yes," she grumbled and reeled away from Tucker and me to run into the house. "Mommy! Tucker ruined my heart!"

I carried my son inside, his tears long since dried. "You're such a faker," I told him, eyes narrowed, but I couldn't keep my tone stern for too long because he clapped his hands on either side of my face, laughing maniacally. "You're being a little shit-stirrer."

"Shit-stirrer!" he repeated happily, and I pointed my finger at him.

"Don't you repeat that."

He curled his chubby little hand around my index finger, pretending to eat it.

"Hey!" I threw him over my shoulder. "Rule number one, no eating Dad."

I stepped into the house, and Neil tipped his chin to me as he rounded the corner to sit on the couch. I nodded back.

Paige followed with a white Stanley cup. "Hey."

"Mommy!" Scarlett screamed from upstairs. "I can't find Macy!"

"Did you look for her?" Paige called back. "With your eyes? Or did you not even look and call for me?"

Scarlett whined, and I motioned in the direction of the stairs. "What's that about today?"

"She's exhausted. Couldn't sleep last night, and today..." Paige waved vaguely. It had been Scarlett's last day of school and now was officially summer vacation. Not much different, except without the kids in kindergarten and preschool, we'd have to shuffle them back and forth between summer camps and Paige's parents.

"Mommy! I looked with my eyes, and I really can't find Macy!"

When Paige started to stand, Neil patted her leg. "I'll get her."

Since it seemed like I'd have a few minutes, I sat down on one of the chairs in the living room, and Tucker climbed into my lap. He took off my hat and set it on his head.

"Who's Macy anyway?" I asked Paige.

"A doll. It was a present from her birthday. One of those ones with really big eyes."

"Oh. Okay." I shrugged.

"You looked tired," she noted and sipped from her straw.

I didn't respond. It had been just last night all my friends were telling me I looked like shit. I didn't need it from her too.

"Oh my god." She hopped up from the sofa and crossed the room to me, roughly grabbing my chin to turn my face. "What'd you do? Get into a fight?"

"No." I pulled away from her.

"You have a black eye."

"I don't have a black eye."

She not so gently pressed her fingers against the bruise that had bloomed slightly purple on my upper cheek and corner of my eye. "Ah, shit, Paige."

I wrenched away from her and covered the side of my face with my hand while Tucker repeated, "Ah, shit, Paige."

She pointed a finger at him. "Don't you repeat that."

He rolled off my lap to the floor then raised his arms up to her.

"Come here, you big lug," she said and heaved him up into her arms before she sat back down across from me. "So, what happened? If you're in trouble—"

"Nate punched me."

"Nate?"

I grabbed my hat from the floor, where Tucker had left it. "He owns Walt's."

"Oh, that bar you go to with your friends?"

I nodded.

"Why'd he punch you?"

"He's Genevieve's brother."

She shook her head at me, and I held up my hand.

"Please don't start."

"I didn't even say anything."

"You were about to."

She pursed her lips, staring at me, a little curious, a little annoyed. When I couldn't stand it anymore, I huffed and gestured for her to have it out.

"I thought you said you and Genevieve weren't a big deal."

I put my hat on then immediately took it off and plowed my fingers through my hair. "It's complicated."

"Because it *is* a big deal."

I couldn't meet her gaze. "I should've told you she was coming to Scarlett's party. I'm sorry I didn't."

"You should've told me because she's important to you. She's important to Scarlett."

I placed my hat on my head and crossed my arms and nodded.

Paige moved Tucker to one of her knees so she could hold my gaze, her voice and eyes kinder than they had been in a long time when aimed in my direction. "What happened?"

"She had never planned to be here more than a year. By the time we met, she only had a few weeks left. She's on her way to Florida. Or, I guess she's there by now." It was after five o'clock, and Nate had said he was taking her to the airport this morning.

Paige rolled her hand, evidently waiting for more. But there wasn't any more.

"Are you still together?" she asked when I didn't say anything.

I narrowed my brows. "She's in Florida. She's going to be working on a cruise for six months."

"Okay." And there was her condescending headshake. "Are you still together?"

I ground my molars. "How the fu— How would we still be together?"

"I don't know. I'm just asking. Is she planning on coming back?"

"I have no idea."

Paige rolled her eyes. "Did you ask her?"

"No," I said with more disdain than Scarlett whenever we asked her to try a vegetable.

"Why not?"

"Because."

"Because…"

"I don't know, Paige. Why are you making this an inquisition?"

She set Tucker on the ground. "Because I could tell you loved her."

"I don't—"

"Don't tell me you don't love her. I was married to you."

I wiped my palm over my mouth, worried my ex-wife was about to turn me inside out.

And I was right to worry, because she said, "I know what you look like when you love someone."

Her words hit me like another punch to the face.

"I know what it looks like when you want to do something and when you don't," she went on, frowning. "And as much as you think I'm still mad about our marriage, I'm not. I'm sorry if sometimes I let my emotions get the best of me, but you know as well as I do that this—" she motioned between us "—is hard. Being divorced and raising kids together and trying to make it all like we're one big happy family is hard."

I leaned forward, my elbows on my knees, fingers laced together. "Yeah."

"I want you to be happy, Dylan. When you're happy, our kids are happy, and if our kids are happy, I'm happy. And I know she made you happy. I saw it. I mean…" She laughed. "Who did you think you were fooling by going early to dance class every week?"

"No one, apparently."

"No one," she agreed. "So, what's the problem?" When I tipped my head to the side, frustrated that I had to keep stating the obvious, she kept going. "Besides that she's got a job on a cruise ship."

I rubbed at my eyes, not really ecstatic about having this conversation with Paige, but then again, if anyone knew what was going on in my head, it was her. "I'm scared."

She waited for more.

"I couldn't do it again."

I didn't have to explain what *it* was. She knew, and she nodded. "Well..." She let out a breath, absently combing her fingers through Tucker's hair as he crashed toy cars together. "Without rehashing what happened between us, I... Well, I think we're both in positions to do better the second time around. We've both grown a lot." She leaned forward too, her forehead scrunching. "We hurt each other. There's no way around that, but the only thing we can do is learn from our mistakes and do better the next time. I wish things had gone differently between us, but what happened happened." She shrugged. "And I don't want you to give up so easily. You always used to take the easy way out, and if you want to be with Genevieve, then you'll have to do hard things."

My first reaction was anger. How dare she tell me what to do in my relationships?

But the more she stared at me—not out of condescension or bitterness, but friendship and love—the more I thought about what she was trying to tell me. We couldn't go backward and change what had happened between us. She couldn't take back her relationship with Neil. I couldn't rewind to be a more supportive partner, but we could both learn from our mistakes and react differently now.

"I don't tell you enough," I said, standing up to offer her my hand, "but you're a really good mom."

She accepted my hand and looped her arms around me. "You're a really good dad."

"I'm trying."

"I know you are. You're doing a great job." She patted my shoulders as she stepped away from me, breaking our first hug in...years. "And I think you'd be an even better dad if you had someone with you. Having someone who supports us and loves us only makes us stronger, right?"

I tugged on the bill of my cap. "Yeah."

She looked over my shoulder at the sound of Scarlett and Neil clomping back down the steps even as she said, "For what it's worth, I really like Genevieve. I think she's really good for you."

"She is."

"I'm ready, Daddy!"

"So," Paige started, meeting my gaze over Scarlett running at me, "why don't you figure out how to make it work? Go talk to her."

I picked up Scarlett. "In Florida?"

"Florida!" Tucker screeched.

"Neil, you've got some frequent flyer miles, don't you?" Paige asked then kissed both kids on the head.

"Yeah, why?"

"Can Dylan use them to go see his girlfriend?"

Neil tipped his chin to me. "Sure."

I nodded back. "Thanks."

Paige clapped. "All right, babies! Have so much fun at Daddy's house. See you on Thursday!"

I'd never thought my ex-wife would help solve my relationship problems, but there was a first time for everything.

THIRTY
GENEVIEVE

'd been in Florida for two weeks and had yet to get used to the heat. I'd already worked up a sweat with morning rehearsal. but the walk to and from the café we ate lunch at made me look like I'd spent a few hours in a sauna. I wicked the sweat away from my collarbone.

"You get used to it," Alex told me with not one drop of perspiration on their forehead.

"Aren't you from Orlando?"

They grinned impishly. They didn't get used to it.

"You were born into it."

They bumped their hip with mine and laughed. I gave in to a smile too. They were about my age and the dance captain. Although I had a lot of professional experience, they had worked on multiple cruises and had given me the lowdown on what to expect.

"Come on. Let's catch up to the kids," they said, grabbing my hand to jog across the street toward the studio.

"The kids" were the other six dancers, named as such because they were all in their early twenties, including my roommate, Ingrid. During these couple weeks of rehearsal, we were offered short-term housing until we boarded the ship, where we'd have our own rooms, thank god. Ingrid was sweet but liked to listen to her spicy romance books at full volume, and I could only take so much. I didn't want to listen to stories about other people getting railed by men, when I was still getting over mine.

But besides that, I liked her. All eight of us got along well, but Alex and I mainly enjoyed long dinners together, bonding over our careers and love of chocolate hummus. Most people thought it was an abomination, but it was actually a really great option for a healthy dessert.

Ahead of us, one of the kids, Mateo, leaped up the steps to the studio, striking a silly variation of a ballet pose with his leg at passé, and Tatum waved her hand.

"Wait, wait, wait, lemme get a picture." She held up her phone, snapping a few photos with her and Mateo pretending they were in a pas de deux. "I'm posting these," she said, a common refrain we'd heard from her over the last two weeks. She was an influencer, popular for her "day in the life of a dancer" TikToks and Instagram posts.

I was on social media, obviously, but since I'd moved back to Pennsylvania, I hadn't posted much. But now that I was in this ragtag crew, I was often tagged in their photos and reels, which convinced me to post more. Pictures of sunsets, my bare feet after rehearsal, a selfie in my newest lounge pants. Real stop-them-in-their-tracks stuff.

"Let's get a group one." Tatum passed her phone off to Jack, who had the longest arms and therefore was relegated to taking the group selfie photos.

Alex rolled their eyes, steadfastly not on social media, convinced that was how serial killers could find a person. But I pulled them in next to me. This was all part of the experience, right?

Except as I lifted my head to look at the phone in Jack's hand, a person stepping out of a car caught my eye.

"Gen, you're not smiling."

Although I had given up all faith of Dylan and me being *Dylan and me*, it had still taken me a good three days after being here for me to stop noticing things that reminded me of him, like a country song or a baseball game on TV or men in gray T-shirts and backward hats.

Like the one coming toward me now, with one hand on the strap of a backpack and the other on his cell phone, eyes squinting in my direction, jaw perfectly unshaven.

"Oh Jesus."

Alex turned to me. "What?"

I stumbled away from the group like a drunk toddler, and Alex caught my elbow. "What's wrong?"

I couldn't answer.

Could only watch Dylan Matthews stride toward me in the blazing Florida sun.

I was vaguely aware of the others taking in the staredown happening between us, murmurs rippling, but I ignored them as he stood in front of me, letting his backpack hit the ground.

"Dylan?" It wasn't so much a question as it was a hope.

"Hi, gorgeous."

"What... How...?"

He grabbed hold of my face and crushed his lips to mine, and behind me, the murmurs became flat-out questions and wolf whistles.

My knees buckled beneath me, and he pulled me against his chest, hugging me so tightly I almost couldn't breathe.

The cement that had dried in my chest crumbled, and my heart once again grew wings.

"You're here," I breathed, barely a whisper.

"I'm here." He kissed my head, my ear, my neck.

"I kept thinking that you would stop me at the airport like a movie or something. I kept seeing you, but it was never you."

He cupped the back of my head in his big hands, his eyes shifting between my own. "I'm sorry I'm late."

My answering laugh was watery. "How did you find me?"

"With help from your brother and Paige."

"Paige?"

He nodded. "She was my social media recon. Somebody kept tagging you in all your rehearsals."

"See, Tatum!" Alex scoffed. "*This* is exactly why you shouldn't be posting your life online. Serial killers!"

It was Alton who said, "Unless he's planning on murdering her by shoving his tongue down her throat, I don't think he's a serial killer."

"Paige helped you?" I asked, trying to comprehend what was happening.

Dylan caressed his thumbs over my cheeks and bent to kiss my lips once. "She was the one who said I had to come talk to you. Tell you I love you."

"You love me?"

He wiped under my eyes. "Don't cry."

"Tatum," someone grumbled, "this is a private moment between them. Put your phone down."

"What if they want it remembered later? What if he's about to propose?"

Dylan finally lifted his gaze to the group behind me, glowering.

I stifled my drunken laugh against his shoulder and turned around once I pulled myself together. Dylan linked his fingers with mine so I couldn't go far. "Everyone, this is Dylan. Dylan, this is everyone."

"Oh, hello," Mateo said with a flirtatious smile and wave.

"How do we know you're not a serial killer?" Alex asked, crossing their arms.

Dylan exhaled an annoyed puff of air from his nose then looked to me, then Alex, and back to me. "We have to do this with an audience?"

"Handsome and grumpy. Good combination," Ingrid stage-whispered to me, and Dylan rolled his eyes.

"We are performers," Jack said, and I shrugged at Dylan.

"What happened to your exhibitionist streak?"

"Kitten," he murmured in warning as the group all broke up in laughter.

"All right, let's get back inside," Alex said, ushering them all away. "Leave these two lovebirds. Gen," they called over their shoulder. "I'll stall, but the best I can do is ten minutes."

I held up my hand in thanks then dragged Dylan around to the back of the building, under the shade of the roof.

He brushed my hair back from my face, his features serious as he started, "I'm—"

I did the only sensible thing and threw myself at him, cutting off his words with a kiss. I slipped my tongue between his lips, and he tasted exactly like I remembered. Not that I could forget.

I burrowed my fingers into his hair, knocking his hat off in the process, and he squeezed my thighs, wrapping them around his waist. He spun us around, my back scratching against the stucco wall, but I didn't care.

"I missed you," I said against his jaw.

"I know. I'm sorry." His fingertips dug into my ass. "I'm so fucking sorry. I love you."

"I love you too."

He smiled against my mouth, pecking tiny kisses on each corner. "What time are you done with your rehearsal?"

"Six."

"I'll pick you up. I got a hotel room for the night." He nipped my bare shoulder. "I have a lot more I need to tell you."

"I have to be back here at nine tomorrow morning."

"That's fine. I'll drop you off on my way back to the airport."

"You came here for less than twenty-four hours?"

He dipped his forehead to mine. "I realized there isn't much I wouldn't do for you. Coming down here for a day was the least of it."

He pressed one more kiss to my mouth then set me on my feet. "Let's get you back inside before they all start thinking I'm dismembering you."

I held his hand between both of mine, tucking my head against his shoulders, smelling his T-shirt as we walked back to the entrance of the building, where he escorted me inside. The crew was warming up, the director and singers chatting up by the mirrors, but as one, they all turned their attention to us.

"Told you," Ingrid said, smiling. "Not a serial killer."

"Nope." I tossed Dylan a smile over my shoulder. "Just a single dad."

He threw me a playful glare that melted into his panther stare, and god, I'd missed that the last two weeks. With a breath that raised his shoulders, he released my hand and stepped away from me, heading out to the exit.

"Okay. You need to tell us everything. Did—"

"Nope. You're back on my time now," Cheryl, the director, said, pointing to the clock on the wall, and Ingrid spun away, making a face.

"Later," I promised quietly, and we got back to work.

Rehearsal was agonizing. Not because it was difficult, but because I knew Dylan was waiting for me on the other side, and Ingrid was relentless in her attempts to wrestle any information out of me whenever we had a minute to spare. Cheryl ran a tight ship, so it wasn't until we were gathering our stuff at the end of the night that Ingrid asked, "I guess you're not coming out to eat with us?"

"No."

"Okay." She shook her hands like a little kid, trying to speed me up. "Quick, give me the TL;DR version."

"Dylan and I had a one-night stand, and he turned out to be the father of one of my dance students."

"No way! Your life is a legit romance trope. Grumpy and hot single dad?" She folded her hands, eyes to the sky. "Lord, I've seen what you do for other people. When will it be my turn?"

I stepped outside into the sunshine. Dylan was leaning against a rental car, waiting for me. "Gotta go. I'll see you tomorrow."

"Have fun with your daddy!"

I sputtered a laugh. Ingrid and Josie would get along great.

Dylan met me with a kiss and squeeze to my hip before opening the rental car door for me. Once we were both settled in our seats, he linked his fingers with mine, driving with only one hand on the steering wheel. "I picked up takeout for dinner. Chicken tacos with some chips and salsa."

"It's almost like you know me or something."

He held the back of my hand against his mouth, not so much kissing it as relishing it. Like he finally could.

"Why didn't you tell me you were coming?"

He dropped our hands to his lap. "Partly because I wanted to surprise you, and partly because I was afraid you'd tell me not to come."

"And Paige really was the one to convince you?"

He nodded and filled me in on the conversation he'd had with her that had made him realize he had to stop being too scared to fail again. "I don't want to hurt you," he told me at a red light. "And I don't want to get hurt, but I want you in my life. I can't promise I won't ever screw up, but I promise to work really hard at keeping us together."

This time, I kissed the back of his hand. "I promise I'll do everything to make sure we don't fail."

"Nah. You're perfect." When I slanted my gaze to him, he raised his brow. "You are."

"Let's see if you think that a few months from now."

"I'll think you're perfect a lifetime from now. You can't do anything to change my mind."

"You want to keep me for a lifetime?"

"Only if you'll have me," he said, turning into the parking lot of a DoubleTree hotel.

After he shut off the ignition, I leaned over the console to kiss him. "I want you for a lifetime too."

"Good." He grinned.

I grinned.

Up in the hotel room, we ate the takeout on the floor, leaning against the bed frame, playing twenty questions. He'd already asked me if I'd ever shoplifted, to which I'd answered, "Yes. By accident. I forgot to pay for the carton of iced teas on the bottom of my cart."

Then I asked him which friend he'd bring to a deserted island, thinking of Liam, Jude, or Nate, but I should've known he'd say, "You." Then he asked, "What are you most excited about for this cruise?"

"Mm, I feel like performing again is too easy of an answer, so maybe, going zip-lining. Alex said we could go on different excursions, and they had already talked me into going with them. What are you gonna do while I'm gone?"

He shoved a tortilla chip into his mouth. "Masturbate a lot." When I choked on a laugh and smacked his shoulder, he shrugged. "What? It's true. What're your plans when your contract is up?"

I dropped my smile, seeing as how our conversation had come back around to the serious stuff. "I'm not sure. I need to talk to Miss Amy."

"You don't want to keep going?"

I toyed with my earring. "This could be my farewell tour."

"Yeah, but Elton John was on a farewell tour for, like, years."

"That's exactly what my brother said!"

He grimaced. "I hate when we agree."

I leaned into him, giggling. "Admit it, you love my brother."

Dylan hooked his arm around me. "He punched me."

Gasping, I pushed away from him. "He *what*?"

"After," he said, then paused meaningfully, almost as if he didn't want to talk about *that* night. I didn't either. "I went into Walt's a few days after, and he coldcocked me. Couldn't blame him, though."

"Oh my god, Dylan. Why didn't you tell me?"

He hauled me into his lap, meeting my gaze. "Because I hurt you, and he's your brother. He's supposed to protect you."

"I can't believe he actually punched you."

He touched the corner of his eye. "Pretty good too. Could tell he used to be an athlete. He had a lotta power behind it."

I kissed the spot by his eye and then his cheek and mouth. "I love you."

"Here." He reached over to his backpack and handed me a small gift bag.

Inside was a construction paper card from Scarlett. More drawings of hearts and flowers, but there were four stick figures holding hands. Tucker, Dylan, Scarlett, and me. I sniffed and opened up the next card. This one came in an envelope and had a pattern of daisies on the front. Inside were a few loopy lines.

Genevieve,

I'm sorry about what happened at Scarlett's birthday party. I hope you don't hold it against Dylan. He loves you, and I would really like the opportunity to get to know you better. Like I told him, whatever makes him happy, makes the kids happy, and when the kids are happy, I'm happy. YOU make Dylan happy.

Good luck with your new job, and I hope to see you again!

Paige

"Wow."

"Good wow?" Dylan asked.

I tucked the card away and laid both of them on the floor. "Yeah. Really good wow."

"Well, wait. There's more." He shook the bag at me, and I stuck my hand into it, retrieving a small car. "From Tuck."

I laughed and placed it down with the cards then looked back into the bag. Inside were a credit card and a key. I retrieved them both, waiting for him to explain.

"This—" he flicked the Visa "—is a reloadable gift card. I've already put three hundred dollars on it, and every month you're gone, I'll add more. I heard the Wi-Fi sucks on cruise ships, so if we're going to talk every day, you're going to need this."

"Dylan, this is—" Too much, I was going to say. Alex had

already warned me about how expensive it was, but Dylan shook his head.

"I expect texts and pictures and phone calls, so I'm going to pay for them. And this—" he held the key between us "—is for whenever you come home. Whether it's at the end of this contract in six months or after another one or years from now. As long as I know you're coming home to me, I don't care when it is."

My vision blurred. "It's for your house?"

"Our house. Whenever you want it to be."

I threw my arms around him, and he skimmed his hands up and down my back, murmuring his I love yous into my shoulder over and over, and when I finally sat up, wiping at my damp face, his eyes narrowed to their panther gaze. "I don't like it when you cry."

"But I'm crying because I'm happy."

His chest rumbled, and I laughed into a kiss. "I love you, and I'm going to come home to you when this contract is done."

He put the Visa, key, plastic car, and cards back into the bag and tossed it on the desk in the corner then gripped my hips with both hands. "You don't have to. You know that, right? Because I know what it feels like to want to keep going, and if you want to keep going, I want you to do that. That's why I couldn't ask you to stay for me."

"I get it."

"Do you? Because it felt like you were waiting for me to ask you to stay."

I nibbled on my lip in thought. "I was waiting. I think because even though I want to do this, I also want to be with you, and if you asked me to stay, then I could convince myself I wasn't giving up on my dreams. I could have used you as an excuse."

His jaw ticked. "Don't use me as an excuse. Don't cut your career short me for me."

"I'm not," I said, and he raised his brow in suspicion. I

smiled into a kiss against his lips. "I liked being back in West Chester. I liked spending so much time with my brother, and I really love teaching. I loved being back in my studio. You're just icing on the cake."

He lifted up my arms and slipped my tank top and sports bra over my head. "Then get on the bed, gorgeous. Can't let you leave without reminding you who this pussy belongs to."

THIRTY-ONE
DYLAN

Genevieve and I spent almost half the night splitting the hours between orgasms and talking. She kept telling me she needed to sleep and then would inevitably wrap those dainty fingers around my dick, and suddenly, I was back inside her again.

I think we finally fell asleep around three and woke up around seven so we could have a proper goodbye with my head between her legs.

When I dropped her off a few hours later, I had trouble uncurling my hand from the back of her neck, but she reassured me she was coming home in something like six months and seventeen days. It would be hard, but I knew I had to let her go so she could come back to me.

By the time I deplaned in Pennsylvania, I already had a voice message from her. "Hi. We're on our lunch break, and I wanted to tell you everyone noticed the hickey you left me. So, thanks for that. I love you."

I texted her back immediately. **UR welcome. I love you.**

———

Five months and twenty-two days to go…

"You're done for the night?"

Genevieve's exhaustion was palpable through our phone call. "Yeah. It was a rough one. Megan caught some kind of stomach bug a few days ago, and it's working its way through the cast."

"Oh Christ. Are you feeling okay?"

"I mean… I'm not currently puking so…"

"And you still performed?"

"The show must go on," she said flatly.

"You got someone taking care of you?"

She sort of snorted and moaned at the same time, and I imagined her lying on her side in the fetal position. "Everyone's either recovering from it, is currently sick, or trying not to get it. But I have water and Gatorade, a few crackers, and I'm about to watch *Footloose*."

I hated to hang up since we only actually spoke to each other every few days, but I knew she needed rest. "Okay. I love you. Try to get some sleep."

"Mm-hmm. Love you too."

———

Four months and ten days to go…

GEN
Did the kids get their packages?

Yea. Scarlett refuses 2 take it off.

GEN
Aww! I'm so glad she loves the dress!

GEN

Send me a picture.

Tucker played w the pupetts for a few minuts and hasnt picked them back up.

GEN

LOL. That's okay. I'm on the hunt for something he'll love.

GEN

Tell them I miss them.

I will.

GEN

I miss you.

Miss u 2.

———

Three months and twenty-nine days to go…

I held my phone up so Scarlett and Tucker were on-screen. Whenever Genevieve was at a port, we tried to FaceTime since the reception was better on land.

"Where are you?" Scarlett asked.

"Santorini. Can you see?" Genevieve flipped her camera so we were looking at a view of the ocean and white buildings with bright-blue tops and doors. Like a postcard. "Isn't it pretty?"

"Pretty!" Tucker repeated.

"Is that the ocean?" Scarlett asked.

"Yep, that's the ocean."

"Are you going to go swimming?"

"No, not today."

"I want to go swimming in the ocean," Scarlett whined. "I love the beach. I went with Mommy and Neil and Tucker."

Genevieve turned her camera back around so her smiling face was on-screen again. "I know. I saw pictures."

"You did?"

"Yeah, your daddy sent them to me. I was jealous. I want to play in the ocean with you."

I crooked my finger so Scarlett would raise her ear to me. I whispered, "Tell her that we'll go to the beach next summer if she'll come with us."

Scarlett screeched excitedly then grabbed the phone out of my hands. "Daddy says—Daddy says that we can all go to the beach! Ah!"

Tucker started dancing too. "I love beach!"

"Daddy says you'll come with us!"

"I can't wait," Genevieve said.

"I can't wait either!" Scarlett spun around a few times then stopped and abruptly fell on the couch. "When are you coming home?"

"I'm coming home at the end of January."

Scarlett sat up, extending her neck to assess the big erasable calendar I'd bought and hung in the hall between the living room and kitchen.

"It's not until next year," I explained. "That's only for this month."

"Oh yeah." Scarlett told Genevieve, "It's September."

"I know."

"September, October, November, December," Scarlett said, counting them on her fingers. "That's four months."

I could hear how Genevieve's pep was fading in her voice. "Yep, and then it'll be the new year."

"Sweetheart, why don't you give me the phone back?" I said, and when Scarlett handed me my cell, I held it up so the three of us were on-screen. "Three months and twenty-nine days."

"Three months and twenty-nine days," Genevieve repeated.

———

Two months and five days to go…

It was trick-or-treat night, and I'd taken a bunch of photos to send to Genevieve. In return, she'd sent me one as I was strolling down the sidewalk in my vampire costume.

Kitten

GEN
Yes?

Im w the kids getting candy.

GEN
I know. I like your fangs.

u sent me a pic of ur tits.

Nice tits btw.

GEN
I'm glad you like them. They miss you.

Gen.

GEN
What?

IM WITH THE KIDS

and now I got a ducking boner.

GEN
LOLOLOLOLOLOLOLOL

Not funny.

GEN

A little bit.

Call me tonite. We can take care of it than.

GEN

K. Love you!

ilu

———

One month and twenty-four days to go…

"How was your Thanksgiving?"

I slumped back against my headboard, already undoing the button of my jeans. "Can we skip this part?"

Genevieve laughed in my ear. "Why? I want to hear about your day."

"It was fine." She knew the kids were with Paige and Neil today, so I'd spent the day at Liam's place.

"You have to give me more than that."

"Why?" I shimmied my pants and underwear down enough that I could wrap my hand around my cock.

"Because I'm…" Her breath hiccupped, and my blood immediately cooled.

"What's wrong?"

"I miss you. A lot. And I'm really homesick today."

I stood up, kicking off my jeans but tugging my boxers back up and sliding under the covers. "Where are you?"

She sniffled. "In my room."

"In bed?"

"No. On the floor."

"Get in bed. Under your covers. Turn on your side."

I could hear her moving around. "Okay."

"Okay," I murmured, "put your phone on speaker and close your eyes." I did too. "You're in bed with me."

She hummed. "Yeah?"

"And I've got my arm around you, your ass is up against me, and you're all soft and warm with only my T-shirt on."

"What do you have on?"

"My gray underwear."

"The Hanes boxer briefs? They're my favorite."

I smiled and nestled my head farther into the pillow. "I can feel you breathing, and I kiss the back of your neck. That spot right at the top of your spine."

"And I pull you tighter around me," she said, playing along. "So you move your other arm under my pillow and lay it flat on the bed."

"My arm falls asleep all the time like that."

"I know, but you do it anyway because you like to let me trace all your veins with my fingers."

"I do like that," I agreed, and she let out a breathy, satisfied sound, so I said, "We stay like that for a long time. Until you're asleep."

It would cost me a small fortune, but I would do whatever it took so she never cried again. I stayed on the phone for a long time, until she fell asleep.

———

Thirty days to go...

Thank u for my gift. I love it.

GEN

You got it already? I wasn't sure when it would arrive.

Opened it in front of my parents

GEN

OMG! NO YOU DIDN'T!

I did.

GEN

OMG I can never meet them. That's so embarrassing.

My mom said ur v pretty.

GEN

OMGOMGOMGOMG

They cant wait 2 meet u.

GEN

That can never happen.

It isnt bad campared to other stuff weve sent each other.

What she'd sent me for Christmas was a framed photo of her on a beach somewhere, naked and lying on her side so most everything was covered up with how her legs were bent and her arm was over her chest. It was super hot. Like something from a magazine.

But since my parents were visiting from Arizona for a few days, and we weren't paying attention as we opened gifts from under the tree, I didn't think anything of opening the package. Now, it was upstairs on a shelf in my little walk-in closet, where no one else but me could see it.

ilu. Cant wait to c u.

GEN

Miss you. Love you. Kiss the kids for me.

———

Five minutes to go…

"I don't see her. Where is she?"

"She'll be here soon," I told Scarlett as she paced around the arrivals area with the sign she'd made.

After crisscrossing the Atlantic, Genevieve was finally coming home to me, and I could barely contain my own jitters, let alone Scarlett's. Tucker was on my shoulders, a lookout from high ground.

In the last six months, I'd learned what patience was. Being physically apart for so long was one of the hardest things I'd ever had to do, but our relationship was stronger for it. It had been a real test, figuring out how to communicate not only as a couple but with so little means. I was sure we could conquer anything from here on out.

And the kids were just as excited as me. Scarlett had loved Genevieve from day one in her dance class, but Tucker grew to know her as the weeks went on through FaceTime calls and the small presents she'd send from every place she went. Now, he was practically shouting, "Evie! Evie! Where you at?"

I checked the time on my cell phone once more.

"Daaaaad," Scarlett whined. "When's she getting here? I'm tired."

I'd recently become Dad to her. The first half of first grade was a steep learning curve for both of us. More math and reading for her, more sassy attitude for me. Genevieve told me Scarlett was just trying to figure out the person she was, echoing what Paige had said.

It was like Genevieve was meant to be part of our family, seamlessly fitting in, even from the middle of the ocean.

"Her plane arrived," I told my daughter. "She's got—"

"Evie!" Tucker wiggled around, kicking his feet. "Evie!"

And then she was there. Running.

I set Tucker down so he and Scarlett could run too.

Genevieve skirted an older couple and almost took a dive over a man's suitcase, but she caught herself, only to be bowled over. By the time I caught up, Scarlett and Tucker were on top of her, speaking over each other like puppies barking at the door for their owner. Genevieve did her best to ping-pong her attention between Scarlett showing off the sign she'd made and Tucker zipping his cars up and down her arm and over her head.

"I know you two are excited, but how 'bout you let Genevieve up off the floor, huh?" I nudged them off and wrapped my hand around her elbow to tow her up. When our eyes finally met, it was like falling into bed after a long day. I cinched my arms around her waist and breathed her in, my nose in her hair, her face against my throat, her fingers curled into my coat.

"Daddy! I'm hungry!" Tucker pulled at me, forcing me to let go of Genevieve.

"Let's get McDonald's," Scarlett suggested, and Genevieve bent down to their level.

"How about we order takeout and eat at home? I'm kinda tired, and I've been dreaming about lying on the couch with you guys while we watch a movie."

"Home?" I repeated, and she straightened, digging into her back pocket, brandishing the key.

"Home."

I draped my arm around her neck and kissed her temple. "That sounds good to me. Scar, Tuck, what do you think? Pizza and movie night at home?"

Scarlett danced ahead of us. "I want pepperoni!"

"I wanna watch Lightning McQueen!"

Genevieve tipped her chin up, offering me her red lips. I kissed her once, twice, and then a third time because I could. "I love you."

She smiled her showstopping smile. "I love you, and I can't wait to go home with you."

I didn't let go of her as I wrangled the kids with my other arm and guided us all toward the luggage carousel. "Pepperoni pizza and Lightning McQueen it is."

EPILOGUE
DYLAN

"Hey, Tuck! Watch what you're doing. You almost ran Finn over."

Imagination seemed extra crowded this morning. Probably because it was the first Saturday in June, and it was finally sunny after a whole week of rain.

"Sorry!" Tucker sent a sheepish smile my way then raced off with the shopping cart while Finn tried to keep up, plastic broccoli and bananas falling out of his arms.

Liam laughed good-naturedly and shook his head. "At least they're getting healthy food."

"What time do you have to leave?" Jude asked me, eyes on his area, where Amelia and Scarlett were pretending to do some other girl's make-up.

"A few minutes." I shook my to-go coffee cup, making sure it was empty then turned toward Sebastian, where he was playing a Switch on a bench. "Hey. Catch."

He immediately put the game down and stood, hands ready. I tossed it to him, and he lunged for it, not expecting the paper cup to fall a bit short of him, but he did catch it.

"Nice."

He smiled and dunked it in the garbage. "You ready for the game tomorrow?"

"Yep!"

I held my knuckles out, and he ran over to tap them before sitting back down.

"What about you?" Jude asked. "Are *you* ready?"

"Yeah. I'm ready."

Liam crossed his legs at the ankles. "How're you gonna do it?"

"I have it worked out with Amy to do it at the end of the show."

Jude eyed me. "Nervous?"

I shook my head. "Not a bit."

I'd known I wanted to marry Genevieve the day I'd picked her up from the airport in January, but I'd wanted to wait until we were both settled in our new life together. We had a few dinners over the winter with Paige and Neil so the kids could get used to seeing us together, witness us all getting along. It was important they knew there was never any competition between us, and that we would all be there for them.

In early spring, I'd talked to Nate about marrying her. Not that I was asking permission, but I wanted him to know what my plans were, especially because I'd need help navigating the rough waters that were their parents. I'd met both Shannon and Tim, and they were nice, but it was easy to understand Genevieve's connection to Miss Amy and her brother. To know who her real problem solvers and supporters were.

Then last month, I'd talked to Scarlett and Tucker about what it would mean for me to marry Genevieve. They were all for it and had a lot of fun running around the jewelry store. They helped me pick out the radiant cut diamond. I had no idea what the different shapes were but Scarlett said it was the most sparkly one and Tucker liked that it was a rectangle, so I was sold.

It was simple, just a white gold band with a single diamond, but there was something about it that reminded me of her. Bright and sharp and glittering.

That was Genevieve.

I had no doubt she'd say yes.

"Scarlett," I called. "Five more minutes then we're leaving."

She started to pout.

"We have to get ready for your recital."

That got her attention, and she threw her fake make-up on the table and ran to me. "Ready!"

I ruffled her hair. "Go get your brother."

She took off, shouting, and I faced my friends.

Jude raised a donut hole to me in salute. "Good luck and let us know how it goes."

I nodded and stood as Liam said, "Guess you'll be out of our club now."

Jude clucked his tongue. "You'll miss out on this year's T-shirts."

"The annual retreat," Liam added.

"Damn," I deadpanned. "What ever will I do?"

"Not hang out with us," Jude said then stuffed a donut in his mouth.

"Nope. I'll be too busy with my head buried between Gen's legs."

Liam covered his laugh with a fist, and Jude reared back. "Please don't say that out loud in front of Nate. I can't handle another fight."

Tucker and Scarlett skipped back to me then, cutting off my retort about how I could kick his ass now that he'd be my brother-in-law, and I asked, "You ready to get out of here?"

"Yes!"

"Let's go!"

"Say bye to Uncle Jude and Uncle Liam."

Tucker swung on my arm, hanging his head back so he was upside down. "Byeeee!"

"Bye, Uncle Jude." Scarlett ran to hug each of them. "Bye, Uncle Liam."

I tapped the brim of my hat in goodbye then headed for the exit, ready to join a new club, the Married Dad's Association.

WHAT'S NEXT?

If you want more Dylan and Genevieve content, use the QR code to have it delivered straight to your inbox!

Loved The Rehearsal Fling? You'll definitely want to check out The Nanny Tenure, the next novel in the Single Dads' Club series, coming 2024!

ACKNOWLEDGMENTS

Indie publishing is a wild ride. Thank you, reader, for coming along with me.

I wouldn't be able to put out these books if not for the encouragement of my friends and the guidance of people much smarter than me, in particular Diamond Dogs of publishing. Big shout out to Echo Grayce for the amazing cover and to Libby and Lisa for editing my brain vomit into an actual book. I'd especially like to thank my street team for helping me spread the word about my books. I'm forever grateful.

If you'd like more information about me, you can find it at https://sophieandrewsauthor.com/

ABOUT THE AUTHOR

Sophie Andrews is a contemporary romance author who writes steamy books that will leave you smiling. As a millennial, she's obsessed with boybands, late 90s rom-coms, and will always be team Pacey. When she's not writing, she's most likely trying to wrangle her children or drinking red wine. Or both at the same time.

ALSO BY SOPHIE ANDREWS

Tangled Series

Tangled Up

Tangled Want

Tanged Hearts

Tangled Beginning

Tangled Expectations

Tangled Chances

Tangled Ambition

Single Dads' Club

The Rehearsal Fling

The Nanny Tenure

Stand-Alones

How to Ruin a Wedding

Love at a Funeral and Other Awkward Conversations

www.ingramcontent.com/pod-product-compliance
Lightning Source LLC
Chambersburg PA
CBHW050755190726
48285CB00005B/1669